the
act of
trusting

Editing: Rumi Khan

Cover Design: Wildheart Graphics

Formatting: Swoonworthy Designs

Cover Image: Wander Aguiar :: Photography

CONTENT WARNING

This book is intended for readers that are 18+. There are
mentions of sexual assault, drugging, and PTSD. While most of
these situations happen off page and are non-explicit, they can
be triggering for some readers. If this is a concern of yours,
please reach out to me.

READER'S NOTE

To all the readers who have been patient with me, thank you. Life got in the way and this book was put on the backburner, as was writing, but I am overjoyed for it to finally be here and the plans I have for future books.

I hope you all enjoy Camden and Blaire's story as much as I did while writing it.

CHAPTER ONE

CAMDEN

Boobs. Boobs *everywhere*. Small boobs, large boobs, perky boobs, saggy boobs—hell, there are even a few fake boobs thrown into the mix. Although, I'm not a huge fan of hard tits. Oh well, still makes for a great sight.

It's the first party of the year and since the weather here in sunny Braxton, Florida, is perfect, what better way to kick off the new semester than a pool party? And of course, it has *nothing* to do with getting dozens of fine-as-hell coeds in as little amount of clothing as possible. That would be downright shameful of us, and we here at Braxton University are nothing but gentlemen.

The party is at the house I share with four of my teammates: Levi, Mateo, Conrad, and Maddox. We all play for the Braxton U soccer team and, if I do say so myself, we totally kick ass. Our team went undefeated last year, but we barely came out winners with only one damn goal ahead at the championship. With us being upperclassmen this year and losing some of our best players after graduation, we have to keep our heads on straight and focus.

"Heads-up," someone yells, right before a beach ball comes

flying toward me, almost knocking the beer out of my hand. They're lucky I have fast reflexes, or I would have been pissed that a perfectly good beer was wasted.

A familiar-looking blonde chick with an obvious fake tan comes strutting up. She bends down, a little too slow if you ask me, and retrieves the ball at my feet. When she stretches back to her full length, I notice a barely-there, bright pink bikini covers her inflated tits. *Hmm, inflated tit girl coming to collect the inflated ball. Seems ironic to me.*

After staring at her boobs for far too long, she must get the impression that I'm impressed by them. I wish I had the heart to tell her I'm an all-natural type of guy. Real boobs, even if they're smaller, are much more fun to play with than hard, fake ones. It just doesn't…feel right to me. Someone should really tell these girls before they spend thousands of dollars on something most guys aren't a fan of.

Someone yells out "Chloe" again and over the chick's shoulder, there is a group of guys in the pool staring at her, including a few of my teammates. She rolls her eyes and turns around to launch the ball in their direction. I'm about to make a quick run for it when a hand latches onto my forearm. Fake boobs, or as I've just learned is Chloe, runs her nails up my arm and starts rubbing my bicep. Most of the time, when a girl shows interest like Chloe obviously is, I'd take them up on their offer. You won't see me turning down no-strings-attached sex. I'm just not feeling it with this one. First, the attraction isn't there on my part. Once again, natural is my type. The fake tits, unnatural spray tan, unnatural blonde hair with purple highlights, and fake nails are actually having the opposite effect on me than I'm sure she thinks. It may be possible that my dick just went into hiding at the thought of going near one of Willy Wonka's employees. Second, I'm not looking to catch any kind of disease that'll have my junk out of commission for an unseen amount of time, and by the looks of this girl, she's a predator on the hunt for her next victim. *Good try, honey, but I'm smarter than you'd think.*

She leans in close, making sure to press her barely-covered boobs up against my arm, and begins rubbing my bare chest. It's a struggle to hold back the eye roll at her obvious moves. Do girls have this shit scripted now? I'm sure this is what Chloe does to every guy she wants to bed. The slight arm touch, then the hand roaming, and I'm sure what comes next is the lip biting while looking up at me through her eyelashes. Then she'll probably say something like, 'What do you say we head somewhere and *talk* for a bit?' and we all know she has no intentions of actually talking.

Chloe licks her lips, then gazes up at me through her long eyelashes. Running her long fingernail down the center of my chest to the waistband of my shorts, she says, "Camden Collins, what a nice surprise it is to run into you. I've never been with a forward before. I'm sure you know all about scoring. How about you show me that big old house of yours and we can have some alone time in your room?"

My body runs cold, despite the ninety-degree weather, when I realize who this is. While I haven't met her in person, every guy on the team knows who Chloe Stevens is. She's a well-known ball chaser and has been making her way through Braxton U soccer players since her freshman year. She usually goes for upperclassmen, although I remember her and Maddox having something going on last semester. Rumor has it she is trying to land a player who will make it past college ball and play pro or for a club team. All she wants is the money and status that come with it.

Ball chasers are what we call girls who go after guys on the team just because of our status as soccer players. Since we're one of the best college teams in the nation, a lot of us go on to play for overseas pro or club teams, and women see that as instant dollar signs. I can tell Chloe sees me like that by the sparkle and excitement in her eyes. No doubt she has plans of trapping a player and making him her sugar daddy. Really, she should have bigger dreams than becoming a gold digger.

Plucking her hand off the string of my board shorts, I take a step back, separating myself from the pro ball chaser. "Sorry, doll, I'm not feeling it tonight." By the look of shock on her face, I'd go ahead and say Chloe isn't used to rejection. I'm sure most guys here, including my roommates, would jump at the easy lay, but I'm getting tired of easy. I'm starting to wonder if there is a girl out there who doesn't throw herself at a guy just because of his status. Sure, I was all for it my first two years here, but it's starting to get old. I would rather a girl want me for me, Camden Collins the guy, and not Camden Collins the soccer player and team captain.

"I'm sorry, but are you saying you don't want any of this?" Chloe says, motioning to her body, making sure she points out the parts that are hidden behind the tiny fabric of her bathing suit.

I shrug my shoulders, seemingly unimpressed. "I'm sure you can find another guy for the evening." And with that, I walk away before I have to deal with the aftereffects of this chick's rejection. For some reason, I don't think she'll take it too well.

Heading toward the back door, I pass by an intense game of flip cup where a young girl is being shouted at by one of the football players because she can't get the red Solo cup to land right. Poor thing, she should have known better than to join a game with the big dogs. Those guys take anything with a winner at the end very seriously. I think it's them trying to make up for being one of the shittiest college football teams. Winning games like flip cup and beer pong make them feel a little better about themselves.

I'm too lost in the game going on in front of me that I don't notice my teammate and best friend, Maddox, come up in front of me and almost walk right into him. "Hey, man, I need you for the next game of beer pong. Levi is a lightweight and's about ready to pass out and you know Mateo's gone for the weekend," he says, shoving me in the direction of the beer pong setup.

There are five white tables set up with different levels of difficulty on each of them. When you have guys as good as Maddox and me playing, the standard ten-cup game isn't enough of a challenge for us. We like to make it interesting, so at one end there's six-cup beer pong, which is usually for the freshman girls who haven't played before, and then two tables of ten-cup games in the middle, and leading up to twenty-one-cup beer pong. The last table is much more of a challenge that most people avoid because with that amount of beer, you start to feel the effects of the alcohol before you're even halfway in. Fifty-five cups filled to the middle with beer will make any man weak. That is, except for Maddox and me. We're the only ones on campus who have won the fifty-five-cup beer pong challenge. Did we pass out after and spend most of the night puking cheap beer into a toilet? Of course. We drank a shit-ton. But it was totally worth it to have that title under our belts.

Two of my other teammates, Rodrick and Aaron, are filling the fifty-five cups with beer from the nearby keg. Maddox is beside me, bouncing on the balls of his feet, trying to get pumped up like he does before a game.

Maddox has always been an energetic guy. While not as competitive as some of the guys on our team, Maddox plays for the love of the sport, like me. We're both forwards, and since we've played together for so long, the two of us are in sync when we are on the field. That bond works when we're off the field also, which is the reason why we're undefeated in basically any drinking game we have at parties. Flip cup? No one can touch us. Quarters? Not a fucking chance. And beer pong? I think being the only ones at any party to win at fifty-five-cup speaks for itself.

Usually, Maddox isn't this excited about a game of beer pong, so to see him bouncing around and rolling his shoulders is unusual. When I turn to see who we're playing against, I know exactly why he's acting this way. Ben and Luis Moore. Seniors and twin brothers who are safeties for the Braxton football team and grade-A assholes. While most guys on the football team are chill, these two are hated by pretty much everyone. They're self-centered jerks who don't give a shit about anything or anyone. We've tried to distance ourselves from the twins after I caught them trying to bring a passed-out freshman to one of our bedrooms last year, but it's difficult to keep people out of an open party.

I grab Maddox's arm and pull him aside, ignoring the yellow-toothed smirk on Ben's face. "What the fuck are you thinking doing anything that involves them? Actually, why the hell are they even here? You know what pieces of shit they are."

"Don't worry, man," Maddox reassures me. "I was sending the douchebags packing, but then fuckface over there"—he points to Luis, the uglier of the two—"started spewing shit and talking about how great he is at life. I had to bring him down a few notches and remind him of the football team's losing streak. One thing led to another, and they challenged me to a game. I couldn't turn it down. It's you and me against the sleazy Moore brothers. We got this in the bag, bro." He holds up his fist, waiting for me to give him a knuckle punch, but I just roll my eyes and turn to face the table.

A small crowd has started to circle around us, waiting for the game to start. I'm sure seeing who the teams are, people are expecting some drama. While I'd love to do nothing more than knock these jerks on their asses and make them look like fools in front of everyone, I'm too frustrated by the fact that they're even here. I won't be taking my eyes off them until they're driving away from my house.

"Are we going to start this or what? Or are you pansies

afraid to lose your precious beer pong champ title?" Luis smirks, showing his crooked, yellowing teeth. Just the sight of this guy has a chill running up my spine.

Grabbing both ping-pong balls, I throw one of them in their direction and get ready for the toss-up to see who throws first.

Ben and I go head-to-head, making sure we don't break eye contact when we try to make a shot. With little effort, I come out the winner.

The game starts off pretty evenly. With this many cups, it is easy to make the first few shots. Once you start taking away the ones you've made, though, the challenge really begins with how many holes there are. I can see the struggle on Luis's face as he focuses on making one of the island shots. I just sit back with a cocky smirk on my face, already having made three of these this game.

He tosses the ball up into the air, letting it sail across the table and...completely misses the target and hits Maddox in the thigh.

The crowd laughs at the lame-ass shot and Luis shoots me a dirty glare, like it's my damn fault he has no hand-eye coordination.

Maddox and I throw next, both making the shot effortlessly, like we always do.

The crowd goes crazy with drunken cheers. Something cold and wet hits my bare back, and I'm sure there are others behind me soaked from someone's tossed beer.

When I glance at the twins, they're both scowling at Maddox and me. I mean, I would be too if I were losing and the other team were six cups away from winning. Judging from the number of cups they have left, the only way they stand a chance of winning is by a miracle. They're not even halfway there and I only feel the slightest of buzzes.

Ten more minutes go by and I'm really hoping we can be done with this game soon. I'm getting tired of having to drink this warm beer and I've had to take a piss for the last half hour.

Maddox and I have one cup left and surprisingly, the Moore brothers only have eighteen to make. They did a lot better than I thought they would, but by the sway in their stances and glossy look in their eyes, I'm guessing someone is going to be calling an Uber after Maddox and I sink this last one.

Maddox makes it into the cup on his shot. Now all I need to do is make it into the same cup and we can have two fifty-five-cup beer pong game wins under our belts.

Channeling out the crowd and everything around me, I focus on the ball in my hand and the cup sitting in the middle of the table on the other side. It's the same way I am when I'm playing in a soccer game. Everyone around us disappears and it's just me, the ball, and the cup. I think that's why Maddox and I work so well in these types of games. We've been trained to tune out screaming fans in stadiums, so a few drunken college kids is nothing to us.

I lift my hand and let the light ball glide through the air, straight for the cup. From this angle, I can't tell whether or not it will actually make it. I'm holding my breath, waiting for the ball to disappear behind that rim and call it a game. One, so I can get the douchebag brothers out of my house, and two, so I can relieve the pressure off my bladder.

The crowd around us is quiet, waiting to see what will happen. Maddox has his hands in his hair, clutching it tightly.

The ball is going…going…and going, until finally the musical sound of splashing beer rings in my ears.

"Holy shit, motherfuckers, we won!" Maddox yells and slings his arm around my shoulders.

Everyone around us is going crazy, splashing beer and hoisting bikini-clad chicks up into the air. You would have thought we won the damn World Cup by how excited these people are, not some college drinking game.

When I look over at the Moore brothers, both have their jaws hanging open, stunned. I walk away from Maddox, who now has his tongue down some chick's throat, and make my way over to the losers.

Crossing my arms over my chest, I make sure to keep my balance now that I'm starting to feel the effect of the alcohol. "We let you guys have your fun, now get the fuck out of my house. I don't want to see either of you at one of our parties again."

Luis goes to say something, but Ben grabs his forearm, dragging him out of the house. *At least one of them was smart this time*, I think to myself.

After I watch them grab one of their football buddies and leave, I make a beeline for the back door, hurrying to get inside and take a piss.

When I reach the downstairs bathroom, I stop at the line of girls starting at the door and leading to the hallway. No way would I be able to hold it for that long.

There are only two other bathrooms in the house, one upstairs that Levi, Mateo, Conrad, and I share. Then there's the primary, which is in Maddox's room. The lucky bastard gets the biggest damn room in the house all because he drew the highest card when we got the place.

The crowd by the stairs is too congested and if I don't find somewhere to go now, my pants are the only option.

An idea comes to mind, and I decide, fuck it, no one will notice. Running out the back door, I make my way to the side of the house and, yes, the coast is clear. Quickly undoing the tie of my bathing suit, I lower it enough to pull myself out and let it all flow.

My head falls back, and I let out a loud moan at the relief. Nothing feels better than this moment.

Ten seconds go by, and I still have a steady flow going. When I feel it come to an end, a loud gasp comes from beside me. Turning to see who it is, I'm jerked to a stop at a hot-as-fuck girl standing there. She has long, dark brown hair that looks soft as silk as it hangs loose down her shoulders. Her skin is pale, as if she has not been spending the summer in the sun like the majority of everyone here. She's not dressed like the rest of the other girls either. Her black, basic T-shirt is flattering, hugging her perky, full rack, but flows down over her stomach and her shorts are surprising since I think the only bottoms girls are wearing tonight are the string kind. Nonetheless, her shorts make those long legs look hot as hell. How is it that this girl is turning me on more than the half-naked ones at the party?

When I make my way back up to her face, her eyes are wide and she's staring at me too. I mean, she's really staring at me... with my dick out...in my hand. Well, this isn't awkward or anything.

I go to make an introduction, but she quickly turns and runs in the other direction. Damn, nothing like having your junk out to ruin the moment.

CHAPTER TWO

BLAIRE

Running through the backyard, I stop when I'm far enough away from the side of the house and try to catch my breath. I can't believe what I saw. That guy was just standing there, right out in the open, doing his business. Is that common for people around here? Doesn't he know there is a bathroom right inside? And another thing, why did I stand there, staring? It was like I couldn't look away. It isn't like I've never seen a penis before. Okay, that's not true. I've never seen one in person, and maybe that was why. Seeing this stranger practically naked was...interesting. I usually avoid men at all costs, but he was sort of cute the way he stood there, unsure of what to do in such an awkward situation.

I make my way back to where I left my best friend and roommate, Emree, only to find her on some guy's lap I don't know. She is straddling him, sticking her tongue down his throat while he runs his hands over her bare stomach, coming dangerously close to the underneath of her breasts.

Watching them, I can't help but wonder what that would feel like. To give yourself to someone voluntarily in such an intimate way. I shake my head, letting go of those thoughts.

Nothing like that would ever be possible. It took me months to let Emree in, and although we have become great friends, I can't imagine doing something like make out with a guy. There's no way I would be able to be that close to someone and not have an anxiety attack.

Grabbing my purse I left on the chair by her, I start making my way to the side of the house, the opposite one where I found Penis Man. I was on my way to leave when I realized I'd forgotten my bag, which was right about the time I saw my first penis. *I really need to stop thinking about it...and picturing it.*

Peeking around the corner, I check to make sure the coast is clear and, luckily, there isn't anyone in sight.

Once I make it to my car, I wipe the small drops of sweat off my forehead. It's been two years since I moved to Braxton, and I still haven't gotten used to the humidity. It's not like I'm from the north or anything, but Texas has a different kind of heat than this tropical weather. I think Florida is in its own category when it comes to humidity and heat.

Starting the car up, I make sure the air is blasting cool and directly in my face, making my long hair fly back. While my budget was extremely limited when I was ready to buy a car last year, my number one requirement was that it needed to have strong air conditioning. I got lucky with my cute, red Toyota Camry that is only a few years old. The air runs great and it has not given me any issues.

After cooling off for a bit, I put the car in drive and check to make sure no one is around before I pull away from the curb and onto the road. The road is littered with cars, and I make sure not to ding someone since the street is so narrow.

Now that I have a chance to relax in the quiet, I can firmly say that my first college party was not a success. It was an outright failure to the tenth degree. I didn't even make it an hour in that place before I was telling Emree I needed to leave. There was no way I could be in that kind of environment with so many careless people surrounding me. I had to get out of there. It has been over a year since I've had an anxiety attack and I didn't want to break that record today.

While my best friend was doing what she thought was helpful, she couldn't have been more wrong. Yes, I have never been to a college party. I know that sounds lame coming from a twenty-year-old junior, but it's by choice. People from class have invited me to them in the past, but I had no desire to go.

Emree always understood my reasoning for not wanting to attend any of the parties. That is until some guy on the Braxton soccer team invited her and she begged me to come with her because she didn't want to be there alone. Emree has had a crush on this guy since she was a freshman and he winked at her in one of their classes. At least, that's what she told me. It wasn't until this year that they exchanged actual words and that was only him inviting her to a party at the house he shares with other teammates. How she ended up making out with him —at least I hoped it was him—in the backyard is beyond me.

Pulling into our apartment complex, I make sure to park under one of the streetlamps. Even though it's lights out, I may end up picking Emree up later tonight. Grabbing my bag, phone, and keys, I exit the car and make my way to the front of the building.

The elevator ride up to the fourth floor is slow and jerky, as usual. We don't live in the newest of apartments, but this is what we could afford close to campus, and it seemed clean and modern enough. When we first rode the elevator, though, I thought we were going to have something crazy happen, like fall to our death or get trapped in the doors, but that could have been from the *Final Destination* marathon we had the night before. Nothing strange did happen. It's just old and makes haunting noises.

Walking through our apartment door, I breathe in the scent of fresh linens, or whatever our newest outlet odor plug is.

Emree is obsessed with everything smelling nice. My best friend's perfume collection takes up most of her dresser, but I have to admit, she always smells great.

Dropping my bag on the living room couch, I head into the kitchen to find something to snack on. After grabbing an apple and water bottle, I settle at the small table we have nestled in the corner and decide to sort through the mountain of mail we've accumulated over the month. Since it's usually bills, I avoid anything else addressed to me at all costs.

Chucking sales crap and flyers into the junk pile, I freeze when I see a letter in familiar handwriting. The perfect cursive and flow of every letter can only be one person: my mother.

I haven't had any communication with either of my parents since moving out here. They continued to try and call me, but after I changed my number, the calls ended. The letters, though, they still come. Somehow, they've been able to always know where I'm living.

I've never responded to any of them or ever read a single one. There's nothing they can say that would make their betrayal go away. Four years later, and the pain is still there. I've tried to let it go, forgive them for being who they are, but how they treated me at a time I needed them the most can't be forgotten. Nothing in a letter or phone call can change that. I've lived a happy and somewhat normal life since I moved here, and I know opening the can of worms these letters will cause is not what I need. Everything in my life is finally starting to come together. I'm on the fast track to graduating with honors, my nightmares are finally starting to come around less, and I'm beginning to feel normal again. Or as normal as I can be.

Leaving the untouched letter and bills on the table, I grab the junk mail and toss it in the garbage. I hitch my purse over my shoulder and gather the rest of my mail, letter included, and bring them to my room. Dropping my bag on the bed, it lands with a plop, and I head over to the desk. I have a special place for the nine—now ten—unopened letters my mother has sent. Even though I won't read them, I don't have the heart to throw them away. I would always live with the regret of what could be written inside of them.

Opening the bottom drawer, I reach for the stack of letters held together by a thick rubber band and add the newest one to the pile. Clutching them in my hands, I can't help but stare at all my mother has written me in two years. A part of me wants to open them and find out what they say, but another part, the young girl who left home at eighteen, can't bear to think of what could be in there. I've made so much progress in my life since moving to Braxton and the last thing I want to do is head in the wrong direction.

Letting out the breath I didn't know I was holding, I place the letters back in the drawer and close it. One day, I might be strong enough to read them, but the indecision I'm feeling right now tells me today is not that day.

Reaching into my back pocket, I fish my phone out to see if there are any notifications. Emree would usually call or text and keep me updated since she knows I worry. Before I get a chance, a new message catches my eye. It's Emree letting me know she's staying the night with some guy named Conrad. I'm only hoping it's the same one she was making out with earlier. After shooting a text, saying 'Okay, be safe' back at her, I toss my phone onto the bed and grab my Kindle off my desk and make my way to the living room. After snuggling in on the couch with a blanket and the new book I downloaded this morning, I enjoy my last weekend before a hectic semester.

CHAPTER THREE

CAMDEN

"Shit!" I yell, throwing the covers over my head, trying to block out the obnoxious screeching coming from the nightstand. Reaching over, I slap around. My hand connects with my phone. After turning the alarm off, I groan. It's too early.

It's the first day of classes and I'm not prepared for the 8 a.m. wake-up call. You'd think after all the years of being in school, this would have gotten easier, but no. I've come to the conclusion that I'm just not a morning person. While some enjoy watching the sun rise and listening to the birds chirp, I'd much rather be dead to the world and hide away in the dream I was enjoying minutes ago.

Rubbing the sleep from my eyes with the palm of my hands, I run everything I can remember about the dream I was in the middle of through my head. I was with a girl, a beautiful girl, but I couldn't see her face. I was dancing with her, which is surprising because I don't dance, and her head was thrown back, laughing. So much of her was a clear vision. The deep throat laughs, her long, chestnut hair falling down her back, and her pale skin.

She seemed too familiar, but I can't for the life of me picture the chick's face. Every time the dream comes back to me, her face is blurred out, which pisses me off because I know she would be even more beautiful with some damn facial features.

Rubbing my hands down my face, I try to forget the girl from my dream and prepare for the day ahead.

The first week of classes is all bullshit. We don't do anything important. It's pretty much a half hour of the professor going over the syllabus and what the semester will be like and then we're out of there early. Not worth my time.

Usually, I would skip the first week and enjoy a few extra days of summer, but Coach has been on our asses about attending every class this year. I guess he found out a lot of the players show up whenever we want and wasn't too happy.

My movements are robotic, just going with the motions of changing into some jeans, a tee, and my old sneakers. Grabbing some gel off my dresser, I put a small dab on my hand and run it through my wavy hair, trying to tame it as much as possible. Once I get it in the perfect messy look, I grab my backpack and head out of my bedroom.

Making my way to the kitchen, I notice the house is strangely quiet. The rest of the guys are probably still asleep since they aren't as dumb as me to schedule a class at nine in the damn morning.

I grab one of the many protein shake mixers we keep on the counter and begin filling it with my liquid chocolate breakfast. After that, I grab three water bottles and some protein bars and stuff them in my bag, then I'm out the door.

Since I didn't know what I was doing my first year here, I selected all my fun elective courses my first two years and now I'm stuck with my requirement classes. Including math, and I hate that bitch. I would have avoided that like the plague. Unfortunately, the time has come to take it, and with my procrastination, I ended up with lovely morning classes.

It takes me no time getting a parking spot, unlike most of the sorry suckers driving around. Being the team captain at a school where soccer is everything, you get some nice perks. One of those being a sectioned-off area for us. It's more of a known thing rather than labeled specifically for us.

Putting my Jeep in park, I check the clock on the dash and silently pat myself on the back for getting here with ten minutes to spare. With the extra time, I scarf down one of the protein bars from my bag and wash it down with half a bottle of water, leaving me now five minutes before class starts. Just enough time.

Luckily, the classroom is in the west building, right by where I park. When I get to the hall my classroom is in, it's empty. The lights are on in the room, and I hear voices coming from inside.

Opening the door slowly, I peek my head inside. There's a loud creak the wider I open the door, causing everyone's attention, including the professor's, to turn my way.

"I'm glad you decided to join us, Mr. Collins." His condescending tone makes me believe anything but. "Why don't you take a seat and enjoy the last half of class since you missed the beginning." Professor Dickhead raises an eyebrow at me and motions with his eyes to an empty seat in the middle of the room.

Entering the classroom, I pull out my phone and check the clock. I'm right on time. "Class starts at nine, though," I say to him.

He points the pen in his hand at me. "I'd check your email, Mr. Collins. One was sent out last week with a time change for this class. It now begins at eight-thirty. Now please, take a seat. You've disturbed the class enough for one morning." Turning, he goes back to the board, dismissing me.

Tucking my phone into my back pocket, I head over to the seat he directed me to take and plop down.

Professor D (aka Dickhead) continues talking as if he didn't just call out one of his students in front of the entire class. Letting out a huff, I pull my notebook out of my bag and start jotting down what was already written on the board before I came in.

Something to my right catches my eye and I see a lot of long hair covering a face. The hair color is familiar. The girl next to me looks like she's doing a bang-up job of trying to avoid my eye contact, which makes no damn sense. I haven't even tried to hit on her yet.

Leaning forward, I try to catch a glance of her face, but she ducks more, blocking any shot of me getting a peek. Which answers my suspicions of her hiding. Her movements cause her scent to waft my way and I get hit with the smell of sweet cherries.

As I go to lean back, I can't help but feel like I know her from somewhere. Most girls I've hooked up with in the past would be more than happy to be sitting beside me in a class, but whoever this is wants to do everything possible to remain hidden.

She glances up at the board, reading what's there to continue her notes. Her focus at the front of the room gives me a chance to sneak a peek at her face and damn if I can't stop the smile that appears. My mystery girl from the party. The one who wanted nothing more than to get as far away from me as possible the other night.

What's the saying you hear all the time? You can run, but you can't hide. Well, looks like I found my mystery girl after her disappearing act. Luck's on my side this time, though, because she's stuck with me for the next thirty minutes and I'm not letting her get away that easily.

BLAIRE

My skin tingles and I know he's still staring at me. My body has been on high alert ever since he sat down in the seat beside mine.

Never in a million years would I have thought I'd see Penis Guy again. Obviously, I knew there was a chance of running into him since we both go to the same college, but I'm a junior, and I figured this guy was a senior. I never would have thought we'd have the same classes since I've never seen him before.

The next thirty minutes go by in slow motion. Professor Darfman continues droning on and on with examples of different types of equations. I've sort of zoned out the last twenty minutes and focused on keeping my face hidden. The last thing I want is for him to recognize me as the girl who saw him with his junk in his hand and then ran away.

Class is dismissed five minutes early and everyone packs their things up and leaves the classroom, wasting no time.

He's still sitting next to me, not moving. With him on my left and the wall on my right, I'm trapped in my seat.

Taking a deep breath, I lift my hand to pin my hair behind my ear and turn toward him. Our eyes lock and the side of his mouth lifts.

"I knew it was you," he says, his smile growing.

I guess my hiding wasn't that great. Obviously, he'd remember my idiot stunt the other day. A quick sweep of the room and I notice we're the only ones left. Even if I wanted to, I couldn't leave. His chair is blocking my only escape route.

"My name's Camden," he says, breaking me from my thoughts.

Camden. I take in his face, from the dark hair that has messy curls on top and is lightly highlighted from the sun to the straight nose and the full lips. His eyes are his most beautiful feature. They are a clear green, but there is a thin ring of dark around the outside, making them appear bigger and his face more expressive. His skin is tanned, like he spends a lot of time out in the sun, and he has a splattering of freckles along his nose that makes him look more boyish. A dark brown beard covers the bottom half of his face, surrounding a pair of full lips.

"You going to tell me your name, sweetheart?" he asks, making me snap my eyes from his lips and up to meet his. He is staring at me intensely and I have to look away, focusing on my hands twined together on the desk.

Taking a deep breath, I clear my throat before speaking. "I-I'm Blaire."

"Blaire," he says slowly, as if feeling my name on his lips. The way his deep voice says my name makes the hairs on my arms stand up. My body has never had a reaction like this to someone simply saying my name.

Standing from his seat, Camden grabs his notebook from the desk and looks down at me. His eyes are boring into mine, his eyebrows drawn together, and I feel vulnerable for some reason, which I don't like.

"It's nice to officially meet you, Blaire. I'll see you around," he says, then makes his way to the classroom door.

I stare at the empty doorway for far too long, confused as hell at the reaction my body had to Camden. I've never felt this...this tingling all over when I was around anyone. I'm not sure how to feel about it yet.

CHAPTER FOUR

CAMDEN

Pushing through the bathroom door, I slam my notebook down on the sink counter and run my hands through my long hair. I really need to cut it, but I haven't had the time to go get it done.

Blaire is in my head, and I wasn't sure how someone I just met could make me feel this way. Her small, fragile form makes me want to protect her from the world. I've never felt this... this fierceness over anyone other than my little sister, Trazia, and my mother. But Blaire? Something inside me is saying that this girl needs protecting. From what, I am not sure.

I close my eyes, remembering the lost look in her eyes as she stared into my own. I could tell she tried to hide it, but there were glimpses when she let it slip. Looking up into the mirror, I stare back at my reflection. I don't know why, but I have this urge to run back to that room and be around Blaire. She drew me in. Not just her looks, but I'm not complaining about those either. Blaire is fucking hot. She has a rockin' body, with a generous chest and nice curves. Her skin is pale, like it hasn't been touched by the sun, and she has these big, gray eyes that look like nothing I've ever seen before. The color is so unique, they practically hypnotize you as they draw you in.

It was the vulnerability I saw when she looked at me. I don't think she meant for me to see it, but I noticed. Something is haunting her, and I want to know what it is.

I use the bathroom before heading to my next class. Without thinking, I search for Blaire, hoping we have this class together too. No luck, though. Someone calls out my name and I turn my head in the direction of the sound.

Fuck. This is not what I needed right now.

Chloe is sitting at one of the desks with the seat next to her empty. There are two girls in the seats ahead of hers turned around facing her, and they giggle as I take them in.

She smiles when I look at her, then points to the empty seat to her right. Yeah, there's no way in hell that's happening. I don't want to be anywhere near that girl and her annoying, high-pitched voice.

Someone slings their arm over my shoulder. Maddox is there with a toothpick hanging from his mouth.

"Well, what the hell are the chances, man? Looks like we get to enjoy some American lit together. Glad I don't have to suffer alone and you'll be here to keep me awake, because I'm betting you right fucking now, this shit is going to be boring as hell." He drops his arm and heads toward an empty table on the other side of the room as Chloe. *Thank God.*

Luckily, it isn't just Maddox and me in this class either. Two of our teammates, Levi, our roommate, and George, are also here with us.

Unlike my last class, this professor didn't decide to actually teach today. Smart man, since I don't think I can handle another hour and a half of boring lecturing.

He lets the class out after he finishes talking about the syllabus, and everyone makes a dash for the door.

Maddox and I are walking down the hallway, heading for the exit, when a slender hand latches onto my bicep. Stopping, Chloe is there to my right, sliding her fake nails up and down my forearm. Maddox continues walking toward the exit, leaving me alone with her. I'm not sure if she's clueless or just hell-bent on adding me to her tally of players she's banged.

"Can I help you?" I ask, making sure she can tell I'm annoyed by the tone of my voice.

She doesn't flinch at my harsh tone, which surprises me. Most girls would bitch me out or huff and stomp away. It didn't even seem to faze Chloe.

One of her hands starts massaging my bicep, and if I didn't want to get away from this chick so bad, it might actually feel good. But all I want is for her to leave me the hell alone.

"I don't have any more classes today. What do you say we get out of here, huh? My dorm is empty. Or we could head back to your place?" She bats her fake eyelashes at me. It takes every bit of self-control I have not to roll my eyes. Her vanilla perfume is overpowering my senses, and I'm suddenly not a fan of the smell of vanilla.

There was a time when this was the norm for me. Take a chick back to her place, bang her, and leave satisfied. For some reason, though, the idea of hooking up with Chloe, or anyone right now, doesn't entice me.

Gray eyes flash in my mind. *Blaire*. The thought of her excites me. Of seeing and talking to her. I want to go and find her, learn more about her. Just hearing that sweet, soft voice would be enough. Last thing I want is to deal with girls like Chloe, who only want me for one thing.

Detaching my arm from Chloe's hold, I step back away from her. "Uh, yeah, I'm going to have to pass on that. But thanks for the offer." Before she can say anything, I head back to Maddox and continue walking out the door with him at my side.

Once I'm safely outside, I can take a breath of fresh air.

"Want to talk about what all that was? You looked like Chloe was going to attack you or something. I've never seen you run from a girl before, and definitely not one as hot as her," Maddox says as he pulls a protein bar out of his backpack.

Shrugging my shoulders, I do a quick scan of the courtyard for Blaire, but she's nowhere around. "Nothing to talk about. She's just not taking no for an answer and I didn't feel like talking with her, that's all."

Maddox and I became good friends when we were paired as dormmates our freshman year. We're complete opposites in how we grew up. Me growing up in a lower income family with a mom who worked more than one job and him coming from money.

The problem with being friends with Maddox is that he is good at reading people, and I wish he'd stop his analyzing of me right now.

He lets out a loud laugh beside me and a hand comes down on my back. "Dude, I know you better than anyone and I know for a fact that you've never given up an easy lay. What's the deal?" Okay, so he may be loyal and down to earth, but yeah, we're both kind of pigs.

I contemplate telling him about Blaire. A part of me wants to tell him about her, but then there's this protective part that wants to keep her to myself. This sense to keep her safe from anything and everything.

"Dude, what's with you today?" Maddox asks.

Clearing my head of Blaire, I grab the protein bar out of his hand and shove the last half of it in my mouth. "Nothing. Let's head to practice," I say after swallowing.

GETTING Blaire out of my head was easier said than done.

All practice she was on my mind. I couldn't stop thinking about her beautiful face, her voice, and then that lost look in her eyes. This girl I didn't even know has consumed my thoughts and it's getting to me. I have always seen women as companions for a nice night. Scratch my back, I'll scratch yours kind of deal. Maybe that's what a need. Just a scratch to clear my Blaire itch.

Coach is pissed because I missed more than a handful of passes, but my head isn't in it. I'm trying to focus on my dribbling and making sure the passes to Maddox are precise, but my mind keeps drifting to Blaire. I need to see her again.

The whistle blows, ending practice for the day. We all head toward the locker room as Coach calls out my name.

He's standing with the assistant coaches but doesn't make any indication he wants me to come over, so I stand there and wait for him to say anything else.

"Don't know what the hell is going on with you today, but if this happens again tomorrow, your ass is benched for the first game, got it?" he calls out to me, then turns to the other coaches.

Freshman year, Coach and I went at it a lot. I was rebellious and didn't like being told what to do, especially by some guy I didn't know.

Growing up with a dad who left his family and a mom who worked too much to be around would do that to you. I grew up fast, having to raise my little sister and myself all on my own. When I got to Braxton, I still had the 'I'm my own boss' mentality. My first practice, though, Coach let the team know who was in charge from the beginning. I, being the rebel I am, wasn't having that. I would show up late to practice, acting like it was no big deal, go against his plays, and do my own thing.

That lasted all of two weeks. I got pulled into Coach's office for a 'talk' that consisted of me sitting there, not saying a word as he went into all the reasons he should have me kicked off the team and my scholarship revoked. That's when it all became a reality. I needed to get my head out of my ass and stay on track and finish what I came here for.

I'm met with the stench of sweat and too much cologne when I walk into the locker room. Most of the guys are in the showers, but some are already dressed and leaving. Walking over to my area, I hurry to get my extra clothes on to get the hell out of here, not bothering with a shower.

Just as I'm lacing up my sneakers, Maddox walks up to his locker next to mine. He's still in a towel after his shower. He grabs the boxers out of his bag and slides them on, making sure not to let the towel slip. Smart man, because if he had flashed me his junk, I'd beat his ass…again. Him being free-spirited and all, he did that shit our freshman year all the time, and I wasn't having it.

Maddox is a carefree kind of guy. He grew up in a filthy rich family and had everything handed to him his entire life. He never went without, unlike my sister and me. When we were paired as roommates freshman year, I was worried this spoiled, rich guy was going to be a bitch and not someone I wanted to be around, but surprisingly, he's one of the most down-to-earth people I've ever met. Practically being raised by a nanny will do that to you. I've met the woman who raised him, and she's a damn saint but doesn't put up with bullshit.

"You going to tell me what's up today or what? You're never off your game like that," Maddox asks as he slips his shirt on.

Leaning forward, I rest my elbows on my knees and run my hands through my hair. "It's this fucking girl. I haven't been able to get her out of my head all day…all weekend, really." I have thought about Blaire since seeing her at the party Saturday night, but now after talking to her and finding out her name, I'm fascinated.

"Hold up, you didn't hook up with anyone that night,"

Maddox states. He tosses the towel into the laundry bin after putting on his gym shorts and a T-shirt.

Opening my eyes, I look up at him. "Not someone I hooked up with, dipshit. I just kind of met her...well, she caught me taking a piss on the side of the house."

Maddox leans down and begins getting his shoes on. "That sounds romantic and all, but I don't see how that little interaction would leave an impression on you."

"She was different, man. She's smoking hot, but in this subtle way. It's as if she doesn't even know she's sexy. And her reaction to me was completely the opposite from the normal girls we see. She seemed almost...embarrassed when she caught me with my dick out. Not turned on or anything."

Maddox bends over, letting out a loud laugh that gets the attention of everyone around us. "What, you mean she didn't jump your bones at the sight of you?"

Fucking asshole. "No, she looked like it was going to attack her and then she bolted before I could even say anything to her."

He grabs his bag off the bench and slings it over his shoulder. "I'm really not seeing the fascination with this chick. Sounds like it's a waste of time. But if she's going to have you playing like that, fuck her and move on, man. We have a championship to win." He heads out the exit. I grab my bag and follow suit.

Part of me thinks it may be a waste of time. She didn't seem at all interested today when we talked for all of three minutes. But then there is this other part of me, the one that is intrigued by her and doesn't want to ignore this gut feeling I have that she's different and I need to get to know her. Blaire seems unlike the majority of girls at this school, who seem to only see me for my status and something they can brag about to their friends. The more I think about how the last two years have gone, the more I start to feel used. Sure, I got something out of it, but sometimes a guy wants to feel seen for more than his body and popularity.

CHAPTER FIVE

BLAIRE

O*h. My. Gosh.*
         Camden. His name is Camden and he's even better-looking with his pants around his waist. It was hard for me to concentrate seeing as how I've *seen him* in all his glory. He didn't act like he was worried about that, though. He seemed nice, kind even. But if I've learned anything, it's that even the sweetest and most trusting of people can destroy you.

My last class of the day is over, and Emree texted me earlier that we needed to go grocery shopping today because the apartment is completely empty. Luckily, we both just got paid, so we can splurge a little.

Emree and I both make good money waitressing at a local college hangout. It's not the most ideal job, but they're flexible with you on hours and the tips are what pay our rent. Most nights, we're both coming home with over two hundred dollars cash in tips alone. I only started a month ago and already have almost five hundred saved up, which is going to help me a lot in the future. Emree has been working there for the last year and scored me an interview the moment one of the girls graduated and moved.

Alongside waitressing, I also tutor math at the library. It isn't the best paying job, hence why I need to waitress, but it's fun for a math geek like me.

I head to the apartment to pick up Emree. I met her two summers ago through an ad on the school website. She had just finished her freshman year, like me, and was determined not to live in the dorms another year. I was planning on getting my own place anyway since sharing a dorm with another person was too close and I felt like I did not have any privacy. A small, one-bedroom apartment was what I was looking for, but I became discouraged seeing how expensive they could be. After seeing her post and considering life with a roommate, I thought it might be nice not to live on my own.

We met and instantly clicked, which is rare for me. Emree is outgoing, the complete opposite of me. Even though she likes to go to parties and hang out with a lot of people, she isn't the kind of friend to leave you out. She always encourages me to go out with her and genuinely seems bummed when I decline. Though she loves getting dressed up and going out, she also enjoys movie nights in with junk food and our coziest clothes. That is more my comfort level. My freshman year, I didn't make any friends, struggling to open myself up to new people. Emree makes it easy with her bubbly personality.

Since we moved in together, I've only gone out with her once. It was to the party I saw Camden at. She was surprised when I told her I would go. If I'm being honest, I was too. I'm not sure why that party was the one that finally made me say yes to her invite, but I'm sort of glad I went. Even though seeing Camden like that was completely uncomfortable and embarrassing, it was nice to get out and feel normal again. I haven't felt that way in years. Although it became too much for me too soon, I'm proud of myself for going in the first place.

Pulling into the apartment complex, I check for Emree's car

and it's in her usual spot. I text her that I'm here so that we can head out to the grocery store.

About three minutes later, she comes bouncing down the stairs in a colorful outfit and her hair in a high ponytail. As she gets closer, I take in what she's wearing. She has freaking unicorns on her leggings. I don't even know where you could get something like that.

She plops into the passenger seat, a big smile on her face when she looks over at me. "What's cooking, good-looking?" she asks.

I roll my eyes and put the car in reverse, backing out of the complex. "Emree, I've gotten used to your free-spirited nature, but what in the hell are you wearing?"

She looks down at her outfit, then back at me. "These are the new leggings I made. Are they not the cutest?" She lifts her leg to show them off better.

"There are unicorns on them," I state.

She gasps from beside me, dropping her leg. "I'm sorry, but are you saying you don't like my taste in fashion?"

"Um, no." I'm more of a neutral colors kind of person. Basic jeans and a T-shirt or tank are my go-to outfit.

Emree makes a tsking sound. "Blaire, my dear friend, you need to branch out. There is a world out there full of colorful outfits and sparkles. I could make some badass outfits for you."

Looking down at her unicorn-covered leg, I can't imagine myself ever wearing something like that. The funny thing is, it doesn't even look ridiculous on her like I know it would on me or the majority of people.

"I will have to just take your word for it, but thank you for the offer," I tell her. Emree's shoulders slump. She knows there is no way she can get me to ditch my staple wardrobe and venture out like she does.

"Fine. It's your loss, though. I'll just be the shiny friend of the group."

After pulling into the parking lot of Publix and putting the car in park, we climb out and she pulls a piece of paper with a list of what we need out of her bag.

"Okay, so I put together all the necessities, such as toilet paper, laundry soap, and of course peanut butter. We've been out for two days and I'm about to go crazy."

"We haven't been out of toilet paper or laundry soap for days," I say, confused, because we aren't out at all.

She folds the list up and tucks it into her purse again. "Not those things, the peanut butter, dork. I feel as if I'm going through withdrawals. We're going to need a backup in case this happens again."

We head into the grocery store on a hunt for peanut butter, and just a few other things.

"ALL RIGHT, that's the end of it," I say to Emree as I drop the last bag on the counter, along with the ten others.

Our small trip to the store turned into enough food to feed an army. She wouldn't tell me why she was getting this much food, just that we needed it for something.

"Go ahead and leave the pizza stuff out. We need to get to baking!" She puts away the rest of the food while I lay out the variety of frozen pizzas.

"You do know that premade pizza isn't cooking?"

Emree's meals are along the lines of cereal, Hot Pockets, and Pop-Tarts. Where I grew up, we never ate anything like that. Even leftovers were a no-no. It was always a variety of foods I could rarely pronounce and probably did not want to know I was eating.

She lifts her head from her bent-over position in front of

the fridge. "What are you talking about? We have to preheat the oven and put it in. Then wait for it to be ready. That's cooking, my dear. Oh, and don't forget cutting and plating. That is a culinary class in itself."

By the look on her face, I can tell she's completely serious. That makes me worried about any future meals that could lead to possible food poisoning. Luckily, I can cook, just not a fan of the actual act and only really know the basics.

Emree grabs two of the pizzas, opens them from their packaging, and places them on the racks in the oven. After she sets the timer, she begins opening chip bags and pouring them into large bowls she pulls down from the cupboards.

Perplexed as to what she's doing, I walk over to her. "So, what's all this food for?"

The bag in her hand pauses. From the corner of her eye, she looks over at me, but then begins to pour the rest of the chips into the bowl. "Oh, I just invited a few friends over."

While Emree grew up near this town and took the opportunity in her first two years here to meet new people, I did not. When she says 'friends,' what she means is hers, even though she would never word it like that. She always wants me to feel included.

Worrying about having people in our apartment, I ask, "How many people is a few? Because you bought enough food to feed at least a dozen," I ask.

Emree bites her lip and avoids eye contact with me. I have a feeling that there are going to be a lot more people than I'd be comfortable with very shortly.

"Emree..."

She lets out a huff and turns to face me. "Okay, I invited that guy from the party. He's super cute and sweet, Blaire. I swear, you'll love him. And he said he was only bringing a couple friends over. We're all in American lit, so we planned to get some studying done."

I'm sure they plan on doing a lot of 'studying.'

Crowds aren't my thing, but I've been working on that. I went to that party, even though I left early. I got a job at a local college hangout that, while completely out of my comfort zone, I have grown to love because of the people I work with. While the party was my big step, and I felt like that was major progress, having people in my personal area feels different.

My therapist has been encouraging me to step out of my comfort zone since I started seeing her my freshman year. She says to always make sure I feel safe, but try to push myself to a certain limit. Looking around my apartment, I feel like this is a place where I'm safe. I'm more comfortable here than I am anywhere else, so this should be fine. It *will* be fine. Maybe it will be better because I'm familiar here.

"Blaire?" Emree calls out, breaking me from my own thoughts. "It's been four years. You're a stronger woman now, not a young, naive kid. And I'm always here for you, no matter what. The moment you want them gone, it's done. They're out of here, okay?"

I nod because my throat is suddenly too dry to use.

Emree smiles and comes over to give me a hug. "You'll have fun, babe, I promise. Plus, you're in American lit also, and you're an English genius. You'll be our savior."

"Oh sure, just use me for my smarts," I say with an eye roll. "I'm going to go change real quick." There's nothing more uncomfortable than being in jeans all day, and if we're really studying, I want to be in something comfortable.

Heading toward my room in the back of the apartment, I shut and lock my door. It's always out of habit for me to lock any door after enclosing myself in a room. I can be home alone in my room, and the door will be locked. Same if I go to the bathroom. It's one of those subconscious actions I do.

After changing into a pair of workout bike shorts, which are my favorite lounging clothes since no actual working out takes place, and an oversized hoodie, I lie across the bed and continue reading from one of my favorite books, *Torn* by Carian Cole. This copy has gotten well-worn over the years, but that's to be expected when you read a book a few dozen times.

Reading has been my escape for years now. It's a way for me to get out of my own head, my own life, for a short period of time. Dr. Warren, my therapist, suggested it and ever since then, I've been addicted. There are several other worlds out there through books, ones that anyone can be a part of. For me, it's the best kind of therapy.

Time goes by as I get lost in the story of Toren and Kenzi, and before I know it, voices drift from the living room. Outside my window, the natural lighting has dimmed. The clock on my nightstand says it's just after seven. I must have gotten too into the book and lost track of time.

Once I climb off the bed, I toss my book onto my desk. Emree said they're planning on doing actual work, but I don't want to look like an idiot if I walk out there and it was all just a ploy.

Deciding to leave the textbooks in here, I unlock the door and follow the sound of the voices. Luckily, there aren't many people here. There are two guys, one being the man Emree was making out with on Saturday, and another girl in the living room, setting down textbooks. Emree is standing in front of the sink, talking to the guy from the soccer team she's been crushing on and was making out with at the party. The oven timer goes off and I wait for Emree to go get the pizzas out of it, but she doesn't move an inch.

Deciding to be a good friend and get the food out before it burns, I head over and grab one of the oven mitts. Just as I open it, the doorbell goes off. I leave that one to Emree since my hands are a bit full.

With two very hot pizzas in my hand, I close the oven door

with my leg and head over to the counter to get rid of these things before they burn a hole through the mitt.

Just as I'm turning around, the sound of a new voice comes from behind me. Everything from that point on happens in slow motion.

The pizza. The *hot* pizza.

The guy who was standing behind me.

Me swinging around.

The hot pizza in my hand colliding with a chest.

That chest belonging to the last person I wanted to see. Camden.

CHAPTER SIX

CAMDEN

I'm not sure what I did to deserve this kind of torture, but whatever it was, I don't think anyone should undergo this kind of cruel punishment.

My chest must be on fire. There is no other explanation for the pain. I've been kicked, studs up, in the balls on the soccer field and even that wasn't half as bad as this. No, this is how they torture people in other countries.

After what feels like hours, but in reality is probably a couple minutes, the pain slowly begins to become slightly tolerable. And I say that mildly. My eyes are shut and I'm lying on something hard. The ground, maybe? I don't remember going from a standing position to being on the floor, but with the kind of pain this shit is causing, anything could have happened.

Slowly, I peel my eyes open one at a time. The first thing I notice is that I am most definitely on the ground, and I have no recollection of how I got here. The second thing, though, well, the second thing is just about the best part of this entire situation.

Blaire.

She's kneeling and staring down at me, biting her full bottom lip and holding a wet rag in her hand. She's not looking at my face, though. She's looking lower…

Oh, right, my chest that was on fire just moments ago. Somehow between trying to figure out how I went from walking into the apartment of the girl Conrad is fascinated with to then seeing my Blaire, the burning chest got forgotten.

Wait, did I just say *my Blaire*? No. Why would I even think that? She's not mine. I barely even know her.

"Dude, are you okay?" someone asks from behind me. Turning to look, I see Conrad with his arm around the blonde he hooked up with a few days ago. Both are staring at the same spot that Blaire was. My chest.

Deciding to see what the fascination is all about, I look down.

What. The. Fuck?

There're blisters and red spots covering what used to be my chest. And the hair? Yeah, that's now gone. Not that I had much, but what little splattering I did have is probably burned off. My chest looks like I should be quarantined. I don't know why any of these people standing around haven't taken off running. If I knew this nasty shit wouldn't follow me, I'd be far gone by now.

Around the room, everyone is still staring at my chest, but no one has talked. "Anyone going to tell me what the hell happened here?" Ah, that got their attention away from the subject at hand. Now everyone seems to be completely fascinated by random spots in the room. Everyone, that is, but Blaire.

"You going to tell me what's going on, sweetheart?" I ask her, raising my eyebrow.

She looks around the room at all the people avoiding me, then her eyes meet mine again. "I—" She stops and takes a deep breath. "The pizza was in my hand, and I didn't know you were behind me and…and it's all just a blur. But I am so, so sorry, Camden. You have no idea how unbelievably sorry I am." Her words come out rushed, but somehow I was able to catch it all.

So, she's the one to cause this ugliness on my chest. I should be pissed. I should feel some sort of anger toward her for causing this amount of pain. But one look at her small body curled into herself like a defenseless little kitten, and there's no way I could be angry with her. She looks genuinely upset about hurting me.

Even though the pain is pretty bad, I don't want to make her feel any worse than she already does. Taking in a deep breath, I shift from my position lying on the ground, to sitting up. I would have made more of an effort to get farther up, but just that simple movement took a lot out of me.

Blaire bends down and grabs my shoulder. She looks back down at my chest, then bites that damn lip again. "Are you okay?" she asks, then rolls her eyes. "I don't know why I would even ask that. Obviously, you're not okay. That's obvious by the look of your chest."

Even through all her worry, she's adorable. Maybe it's the worry over me that makes her adorable.

Using every bit of strength I can muster up, I force myself to stand up. Blaire keeps a light touch on the back of my arm. I decide not to tell her that there's no point in doing that because it's not helping at all. Sometimes people just feel the need to help in any way they can.

Once I'm standing on both feet, I take in my appearance. My plain black, V-neck T-shirt is ripped right down the middle. Guessing one of the guys did that so they could assess the damage. The sores on my chest aren't looking any better and the pain has turned into a steady thud. It's like the burn has its own heartbeat. These are for sure going to look nastier in a day or so.

"There a bathroom?" I ask Blaire. Everyone else has drifted

their attention to conversations going on around them. The only ones still near me are Blaire, Conrad, and the chick Conrad has been seeing, who is Blaire's roommate.

She nods and points in the direction of the hallway. "It's that way. I'll show you." She sounds hesitant.

Before she moves, Blaire's friend gives her a strange look. I'm not sure what kind of girl signal that was, but Blaire gives her a reassuring nod back. She turns around and leads the way through the crowd of people toward the hallway.

Everyone watches us. No, they're watching her.

While most girls thrive off the attention they get, Blaire doesn't give any of them a second look. It's as if she doesn't even realize she's being watched. Not once on the walk to the bathroom does she look around. Her head stays straight the entire way. My roommate Mateo's eyes drift down toward her perfectly round ass, and I have to suppress the growl that wants to come out of me. Deciding not to call him out on it, I move slightly to the left to block his view. His eyes lift up and when he sees the look on my face, he laughs.

The bathroom is the last door on the right, and Blaire steps to the side to let me in. After turning the light on, I look in the mirror and assess the damage. The pain has become bearable. The light thud is still there, though. From the looks of my chest, you'd think it would hurt more.

The area that was exposed at the top of my shirt is the worst. Blisters have begun to form throughout the redness. There's still some lingering red sauce around my nipple, which makes me wonder if someone else wiped the burning, hot pizza off of me. When I look over at Blaire, I notice for the first time she's holding a washcloth with red spots and crusted pizza on it...and she has that same rag I saw earlier wrapped around her hand.

"What the fuck happened?" I reach forward for her hand, but she jumps back, slamming into the doorframe behind her.

Her face says it all, even if her body language didn't already. I scared her. Shit, I wasn't trying to, but I'm pissed as hell that she got hurt.

"I'm sorry," I say, making sure my voice is soft. "Will you let me see your hand? I just want to make sure you're okay."

She looks around, unsure of what to do, but after taking a shaky breath, she unwraps her hand.

Blaire is a timid person. She doesn't trust me, which makes sense because I am basically a stranger. I don't know what's happened to make her nervous, but I can tell letting me examine her hand is making her uncomfortable.

Ever so slowly, she lifts her arm until her hand is out in front of me. I take it, making sure to be careful of where she was burned and try not to startle her again.

Our hands touch. Blaire flinches.

I don't know if it's from the burn or the physical touch, but she doesn't pull away. With a small boost of confidence, I slide my hand around her wrist and flip it over so her palm is facing up and I unwrap the wet towel.

"Shit," I whisper.

Her hand is a bright red, much like my chest. Luckily, it doesn't look too bad. She has a light bubbling forming on her upper palm, but it's not horrible.

"What happened?" I ask. My fingers run along the edge of her palm, barely touching it. When they graze the aggravated skin, my fingers burn from the heat coming off of it.

Goose bumps form on Blaire's forearm. I lift my head to come eye to eye with her and she's biting her lip, staring down at her hand in mine.

"I grabbed the pan," she mumbles. It's barely above a whisper, and I'm confused by what she means. Pan? What pan?

Oh, my question.

"You grabbed a burning hot pan with your bare hand?" She

had gloves on when she ran into me with the pizza, so I'm not sure why she didn't then.

Blaire ducks her head, so I can't see her eyes. "The mitts fell off when I ran into you. The pan had fallen on your chest. I grabbed it so it wouldn't burn you worse than it already did." Her voice is low, but I hear every single word.

"Why would you do that?" I ask, completely shocked.

That full bottom lip makes its way between her teeth again, and Blaire shifts from foot to foot. "I just...you were burned, and I didn't know what to do."

There is a man with burning hot pizza on his chest and her first reaction is to go in with bare hands and grab it off his chest? Rational, I think not.

"That was really...stupid, you know that?" Her head snaps up as if I just insulted her. "What? The last thing you should have done was grab it without any mitts. Why create more damage by injuring yourself in the process?"

Letting out a little, adorable huff, she removes her hand from my grasp and crosses her arms over her chest, still clinging to the rag. "I'm *so* sorry for trying to help you. Next time I'll just let you lie there with hot pizza burning into your chest."

My eyebrows rise. "Next time, huh? You plan on burning me again?"

She uncrosses her arms and the rag slips between her fingers. "No, no. I just...I meant—"

"I'm only messing with you," I cut her off. The nervous stuttering wasn't what I was going for. "Why don't we get these burns cleaned up a little, yeah?" I ask, trying to do anything to get her to relax around me. I want Blaire comfortable in my presence.

Reaching down, I grab the discarded rag and turn the sink on, running it under the cold water. As I'm wiping the pizza sauce and cheese off my chest, I notice from the side that Blaire is still standing there, completely silent. Her hands are interlocked together, and the corner of her bottom lip is between her teeth.

Her gaze is focused right on my chest. And that look in her eyes, I know it all too well.

"Like what you see, baby?" I ask, not being shy about catching her checking me out.

Her head snaps up, that plump lip is released from her teeth, and her jaw drops. "No, no. I was...I was just checking out—I mean, looking at your chest—the burns! I was looking at the burns."

Making Blaire nervous might have just become my new favorite hobby.

"It's okay, baby, you can stare all you want." I give her a wink and hand her the rag, heading out the bathroom door.

She's still standing there as I head to my car to get the first aid kit. Being a soccer player means you always have some kind of injury. Keeping a first aid kit is survival 101 for us.

When I get back into the apartment, Blaire is now in the kitchen. She sees me and her cheeks redden as she ducks her head. Her friend—still haven't gotten her name—is beside her, checking out the burn on her hand.

Holding up the first aid kit, I say, "I come bearing ointment."

"Dude, you're such a Boy Scout." Conrad laughs from the far side of the couch. He rummages through his backpack for a second and comes out with a blue T-shirt. "Here, man, do us all a favor and cover up."

After removing the supplies I need from the first aid kit, I chuck the bag at his head. It hits him right above the ear. "There's some aspirin in there for that headache you're gonna have."

He flips me off and tosses the bag beside him.

"Here you go," I say, handing the cream over to Blaire's friend. "I'm Camden, by the way."

"Emree," she states, then begins applying the ointment to Blaire's hand. "So, how do you two know each other?"

I go to tell her the party story, but Blaire cuts me off. "We have a class together."

Ahh, so Blaire doesn't want to be completely truthful with how we really met. Well, I happen to love the story and feel the need to tell the world about our unusual encounter. "You're not going to tell her about the party, are you, Blaire?"

Her eyes widen and she tucks a piece of loose hair behind her ear.

Emree looks between us, analyzing. "Tell me what, exactly?" she questions.

There's a twinkle in Emree's eyes and nervousness in Blaire's.

"Your friend here caught me a bit...exposed that night." There's no classy way to explain a chick finding you mid-piss with your pants down.

CHAPTER SEVEN

BLAIRE

My face could not be any hotter than it is at this very moment.

"Care to explain?" Emree questions, leaning back and crossing her arms.

How do you explain walking around a corner and catching a guy with his pants down, and him doing nothing to cover his...stuff? Oh, and all while he is standing right in front of you.

"Pretty sure he said it all just a second ago," I snap. Emree's mouth drops and I don't blame her. I don't snap. Ever. Something's come over me. I didn't want to give Camden the satisfaction of my embarrassment that I know he would enjoy.

From behind me, someone blows out a drawn-out whistle. "Damn, this girl has got spunk."

The man Emree has been crushing on comes up beside me and reaches his hand out. "Hi, I'm Conrad. Nice to meet you, Blaire."

Biting down on my lip, I go to shake his hand, but Camden comes forward and grasps his friend's shoulders. Conrad drops his arm, and my jaw relaxes.

"Come on, man, let's get to that studying we came here to do," Camden says, directing his friend toward the living room where some other guy and a girl are sitting. He grabs the T-shirt his friend offered him and the ointment Emree applied to my hand, then heads to the bathroom, reappearing changed.

As I'm about to follow them, Emree grabs my non-burned hand. "Want to tell me what that was all about?" she asks.

"I can't," I tell her honestly. "I don't even know myself."

AN HOUR later and my brain is officially fried from all the bits of knowledge.

We've been studying American lit and calculus, because those are the classes we all have in common, and apparently, I'm the only one who enjoys school and has reviewed the syllabuses before the start of the first week. Our professor had assigned an assignment before the semester started. It was to write a paper on the most influential American authors' novels and why we think these works are still deemed classics. I, of course, chose *The Scarlet Letter*, one of my favorite classic novels.

No one else here read any of the suggested material or even looked at the reading assignment, so we've spent the majority of the time going through the different authors and poets on the approved list. Glad our professor clarified, because the moment Emree heard we had to write about an author, she ran to grab her *Fifty Shades of Grey* collection. I don't think our middle-aged male professor would enjoy an erotica novel. Or maybe he would. Who am I to judge? Plus, the author isn't American, but I doubt Emree knows that.

Emree leans back from her seated position on the floor and

lets out a dramatic yawn. "All right, guys, as much fun as it's been having you here, I'm exhausted."

Conrad leans forward and bites her shoulder. "You kicking me out already?"

She giggles, and I swear I have never heard anything close to that sound come out of her mouth before. "You're more than welcome to stay, but I really am tired," she tells him honestly.

He pouts.

I just witnessed a grown man pout for the very first time.

"Fine, fine. We'll get out of here."

Everyone starts packing up their things, and I can't help but notice Camden. He's sitting on the couch alongside me, but on the opposite end, leaving a cushion of space between us. While Mateo and Jules, his other friends I was introduced to earlier, load their backpacks up with books and notes, he doesn't move a muscle. He's looking down at his phone.

Without breaking eye contact from his device, his position changes from sitting upright to lying on the couch. With the shift and his closeness, I get a whiff of his scent. It's spicy and I get the faintest smell of sunscreen mixed in.

His head is right beside my leg and the top of his hair is tickling my lower thigh that is exposed in the shorts I am wearing. I try to move away from him, but I'm already practically hugging the armrest. "Blaire, darling, what's your last name?" he asks me, still not looking away from his phone.

Confused by the random question, I ask, "Why?"

He lets out an exaggerated sigh. "Because, Blaire, I need it."

"No."

The phone he has glued to his face lowers, and he looks into my eyes from his upside-down position. "Did you just say no?"

I nod.

"What do you think I'll do with your last name? Honestly, what kind of crap can I do to you with just knowing your full name?"

Good question, and I don't have an answer for it. "I don't know, but I'm not giving it up unless you tell me why you want to know it."

He lifts his phone and shows me the screen. "I'm looking you up on Facebook, dork." On the screen is a list of girls named Blaire in the search bar. None of them are me.

"I'm not on Facebook."

The phone falls from Camden's hands and lands on his stomach. "You're joking," he states.

That's basically what every person's reaction is when I tell them this. Apparently, you can't be normal if you don't have some form of social media. I mean, I get it because I used to be glued to my phone, but now I love the freeness I feel without that.

"Nope, so you can stop searching the millions of Blaires you're going to come across. I'm nowhere there."

He sits up and stretches. "Fine, don't tell me your last name. I'll just have to woo you into giving it to me." He sits up, tucking his phone into the front of his jeans.

"Woo me?" I ask, confused.

He runs his hands down his thighs and stands. "Yep, woo. You know, impress you and stuff. You'll be completely wooed."

"You're crazy," I tell him, stifling a laugh. I have never met anyone like Camden before. He oozes confidence, but not in an arrogant way. He makes me feel somewhat relaxed, and it's been a long time since I have felt that way around a guy. Trusting men has gotten me into trouble in the past and I have put up these walls to protect myself for so long, I forgot what it is like to feel...normal.

"Let's go, Camden," Conrad calls out.

"You'll be wooed by my crazy in no time, Blaire 'no last name.'" He winks, then slings his backpack over his shoulder, heading toward the front door with his friends.

Once everyone is out of the apartment, I start picking up

the empty plates and bowls of chips. There's spilled salsa under a bag of chips that I'm going to guess someone tried to hide. I'll leave that one for Emree to pick up.

"Blaire Elaine Wentworth, you have some explaining to do," Em says from behind the couch.

I shiver at hearing my middle name. My mother's name. "You know how much I hate being called that." I stick her with my not-so-serious face, and she laughs at my attempt of being tough.

"Oh, I know just how much you hate when I pull out the full name, but the situation calls for it." After wiping up the salsa spill and tossing the dirty paper towel in the sink, she plops down on the couch, the very one Camden and I were just on, and tucks her legs under her. "Now explain to me this Camden guy and the flirting I witnessed tonight."

"Oh no, no. There was definitely no flirting going on." Shaking my head, I sink into the couch on the other side of her. "Flirting isn't even in my vocabulary, Em." To be honest, I can't even remember the last time I flirted. If there was ever a time.

Blowing out a breath, Emree rolls her eyes at me. "I've seen flirting, Blaire, and it was for sure going on tonight. Him too. He is totally into you, and I saw the way you were checking out his chest when that shirt was ripped."

The heat coming off my face is hard to hide, because I can't help but think of Camden's chest at the mention of it.

Being twenty, you're supposed to have all these experiences with the opposite sex. Unfortunately, I'm lacking in that department. I have been on exactly one date when I was sixteen and it has haunted me for the last four years.

"I'm not a nun, Emree. Of course, he is an attractive guy, but that doesn't mean I was flirting or that I even like him." Does it? Is it even flirting if I don't have the slightest clue what flirting looks like?

Stretching out her legs after sitting on them, Emree stands

and twists her back, letting out a crack. "You keep telling your-self that, babe, but I know what I saw. You may not think it was flirting, but I saw you with Camden. There are for sure sparks there, whether you want to deny it or not." She gives me a soft smile and squeezes my knee. "He seems like a nice guy, Blaire. Maybe this is it, the next step. I'm not saying go out and maul the man, but maybe start out as friends? Let him gain the trust you gave me."

She leaves me sitting there with a million and one thoughts running through my mind. Trust is something I gave away too easily before. It was broken by people I thought were my friends. People who were supposed to be there to support and love me.

CHAPTER EIGHT

BLAIRE

Thursday morning, I wake up feeling better than I have in a long time after a peaceful night of sleep. While the nightmares have been far less present with the help of my therapist, I still wake up startled and covered in my own sweat, soaking the sheets. This morning, though, there is no nightmare, but instead, I had a peaceful dream. Today I woke with a brand-new thought: Camden Collins.

In my dream, I was reliving the events of last night. It was my closest interaction with a guy since high school. Even if it did result in bodily harm, I can't help but smile at the feeling of how...normal it was. Being around Camden made me feel like any old average college kid. In the two years I've been at Braxton, it was a first. During my time here, I have alienated myself from most people at school, until Emree. Since we have known each other, she has wanted me to come out of my shell and meet more people. All at my own pace, of course. She has never pushed me, but some slight nudging has occurred.

Over the two years here, I have kept to myself, but in the back of my mind, I have been yearning for a normal college experience. Maybe it's finally my time. I trust Emree not to steer me in the direction of something bad. I should be able to be friends with the people who she thinks are good people and is comfortable around.

Thursdays and Fridays are the only two days I don't have classes, so I use this time for studying and tutoring. Last fall, my math professor was impressed with my assignments and test scores, so he asked if I wanted to work in the library and make a few extra bucks tutoring. Spending my time in the library sounded perfect to me. Gives me time to catch up on my own studies, as well as the hundreds of unread books on my Kindle.

The four-hour shift starts out slow, and by hour two I'm all caught up on assignments for the first week of class. Just as I'm about to dive into my Kindle, the tutoring leader, Michael, comes over to the table where I made myself at home.

"How's it going, Blaire? Exciting stuff, huh?" he jokes. When I signed up to tutor, Michael had cautioned me that this wouldn't be the most thrilling job, especially in the beginning of the semester. Not many students are looking for a tutor until they realize how difficult the class is, which is usually after the first test. In all honesty, getting the help in the beginning to give yourself tools for the rest of the semester would be smarter.

"Not too bad, actually. Was able to catch up on my own studies, so that's a plus," I answer him, pointing to my stack of books.

He laughs. "That's great you're all caught up. We have a student looking for some tutoring in American literature, and since Selena just left, I was wondering if you'd be able to help him out?"

Math was the only subject I signed up to tutor in since it's my strongest. Though English is a close second. "Sure, no problem, Michael."

His face lights up. "That's great. The only other tutor I have here is a science major and, well...he was one of the students going to Selena for English tutoring last semester."

I let out an awkward laugh, not sure what else to say to that.

"I'll go ahead and grab his paperwork and send him your way."

After Michael walks off, I put my Kindle away, slightly bummed I wasn't able to catch up on some fun reading. Too distracted gathering my American lit books and notes, I don't notice someone has approached until I hear the clearing of a throat.

"Well, if it isn't my lucky day," a familiar voice says.

My body freezes and my head snaps up. Of all people who could walk in here looking for help in a class, of course it is Camden Collins who shows. And just as our English tutor has left for the day.

After staring at him for an awkward amount of time, I finally speak up. "You're the student I'm tutoring?"

"Sure am, Teach," he says, plopping down in the seat across from me. He's flashing me the warmest smile, and I can't help but get lost in his features. The tanned skin, white teeth, and those bright green eyes. He was the last person I wanted to see today, yet here he is. The universe works in the crappiest of ways.

"Um, okay then." Taking a deep breath, I slowly let it out, trying not to make a sound and have him notice. My nerves are all jumbled around, and I've forgotten what subject we're supposed to be studying.

Camden grabs the American lit textbook from his backpack, and I follow his lead, grabbing my own. Luckily, I'm taking the same class, so it will help with the assignments he has any questions about. Not my luck that I now have to spend an unknown amount of time with the guy I have not been able to stop thinking about for days and would like to avoid.

"You know, when I came here, I assumed my tutor would be

some pimple-faced, glasses-wearing nerd. This comes as a surprise, Miss *Wentworth*," he says my last name with a cocky tone.

My eyebrows rise in surprise. "How'd you find out my last name?" When I told him I wasn't on social media, it was not a lie. No Facebook, Instagram, or Twitter. All that was gone the moment I started college and wanted a fresh start.

"Professor Darfman's discussion board," he says in a matter-of-fact way. "Since you were sticking to your guns and wouldn't tell me when I asked at your apartment yesterday, I had to resort to snooping. Our lovely professor has all the students' names and emails on there. Took me some time, since the Ws are so far at the bottom and he had a ridiculous amount of students, but I eventually got there."

Wow. Can't deny he is a determined one. "I applaud the use of resources and creativity," I tell him. "Now, Michael told me you're here for English. That's not my strongest subject, but I'm sure I will be able to help."

Camden stares straight into my eyes while I talk, without breaking contact. Something tingles in the depths of my stomach at the way he looks at me. An almost awkward amount of time goes by before either of us says anything.

"I've never seen someone with such unique eyes," he says. "Are they…gray?"

I can't help but drop my head down. My eyes have always been my most unique feature, one I got from my mom. When I was younger, everyone—from strangers to friends—would comment about how my mother and I were twins with our gray eyes and dark brown hair with natural highlights. That was, until my mother started graying and went mostly blonde.

Warm fingers clasp my chin, and he slowly lifts my head up, bringing my face back in front of his. I can't help but notice I do not have the normal repulsed feeling I get when people touch me.

"Don't do that," he says. "I like looking at your eyes. They're so unique, I was starting to wonder if they were contacts."

I smile and he releases my chin. "You would be surprised at how often people say that to my mom and me." I laugh, thinking about a time my mom got up close and personal with someone who didn't believe her, and my mother, who has put etiquette above anything else, made a point to touch her eye to prove there were no contacts there.

Camden smiles. "Definitely nice to see."

I grab my English textbook. "Well, seeing as the semester just started, I'm going to assume you don't need help with assignments?"

Shaking his head, Camden lets out a laugh. "No, no. I only have two difficult classes this semester and struggled with English last year. Wanted to get ahead of it. Coach has been on my ass about my grades since freshman year. Hoping to impress him this year."

"What is your major?"

The excitement on his face is cute. "Kinesiology. The human body is fascinating, and I would love to do that if my plan A doesn't work out."

My interest is piqued at the mention of his plan. "You play a sport for the school." It's more of a statement and less of a question.

He answers anyway. "Yeah, soccer. You're looking at the team captain and left striker, baby." He leans back in his chair and clasps his hands behind his head, smiling proudly. "You should come to our first game. Seeing as how our two friends seem to be all over each other, I assume she'll be going as well."

"I've never been to a sports game," I tell him quietly.

He smiles. "Well, we're just going to have to rectify that now, aren't we?" After a short pause, he asks, "What about you? What degree are you working for?"

Smiling, I answer, "Teaching. Hopefully, middle or high school math."

His eyebrows widen. "Wow, that would be great. I guess this tutoring is good practice for you then."

"Pretty much. I have always felt this urge to teach and help people and would love to be able to work with kids."

He smiles and studies my face but does not respond. The corners of my mouth lift, matching his. Camden has an infectious smile and by the look in his eyes, I can tell he knows this.

Clearing my head, I grab the class syllabus. "Enough chitchat. How about we get an early start on the final class assignment since it is worth thirty percent of your grade? We talked a little about it during our study night, but I'm assuming you haven't picked a book yet?" I ask him.

The class assignment is something we discussed last night. The same assignment that only I knew about. Camden, especially, seemed less than enthusiastic about the essay on an influential American author novel.

"All these books sound boring as hell," he says after reading through the list our professor provided. "I don't get why we have to continue reading these books from over a hundred years ago. I'm sure there're newer authors we could be studying who are much more entertaining."

I can't help but smile at his mini rant because he has a valid point. "Yes, but then we wouldn't sound as sophisticated if we didn't read a classic like *The Catcher in the Rye* or *The Scarlet Letter*." Glancing down at the list of novels, one catches my eye. "Hey, what about *The Great Gatsby*? That may keep your attention. Millionaires, extravagant parties, and sex? What guy wouldn't enjoy that? Plus, F. Scott Fitzgerald is an excellent writer."

He thinks it over. "Wait, is that the one about that guy who snorts coke off a chick's ass?" he asks.

I roll my eyes. "No, that's another Leo DiCaprio movie."

70

His shoulders slump just slightly. "Damn, that would have made the novel more enjoyable." After reading the short description of *The Great Gatsby*, he sets the paper down. "Okay, you've piqued my interest with the millionaires, extravagant parties, and sex that you so surely think I will enjoy." His smirk at the word sex makes my breath hitch and he takes notice.

Ignoring the enjoyment he is getting from my reaction, I say, "Why don't we go check it out from the library and get started with how to prepare for your essay?"

We stand at the same time and head toward the books, leaving our stuff at the table. There are very few people in here, so I don't worry about someone taking our things.

As we walk toward the classical fiction section of the library, I can't help but notice Camden's arm grazing mine as we walk side by side or the goose bumps that appear at the simple touch. My normal reaction would be to step away. Physical contact has been something I have avoided for four years. At first, it made me physically ill. A simple hug would send me running to the bathroom, retching into the toilet. Over time and with the help from my therapist and Emree, I have gotten better. I still don't initiate physical touch, but now it makes me only slightly uncomfortable.

Camden's simple touch doesn't send me running, though. The hair from his tanned arm tickles mine and every so often I feel a slight static shock. He's warm. I can feel his body heat beside me, like a human space heater.

We stop in front of the classical fiction section. I take a slight step away, needing the distance. He starts looking through the books on the row at eye level. "What's the dude's name again?" he asks.

"F. Scott Fitzgerald."

He turns to me with a questioning look. "You think he'd be under the Ss or Fs? Man has to make it difficult having two last names," he scoffs.

His question makes me wonder too. Two last names do make it difficult when categorizing an author's name in a library. "Not sure," I say. "How about you take the Ss and I'll take the Fs."

He nods in agreement, and we part ways in search of the novel.

AN HOUR LATER, Camden has all the tools he needs to write an A+ essay. He is still skeptical about the novel, but I think that is just because he isn't much of a reader. I wrote out a guide for him on what notes to take while reading *The Great Gatsby* and specific questions to keep in mind that he can incorporate into his essay. If he focuses on the tools I provided for him, he'll be fine.

I start closing my textbooks and stuffing them into my backpack. "Well, I'm glad I could be of help to you. I truly hope you enjoy the book. It really is a great classic."

He leans back and his eyes are slightly squinted as he watches my every move. "You should go out with me," he says casually.

I pause. That was not something I expected to come out of his mouth. I haven't been asked out in…well, four years.

"Oh, um," I stutter. Words are not forming correctly and I'm having a hard time coming up with a response.

He grabs his textbook. "Just think about it." He smiles and heads out of the library, leaving me completely speechless.

CHAPTER NINE

CAMDEN

Sweat drips off my forehead and is streaming down my face. I lift the bottom of my shirt and swipe it from forehead to chin. Coach is running us hard during practice with the most brutal drills. Two of my teammates are off on the sideline, vomiting up their breakfast, Maddox is by the benches, drenching his head with his water bottle, and Conrad is lying flat on his back, trying to catch his breath.

Suicides are the most perfect name for the drill we just completed.

Our team was on a winning streak last year, ultimately gaining the title of NCAA Men's Soccer Champions. A title I so proudly wear.

This year is different, though. We lost three of our best players as well as our team captain due to them being seniors and graduating. To say our team took a shift in our performance would be putting it lightly.

We have lost our dynamic, and with our first game coming up, we need to get it back. Like now.

Coach blows his whistle, gaining everyone's attention. We've been at this practice for over two hours now and I know all the guys have reached their limit. "Get your sorry asses over here," he shouts.

Not wanting to piss him off and get on his bad side, we all drag our bodies toward Coach by the goal and I drop my body to the ground in front of the team. Coach goes on about how we need to come back from the loss of our last year's seniors and get our heads out of our asses to win another championship this year. I understand the need for a pep talk, but it's not like all of us don't know this.

"All right, men, hit the showers. Today was better than it's been the last few weeks. We need to get it perfect before the game against Cornwall. We nearly let them win last year and I'll be damned if I give their sorry excuse of a coach any hope for that championship," he says. Coach Walters and the Cornwall coach, Brian Hanson, have had beef between the two of them that none of us can understand. Maddox thinks it has to do with some chick since Hanson is known for being a player, even well into his forties.

We all moan and groan as we head into the locker room. No matter how many times the janitors clean this place, it has a permanent stench of sweat, BO, and Icy Hot.

Stripping out of my sweat-drenched uniform, I wrap my towel around my waist and head for the showers. They are all divided by a wall a little over waist height and I silently thank whoever designed this locker room because it's better than the ones where we're all just standing around naked, just a few feet away from each other. I love my teammates like family, but some things are just...too close.

After washing off the sweat and dirt and rewrapping my towel, I head back to my locker to get dressed. Maddox, Conrad, Levi, and Mateo are all hanging around talking. Maddox is the only one fully dressed and running a towel through his long, dark blond hair, then securing it back in his usual bun. I slip on my boxers under the towel and once they are secured, I toss it into the rolling hamper in the corner.

"We heading to Whiskey Joe's tonight?" Maddox asks.

It's Friday night and since Coach has a conference this weekend, we get two free days of no practices. During the season, we are all pretty good about not overdoing it with parties or drinking. If we go out tonight, though, we should all be fully recovered by Monday's practice. Next week's practices are sure to be strenuous with our game being that Saturday.

I tug my jeans on and grab a shirt out of my gym bag. "Whiskey Joe's sounds good to me," I say. Hanging with the guys and having a drink or two sounds like a better night than going home and thinking of reasons not to drive to Blaire's apartment.

When I blurted out that she should go on a date with me, I wasn't thinking clearly. It was on impulse. Not that I wouldn't jump at the chance to take Blaire out, but I get the feeling she hasn't dated much, if at all. She's timid and shy, two things I don't particularly look for in a woman. I have always been more interested in the experienced and confident type. But there is something about Blaire that draws me to her.

Conrad slings his gym bag over his shoulder after tossing his towel in the hamper. "I think Emree is working tonight, so you know I'm down," he states.

Emree. As in Blaire's roommate. "Your girl works at Whiskey Joe's?" I ask, trying not to sound too interested. Gaining any information about Blaire's life is all I'm after.

He doesn't seem to question why I'm asking about the girl he's been hooking up with the last week. "First off, not my girl. Second, yeah, she's been working there for a while."

Conrad has never been the dating type. Hell, neither have I, but at least I don't string girls along like he does each semester. Usually, he will find a girl at the beginning of the semester and keep her as a casual hookup, although every time they think they can get him to settle down and finally be in a relationship. I don't see this one being any different than those of the past.

"All right, y'all want to leave around what, eight? I can schedule an Uber to pick us up," says Levi. He has always been like the dad of our group, making sure we are being responsible.

"Fuck yeah, I'm ready to get plastered tonight, boys," Maddox shouts.

I wince, hoping none of the coaches heard him. "You want to say that a little louder so the coaches come in here and kick our asses?" I whisper to him.

He shrugs his shoulders. "What're they going to do? We're college students. We are expected to drink, party, and have sex. It's a rite of passage."

There is no stopping Maddox when he's in this mood. Guy came to college and decided to live this worry and carefree life. Part of me thinks it's because of his life before college living with a strict, yet distant, family.

"You know Coach Walters has a zero-tolerance policy for drinking during the season," Mateo says. Out of the five of us, Mateo is the one who takes soccer the most serious. Don't get me wrong, I keep my head on straight, but Mateo's entire life has been soccer since he first touched a ball.

Maddox rolls his eyes and grabs his bag. "Whatever. We have two days off. I'm getting hammered tonight. Meet y'all back at the house. Going to see if Chloe is available to blow off some steam." He walks out of the locker room.

Levi schedules the Uber to pick us up at eight tonight and after we're all dressed, we grab our bags and head out to the parking lot.

Whiskey Joe's is a popular hangout near campus. It has been owned by the same guy—ironically his name is Brad and not even Joe—for the last thirty years. He is older now, well into his sixties, and isn't around the bar as much. His son, Garrett, manages it now and does a fine job of hiring mostly college kids, especially hot girls, and avoiding the cops with the number of times he lets it slide that many of us are under the drinking age. His lax rules on serving people under twenty-one is probably why it is such a popular place for Braxton U students.

The Uber picks us up just after eight and the five of us squeeze our bodies into the tight Honda CR-V. Maddox ends up sitting in the trunk since Levi didn't think to order a vehicle that can fit more than four passengers.

Levi's elbow is jammed into my ribs, and I glare at him. "You realize there is a fucking option to list how many passengers you have, right?" I grind out through my teeth.

He shrugs his shoulders, relieving the pressure of his elbow in my abdomen. "Didn't really consider the driver when I said a five-person vehicle," he says innocently.

The driver jerks to a stop once we are outside of Whiskey Joe's. I look back at Levi. "Remember that before we leave or I'm making you walk home," I say before exiting the SUV.

Eight is still early for there to be a lot of people at the bar, but there is a good-sized crowd filtering outside. It is August and Florida's humidity has been brutal this summer, so there are several fans out on the patio.

After the rest of the guys exit the car, Maddox having to wait for someone to open the trunk, we head toward the front door. Once inside, the music is loud and there are bodies everywhere.

Whiskey Joe's vibe is a mixture of a sports bar and, on the weekends, a tame club. On the right, the bar runs along the length of the wall and is filled with stools and a variety of liquors displayed on shelves in the back. That area is more lit than the rest of the place with hanging light fixtures above. The open space in the middle and the right side of the building is littered with red leather booths and tables that don't have matching chairs. Most are occupied by groups of people leaning together in conversation. Straight ahead, past the tables, is a large open area with a stage that has a DJ on weekends. The open space is filled with bodies grinding against each other under the multicolored lights.

Outside the doors by the booths, there is an area that has fake grass on the floor and a few different sets of patio furniture. Games like cornhole, table tennis, and giant Jenga are set up for people to play.

We're able to snag a table far enough away from the loud music on the dance floor. Conrad is looking all over, I'm assuming trying to find Emree. There are a few staff walking around with trays of drinks or food, but I don't spot Emree's long, blonde hair anywhere.

"She a bartender here or something?" I ask.

He doesn't look my way, still trying to find her. "Waitress, I think." Something catches his attention. "Oh, there's her roommate. I'll go ask her where Emree is."

At the mention of Blaire, my body tenses. When I glance in the direction Conrad is now heading, my jaw drops. Unlike the rest of the waitresses working here who wear the tightest clothes that reveal the most cleavage, Blaire is in a loose-fitting pair of dark blue jeans with large holes in them and a green tank top that ends right where the top of her jeans starts. She has very little makeup on, but what she is wearing makes her eyes pop even from where I'm sitting. Her hair is hanging in loose curls past her breasts and the top half is pulled back away from her face.

When she sees Conrad approach her, I can tell she tenses up just for a moment before becoming more relaxed. She gives him a small smile and after he says something to her, she points to the side of the bar. Over there, Emree is picking up an order of drinks I'm assuming is for the table she is waiting on.

Conrad heads in her direction, giving a wave to Blaire as he walks off. She smiles back and when she turns to walk away from him, her gaze meets mine and that smile grows even wider before she ducks her head, hiding those gray orbs from me. She grabs a few menus from the side of the bar and approaches us.

"Hey," she says to me, "what are you all doing here?"

Leaning forward, I can't help but smile at her. Now that she is closer, I can see the hint of red lip gloss on her lips and if that isn't the sexiest thing a girl could wear, I don't know what is. "The guys and I have a practice-free weekend, so we figured we'd come here for a few drinks. Plus, Conrad wouldn't shut up about your roommate over there." I point toward the two of them making out, the drinks on Emree's tray forgotten.

Blaire looks over as Conrad pins Emree to the wall. "Oh no, she better not get caught. Garrett's already in a bad mood after having to throw out a group of guys for groping her earlier." Blaire sighs, shuddering at the end.

At the mention of someone groping Emree, my body goes ridged. "Are you shitting me?"

She flinches at the harsh tone of my voice.

I take a deep breath, not wanting to scare her. "I'm sorry, it's just...do guys mess with you here?" I ask quietly. The thought of someone touching Blaire, especially without her consent, infuriates me.

She stares at me for a moment, her eyebrows drawn together. "Um, we sometimes get people who drink too much and are rowdy. Garrett is pretty good about keeping an eye out for groups that are heading in that direction. The guy who grabbed Emree's butt tonight has been hitting on her for a while now and hasn't taken no for an answer. Garrett banned him from the bar and threatened to call the police if he ever came back."

I'm glad to hear Garrett takes the safety of his employees seriously. Some fucked-up shit happens to women on college campuses—hell, anywhere really. The school has put in a strict buddy system policy in place and campus security is more alert during nighttime classes and around the dorms.

Reaching forward, I rest my hand on Blaire's hip. She stiffens but doesn't pull away. "You feel safe working here, right? Nobody's fucked with you?"

She glances down at my hand, and I tighten my grip. She bites her lower lip and looks back up at me. "Yeah," she whispers, "I really don't even get hit on. Pretty sure I dress like a prude compared to what the rest of the girls here wear." She doesn't say it in a slut-shaming way, laughing lightly.

This chick has no idea how unbelievably attractive she is. Maybe that is part of her charm. She doesn't stick her chest out or flutter her eyes like some girls do. She's just herself. "I quite like the prude look, if I do say so myself." I wink at her and the lightest of pink creeps across her cheeks.

Blaire drops her head and takes a step out of my grasp. "Please don't say stuff like that," she says quietly. Her fingers are gripping the menus she hasn't passed out to the table yet.

"Did I make you uncomfortable?"

She takes a deep breath. "No. Yes. I mean, I don't know. I'm just...I'm not used to that kind of thing," she says honestly.

"What kind of thing? Compliments?" I ask.

"No. Flirting."

"Blaire, baby, you think I was flirting with you?" I tease her.

Her eyes widen and her mouth drops open. "Wait, um, no. No, I didn't think you were flirting. I—"

"Blaire, I'm messing with you," I cut her off.

"Hey, babe, we ever going to get those menus and be able to order some drinks?" Maddox asks from the other end of the table. "You and my boy are cute and all cuddled up over there, but some of us aren't getting any from you and need some booze and food before we hook up tonight."

I groan. "Shut the fuck up, man, and watch what you say to her."

Blaire scrambles to hand the menus out and grabs her notepad and pen to take our drink orders. Conrad reappears, his hair more disheveled than before.

"Blaire, you our lovely waitress for the night?" he asks before sliding onto a stool across from me.

She quickly scribbles down the bucket of Corona, a beer pretzel, and five tequila shots that Maddox orders. "Yeah. Sorry it isn't Emree, but seeing how Garrett is probably lecturing her in the corner over there, I am going to assume it's for the best. What can I get you?"

"How about whatever IPA you have on tap and an order of pork nachos?"

She writes down his order, as well as Levi's Jack and Coke and Mateo's Budweiser and chicken quesadilla.

She takes a deep breath and turns to me. "What can I get you, Camden?" Damn, my name on her lips sends a jolt to my dick.

"I'll take some buffalo wings and an old fashioned," I tell her. She writes it down and leaves our table as quickly as possible.

"Dude, you tapping that or something because I figured if you're banging the chick, she'd be a little less skittish around you?" Maddox asks. "Also, your drink and food combo is vile and I don't understand how you eat those two together." His gaze is focused on a blonde grinding against her friend on the small dance floor near the stage where they sometimes have live music, unlike tonight.

Something has crawled up Maddox's ass because he's being more of a dick lately.

"You want to cut the shit, man? Don't know what is going on, but you are seriously starting to get on my last nerve. I'm not banging Blaire. I like her. And yeah, you can like a woman without fucking her," I say harshly.

"Whatever." He stands and heads toward the blonde and her friend. Both girls smile when he approaches and sandwiches himself between them, grinding his hips into the blonde as he snakes his arms around to rest on her hips. The friend runs her hand up and down Maddox's sides and he throws his head back, resting it on her shoulder.

Something is going on with him. He's drinking too much, sleeping around more than usual, and based on his carelessness in the locker room today, he's getting sloppy around Coach. Whatever it is, he needs to get it together before our first game.

CHAPTER TEN

BLAIRE

After putting my orders in with the bartender and kitchen, I head to the bathroom to collect my thoughts and take a few deep breaths.

My heart is racing too fast, and I feel like I can't catch my breath. Not because of being scared or nervous around Camden, but because of the way my body reacts to him being close to me, like touching my hip the way he did. Something like that shouldn't make me feel hot all over. I haven't ever felt like that with a guy being close. Normally, I break out in a sweat and want to make a run for it. When Camden touched me, I wanted to lean into it.

For so long I have felt broken, unable to move past what happened to me when I was sixteen. Maybe this is what my therapist told me about. The moment I find my safety. The person who feels like home to me. She said I needed to trust my instincts when it came to meeting new people. I did it when I met Emree and got a best friend out of it.

I'm not sure if I feel safe around Camden, but after seeing his reaction when I told him about the guy groping Emree, I know he won't hurt me. He was angry, and at first it scared me until I realized he was angry *for* Emree and at the guy who touched her. His friend, Maddox, was kind of a jerk, but one of the other guys was at our study session earlier this week and seemed nice. Conrad and Emree have been seeing each other and he has been by the apartment occasionally to pick her up or hang out in her room. I haven't spoken to him too much, but he seems nice too, and Emree seems to like him a lot.

As I'm dragging a cold paper towel across my neck to cool myself off, two girls walk in. They're giggling and leaning against each other and the blonde stops when she almost bumps into me. "Oops. Didn't see you there," she says, although she doesn't sound the least bit sorry.

The blonde heads into one of the stalls while her friend fixes her makeup in the mirror beside me. "You are so lucky Maddox is into you tonight. I'd do anything to get his attention," she says with a dreamy look in her eye.

"You could always go after one of his friends. You know how easy Levi and Conrad are. Camden is a little more difficult, especially with Chloe telling me he has turned her down twice this semester already." At the mention of Camden, the hairs on my arms stand up.

Are they talking about…hooking up with him? The thought of him being with either of these girls weighs heavy in my stomach.

"That's a damn shame," says the friend beside me. "Chloe said he's the roommate she really wants to hook up with and if the rumors are true, he's a great lay."

I've heard enough of this conversation. After tossing my paper towel in the trash can, I storm out of the bathroom a little too forcefully. As the door is closing, I hear "What the hell is her deal?" from one of the girls in there.

What the hell is my deal?

As I approach the bar, I see Riggins, the bartender I gave the boys' orders to, placing the last drink on my tray.

He smiles when he sees me. "Hey, I was just about to call a search party for you," he jokes. Riggins is a nice guy. He is a little bit older than us and an almost giant with his tall height and large build. He said he graduated two years ago but decided to go after his master's degree, so he has been bartending here for a while now. "Your drinks are all ready and the kitchen said the food should be out in a minute or so." Someone from the other end of the bar calls his name and he winks at me, turning his attention to a new customer.

Balancing the glasses filled with liquid as best I can on my tray, I head over to Camden's table. The blonde from the bathroom has taken up residency on Maddox's lap, whispering in his ear and nuzzling his neck. Her friend is doing everything to gain Camden's attention, including pushing her impressive cleavage in his direction, but he isn't giving her any of his time. His focus is solely on me as I walk across the bar.

I wonder what it would be like to be in the position of the blonde woman on Maddox's lap. To be so comfortable with a guy you barely know, one you aren't even dating. To meet a guy and spend a nice night together. Maybe kiss or even let him take you home.

It isn't like I haven't thought about those things. I have, and sometimes I wish I were a different person and could be able to do that. The problem with traumatic events in our lives is that often they stick with us, lingering in the background. Everyone lets their trauma affect them differently. My trauma has left me with the inability to trust.

Camden helps me as I lower the tray to the table. I smile at him, silently thanking him because it was pretty heavy. As I pass out the drinks, I can't help but notice that the blonde's friend is staring at me like I kicked her dog. I try to ignore her, but it's hard when she is so close.

Deciding to keep my attention on everyone besides her, I grab the tray and tuck it under my arm. "Your food should be out in a few minutes. Can I get anyone else anything?" I am really hoping they all say no.

"Actually," the blonde girl says, "I would very much appreciate a green apple martini. How about you, Stacy?" she asks her friend.

Taking a deep breath, I turn my attention to the woman who seems to not like me very much. She walks to Camden, dragging her manicured finger along his forearm, up to the spot where his button-up sleeve is rolled up. "How about sex on the beach? That sound good, Cam?" She runs her fingers through his hair, and I grip the tray under my arm tighter.

He shakes her off, looking disgusted by her touch. "Get whatever the fuck you want, and my name isn't Cam." His tone is angry, and he moves away from her.

I turn and head toward the bar to order their drinks. I shouldn't be happy with his reaction to her, but I can't help it. I like that he didn't want her attention but am confused by my reaction to her touching him.

As I reach the bar, I feel someone behind me. When I look back, Camden is right there. He comes to the bar and stands beside me, his arm molded to mine. I don't flinch at the touch. My body's normal reaction to recoil isn't there and instead, his body heat makes me want to move closer. I resist.

"I'm sorry about that. I don't even know that girl," he says. I can feel him staring at me, but I keep my head forward, waiting for Riggins to come over.

"You have nothing to apologize for," I tell him.

"Hey," he says, grabbing my hand from where it rests at my side. "I know I have nothing to apologize for, especially when her advances were unwanted, but I meant what I said in the library. I think you should go on a date with me, Gray Eyes."

I smile at the nickname.

"I don't know…" Dating is foreign to me. Dating someone

90

like Camden, someone who I'm sure has experience and expectations of the women he dates.

I can't meet those expectations. I'm a broken, scared girl with a past I'm ashamed of, that I'm sure will send him running.

"Just one date. You can pick the day, time, and location. Whatever you're comfortable with. I want to get to know you. Away from our friends, class, and studying. Come on," he pleads.

"I've never...dated before," I tell him honestly. It's embarrassing to admit that at twenty years old I have never been on a date.

He smiles. "You really think that is going to stop me from chasing you?"

Riggins comes over, saving me from having to answer Camden's question. "What can I get for ya, good-looking?" he asks.

Camden releases his hold on my hand, tensing beside me.

Riggins is a sweet guy. He is a major flirt, but that comes with the territory of being a bartender, I guess. His charm is always on, even when it's as innocent as a wink my way.

"Could you get me an apple martini and a sex on the beach, please?" I ask.

He nods. "Sure thing, gorgeous." He turns to another waitress and gets her table's order so he can make them all at once.

"Anything going on there?" Camden asks from beside me.

I can't help the laugh that escapes. "Did I not just tell you that I haven't dated," I say more as a statement and less as a question.

"Your laugh is beautiful," he says, making me blush. "And just because you haven't dated doesn't mean there isn't something else going on between you two."

He can't be implying what I think he is. "Camden, there is

nothing going on with Riggins, or any other guy for that matter."

My response seems to make him happy. "Then what's stopping you from saying yes to a date with me?"

"So much," I whisper.

Riggins comes back with my drinks and glances between me and Camden. There is a silent question in his look, and I shake my head, letting him know this guy is okay.

"Kitchen says your food is ready. Want me to help you get it to the table?" Riggins asks. He keeps glancing between Camden and me.

I nod. "Sure, thanks." As I bring the drinks back to the table, I can feel Camden following me. I set the drinks down in front of the girls. Stacy has moved on to Levi's lap and they seem happy with the change.

A hand grabs my wrist and I'm forced to turn toward Camden. He's staring down at me. While I have never considered myself a short woman at five-six, with him right in front of me like this I am having to strain my neck to look up into his eyes.

"One date, Gray Eyes. Trust me, it will be fun. And if for some earth-shattering reason it isn't, I'll leave you alone. We won't have to talk about the horrible date, although I don't see how it could go wrong, and I won't ask you out again." His eyes are serious. He wants this. Wants me. I have no idea why.

Camden has asked me to trust him on multiple occasions now. I feel as though he can sense that is difficult for me. Trusting him and going on this date would break every rule I have set up for myself. I haven't allowed myself to be vulnerable around people in four years. Maybe this is the chance, the moment my therapist said would happen eventually.

I find myself letting out a quiet, "Okay."

Camden's eyes widen in shock at my answer.

"Blaire Wentworth, you are not going to regret this," he tells me with a smile on his face. After giving my wrist a squeeze, he releases it and takes a small step back. "And I won't even make it an uncomfortable date like some movie or something. It'll be fun, I swear."

The small smile on my face can't be stopped. I like that this is important to him.

He adds my number to his phone just as Riggins comes over with their food. Camden takes his vacated seat on the stool as I'm passing out their dishes. He hasn't stopped staring at me, and it partly scares and yet excites me.

After grabbing my tray and asking if anyone else needs anything, I turn to Camden. "I'll, um, talk to you later?" It comes out more as a question.

"I'll text you," he says with a promise in his eyes.

Once I check on another one of my tables that have finished their food and have been nursing the buckets of beers I brought them earlier as they watch some sports game on the TV, I head back to the bar. Emree is there and raises an eyebrow when she sees me.

"What's got you all smiling?" she asks.

I hadn't even realized I was smiling. I contemplate telling her because I know Emree will make a big deal about it. But seeing as she and Conrad are kind of together, she is bound to find out. "You are not going to believe me," I tell her.

"Try me, babe."

"I have a date," I tell her quietly.

Her mouth drops open. "No. Way," she says. "Blaire, I am so happy for you. Who is it? Where is he taking you? It is a he, right?" Giving my lack of dating history or really any interest in anyone, her last question does not shock me so much.

"Yes, it is a he. It's Camden."

Her eyes go wide, and she is clapping and jumping up and down.

"And I don't know where he's taking me. He just said it

would be fun." Just talking about it excites me. There is a small bundle of nerves in my stomach, but I try to push past it.

"Oh, Blaire." Emree sighs. "I am so happy for you. See, I told you that boy was flirting with you." She winks and nudges my shoulder before grabbing some drinks Riggins dropped off.

Maybe she was right all along and there was some sort of flirting going on between Camden and me. I have been so shut off from forming any kind of connection with a guy in the past, I don't even realize when one actually likes me.

After four years, perhaps I'm finally able to open myself up and put my trust in a boy's hands. I just hope he doesn't crush it, and me, in the process.

CHAPTER ELEVEN

BLAIRE

UNKNOWN NUMBER

Morning, Gray Eyes. Are you free today?

S ince I woke up, I have been staring at the text message I can only assume is from Camden. I am free today, but now that bundle of nerves that was in my stomach last night after I agreed to the date has taken over my body and pushed the excitement down.

Four times I have typed out a different response to him from the truth, that I am free, to a lie, that I have work. I can't do that to him, though. It feels wrong. Taking a deep breath, I type out a message to him.

BLAIRE

Good morning. I'm free today.

The bubbles that indicate he is typing appear within seconds.

CAMDEN

Get ready and dress in something comfortable and casual. We're having our date today, Gray Eyes.

BLAIRE

Where are we going?

CAMDEN

If I told you, it would ruin all the fun. Get dressed and I'll pick you up at 11.

Glancing at the time, I have two hours to get ready. I jump up and grab my towel that I left hanging on the back of my desk chair and head for the bathroom. While I wait for the water to get hot, I check on Emree and realize she isn't in her bed.

Grabbing my phone, I look at my other messages to see if she told me she was staying out. We got off at different times last night and she unfortunately had the closing shift at Whiskey Joe's. There's a message that came in around two in the morning, well past when I got home and fell asleep. She let me know she was going home with Conrad and would call me in the morning when she woke up.

The bathroom is filled with steam and the water is at a painfully hot temperature. Just right. I undress and step into the shower, letting the hot water cascade down my body. The heat helps to relieve some of the tension in my shoulders with the thought of going on my second date ever.

My mind flashes back to my first date. I was sixteen and Harvey Galloway was the son of our town's police chief and his mom was on the board of many notable charities with my mother. Our families had been friends since we were kids and we became close by proximity, even though we drifted apart in middle school when girls became gross to Harvey and his group of friends.

When Harvey asked me out, I was excited. I had never been asked out before and Harvey was attractive and nice. He had the bluest eyes and blond hair that was always styled to perfection. He was on the football team, the debate team, in all honors classes, and had the respect of all the teachers and administrators at our school.

Our date was at the beginning of our junior year and at his friend's party. The house was adult-free and filled with alcohol and sweaty teens dancing together. It would not be what I consider the ideal date, but being on Harvey's arm was nice. He was popular and while I had a few friends in school, it was nothing compared to him. Being the police chief's son gave you some sort of importance in a town as small as ours. My father is a successful lawyer and had been good friends with Harvey's dad since they were young. He was happy about the potential of the two of us becoming a couple. Plus, Harvey was charming. He had a smile that won over anyone he flashed it to, and he knew how to use that charm to his advantage.

Harvey asked me if I wanted to go somewhere quiet to talk. It was hard to get to know each other like I thought people did surrounded by loud music and other people. Many of our classmates were hooking up, but that was not the first thing on my mind, especially on my first date. I didn't think anything of it when he brought me to his friend's guest bedroom, truly believing he wanted to get to know me better away from the crowd.

I shake my head before my memory is brought back to that bedroom.

Today is not going to be like that date. Looking back, I can't help but think that what I thought was charming when it came to Harvey, I now see was slimy. He didn't take no for an answer, especially when it came to the debate team. He knew how to get people to do what he wanted by being persistent, even pushy. It is sad the things we realize years later after our life experiences teach us.

Camden is not like Harvey. He isn't pushy in an arrogant way. He is sweet and he likes me. Even though I am shy and quiet, he likes me and I can't help but smile at that fact. I have closed people off for so long, I never thought forming a connection with a guy would ever happen.

The smell of my lavender-scented shampoo fills the bathroom and after I scrub my body clean with the new body wash Emree got from Target, I rinse the soap away and turn off the water. Grabbing the towel, I dry off most of my body and head out of the bathroom and to my bedroom where I shut and lock the door. My plush robe is hanging off the back of the door and after I shrug it on, I go to sit at my desk.

While our bedrooms in the apartment are not exactly large, they leave just enough room for a queen-sized bed, a dresser, a desk, and for me a bookshelf. Emree isn't a book lover like I am and instead of a bookshelf in her room, she opted for a craft corner. With being a fashion design major, Emree uses much of her time experimenting with her sewing machine and the plethora of assorted fabrics in her room.

Back at my childhood home, my bedroom had been at least twice the size of my bedroom now. There was a large, canopy king bed, a solid wood desk, a walk-in closet, and a vanity that I would spend far too much time getting ready for school at in the morning.

My mother taught me at a young age that the Wentworth family does not leave the house looking anything less than perfection. My hair was never allowed to be out of place or dirty and my clothes were to be wrinkle-free and conservative. While my mother was not a fan of much makeup, she did have me wearing the minimum before starting high school. A little bit of concealer, a few swipes of mascara, and a dab of lipstick, but never anything more than a neutral color.

THE ACT OF TRUSTING

Since leaving home, I have foregone all the rules my mother instilled in me from such a young age. Well, besides the minimal makeup, but that is by choice. I have never been one to have the talent or desire to wear more than a little bit of mascara and concealer. Now instead of the stuffy dresses and matching co-ord sets my mother would have me wearing, I opt for more comfortable attire like loose jeans and T-shirt ensembles. Sometimes I will wear a dress, but it is more of a summer casual one. My hair is often in a messy bun or hanging naturally down my back.

Today I want to look nice. Camden said to dress comfortably and luckily that is my entire closet. After blow-drying my hair, I use the curling wand to put in a few loose curls and secure them with hair spray. My hair is long and even with the curls, it hangs far past my breasts.

After finishing my hair, I check the time and see I still have forty-five minutes until eleven. Opting for my usual minimal makeup, I apply concealer under my eyes, above my cheekbones, and in the center of my forehead. Once I swipe on a few coats of mascara, I take in my appearance and smile. My eyes stand out more since I put on a few extra coats, and I know Camden is going to notice.

Taking in my limited clothing selection, I decide on a simple flowy wrap dress. It is a sage green with small, white daisies on it. The dress hits just above my knees and has cap sleeves. The top doesn't dip too low but is tighter until it gets just below my breasts, where it flares out. Since I don't know where our date is, I grab my light brown cardigan in case it is cold.

Just as I am slipping on my cream-colored ballet flats, there is a knock at the door. He's five minutes early and I can appreciate his punctuality.

On my way to the front door, I grab my small crossbody purse from the couch. After opening the door, I let out a small gasp that I hope Camden didn't hear. He stands there wearing a perfectly fitted pair of dark-wash jeans, a maroon T-shirt with a pocket on the breast, and a baseball cap sits backward on his head with pieces of his hair flipping out. His green eyes are brighter today, and I wonder if it's because of the way the sun is hitting them or the color of the shirt he is wearing.

In his hands is a bouquet of blue, orange, pink, yellow, and white wildflowers, and I smile when I spot my favorite flower. Sweet peas. Camden's smile matches my own and he ducks his head.

"I know flowers are kind of cheesy, but I was on my way here and passed this guy on the side of the road selling these. I thought you would like them," he says, thrusting the bundle of flowers at me.

Taking them from his hand, our fingers graze each other's and the spark I feel does not go unnoticed. As I bring the bouquet up to my nose, I capture their scent. They smell fresh. I step back from the door and let him inside. "They're beautiful, Camden. Thank you. You didn't have to," I tell him. I head into the kitchen to find a vase and he follows.

He mumbles out a "You're welcome" as I grab a vase from the back of the cabinet under the sink. "You look beautiful, by the way. I don't think I've ever seen you in a dress."

He's probably right. In class, I usually opt for jeans or leggings and a T-shirt. "You said casual and comfortable and what can be more comfortable than not having to wear pants?" I say with a slight laugh at the end.

After putting the flowers in the vase and filling it with water, I give them one final sniff before heading toward Camden and following him out of the apartment, then lock the door.

As we walk through the apartment complex, I can't help but wonder where we're going. "You're really not going to tell me where you're taking me?"

Camden chuckles. "I'm going to guess you aren't one for surprises," he says more as a statement.

"Personally, never been much of a fan. I would rather be the one doing the surprising than being the surprised." Though I don't throw much of them anymore, my friends and I had done a good job of throwing each other surprises for each other's birthdays. Well, back when they were my friends.

Camden reaches for my hand and intertwines our fingers. "Tough because apparently I like being the surpriser also." He smiles down at me. I decide to give up on trying to get him to budge on telling me where we are going since he seems adamant about not letting the secret out.

He reaches into his pocket and retrieves a key fob. In front of us, the lights of the tallest vehicle I have ever seen flash. It's a four-door Jeep Wrangler and by the added height, I can assume Camden has done something to make it several inches higher than it was when the car manufacturers made it.

"And how do you expect me to get into that monster truck?" I ask him as we stop beside the passenger door. There isn't even a step for me to get into. I am sure with Camden's height he has no issues getting into his car. He stands at least more than six inches taller than me. Plus, he has long legs.

He opens the door and looks at me and the seat. "Yeah, you know, I never really thought about that. My sister is the only other girl who has been in here and she usually gets a running start and just dives in," he says, laughing at what I can imagine being a comical image.

"Maybe I can give that a try." Although the thought of leaping into his Jeep in a dress makes me think I will flash anyone around.

"Here, let me just..." He reaches forward, his hands hovering around my waist. The shock on my face must stop him. "You okay if I lift you in? I promise I won't cop a feel or anything," he jokes with a smirk on his face.

I like that he makes light of groping me because it makes me think he wouldn't actually do anything that would make me uncomfortable. "Yeah. That would be fine," I tell him, slightly breathy, but I don't think he notices.

He closes the distance and engulfs his large hands around my waist. As he lifts me into the passenger seat, he makes sure not to touch his chest against mine. I watch his forearms and the muscles beneath his tanned skin as they flex. I have never thought something like forearms could be attractive, but I have come to realize just about everything to do with Camden attracts me.

He releases me and steps back, clearing his throat. "Maybe I can get a step stool for next time," he says.

"Already confident there is going to be a next time," I tease him.

His eyes light up and he leans forward, coming just inside the door. "Oh, baby, I can guarantee there will be a next time," he says. The minty scent of his breath greets my nose. Stepping back, he closes the door and walks around the front before I can respond.

CHAPTER TWELVE

CAMDEN

S he smells like the lavender bath soap my mom used to buy for my sister and me to help us sleep at night, and it takes everything in me not to reach across the center console and nuzzle my nose in the crook of her neck and capture more of that scent.

Having Blaire in my Jeep shouldn't excite me as much as it does, but aside from my sister, she is the only girl who has ever been in here. She looks damn sexy too. Her long legs are stretched out in front of her and her hair whips around from the rolled-down window as "Heat Waves" by Glass Animals plays on the radio.

The weather is in our favor today, so I had the windows down on my way to her apartment, but I'm regretting it now because it leaves little room to talk. But seeing Blaire enjoy the fresh air is worth it.

Our date destination isn't too far, but I take the back road to avoid any billboards that would have an advertisement for the place. I want it to be a surprise as long as possible.

After talking to my mom last night when I got home from

the bar, I was able to get some womanly advice on where to take a girl for a first date. I wanted it to be something better than the generic dinner and a movie. It needed to be a date Blaire will remember and make her want to go on another one with me.

Asking my mom for dating advice was more awkward than I thought it would be, but I guess that is partly due to my lack of really dating in the past. Before, a date for me was a step toward getting a girl into bed. I wasn't a complete asshole. I would wine and dine a girl first, but it never led to a second night out. Never did I want it to be something more.

With Blaire, I want it to lead to more dates. More conversations. More of us.

Mom said to do something during the daytime to lessen the expectation of sex at the end of the date and I almost hung up on her on the spot. Does not matter how old I am, talking about sex with my mother will never be okay. After some suggestions, we came up with the perfect day planned and my mom made me promise to bring her by the house to meet her and my sister, Trazia, if our relationship progresses.

As I pull off the highway, Blaire rolls up her window. "We aren't in the best area of town, and we are moving farther away from the city, so I can only assume there is no date and you're taking me away to murder me and hide the body," she says.

A deep laugh comes out of me, and I look over to see a smirk on her face. "I think you've been watching too many murder mysteries," I tell her.

"More like reading murder mysteries. I don't watch much TV," she tells me.

I add that little fact about her for future reference. "So, you're more of a bookworm."

She gives me a questioning look, probably curious why I know the term used for people who read a lot.

"My sister is a hopeless romantic and reads probably just as much as she breathes."

"You've talked a little about her. How old is your sister?" she questions.

"Trazia is seventeen going on thirty. I swear she is going to give me a heart attack one day. Just last week she told me about going cliff jumping with friends of hers from school. I mean, I did that shit in high school too, but it's different when it's my little sister, you know?"

"Yeah, I know. I mean, I don't have any siblings, but I can image her keeping you on your toes, especially with something like cliff jumping. I can't image doing that. It sounds terrifying."

I smile at the thought of getting this beautiful woman in a bikini at the springs.

I look over at her. "You should try it, you know. It's scary as hell, but a complete adrenaline rush. Plus, at the springs they have cliffs of all sizes, so we could try out the baby cliffs. I wouldn't even call them cliffs, more like big rocks."

Florida isn't as exciting as someplace like Washington or Oregon would be for cliff jumping, but our springs have a few good spots for it. Apparently, Trazia's friends found out about Devil's Hollow Springs and decided to make a trip of it. When she posted the video of her and a guy jumping off the highest cliff, I about drove out to drill some sense into her. I also almost drove to the little prick's house she jumped in with because the moment Trazia yelled she lost her top, he was more than comfortable swimming up to her to 'help.' She got a mouthful about that from me as well.

"Maybe. How about we get through this first date before we plan anything else, buddy?"

The fact that she still doubts whatever this is between us will make it past this date makes me smile.

I decide not to respond to her since we're one street away from our date destination. I'm surprised she hasn't guessed it the entire drive. There isn't much out here that could be worthy of bringing someone on a date.

As I turn the Jeep to the left, a giant sign comes into view and Blaire gasps beside me. "No way. Camden, are you taking me to the aquarium?" she asks with excitement in her voice.

Based on her reaction, my mom's suggestion to bring Blaire somewhere we could walk around and talk was great. At first, I thought maybe the pier out by the beach and my mom suggested a museum, which I would fall asleep at, but the aquarium downtown has been a place I loved visiting since my first school field trip in fifth grade.

"Sure am," I tell her. "It's not stuffy like some fancy restaurant, and who doesn't love looking at all the funky sea creatures?" That part is my favorite because Tampa has one of the largest aquariums in the state.

As I pull into the parking garage, I can sense Blaire's growing excitement. "You know, I've never actually been to an aquarium. We didn't have one close by in the town I grew up in, so there were never any school field trips. The administration tried fighting for funding to get the students to the Dallas aquarium, but that was way out of budget for our small school."

"You're from Texas? I could hear a bit of an accent but couldn't pinpoint which state." She doesn't have a strong Southern accent, but it's faintly there. Sometimes it comes out more when she rambles.

"Yeah, born and raised in a small town there," she tells me as I take our parking ticket from the machine. The gate goes up, and I drive through to look for a spot.

Once I find a spot, we jump out of the car. Blaire has an easier time getting out than she did getting in. "What made you want to come to Braxton U?" I ask her as we round the back of my car. I resist the urge to grab her hand as we walk, knowing that would probably be too much for her too soon.

She bites her lip before answering. "Oh, you know, just

wanted a change of scenery. There wasn't much left for me in Texas, and Florida seemed like a great place to start over."

"You don't miss your family or anything?"

She laughs. "No. My parents and I have been estranged for quite some time now. There was nothing left for me back there. Braxton has become my home these last couple years." Blaire says every word with such honesty even though I can't imagine not seeing or talking to my mom or sister.

"I can understand estranged family relationships. Don't get me wrong, I'm close as hell to my mom and Trazia, but my dad walked out on us when I was eight and my sister was only five for some twenty-something-year-old assistant at his job. He tried coming back into our lives when I was fifteen and after the girlfriend had drained him of all his money. None of us were having any of it. My mom threatened to call the police on him." I laugh at the memory of my mom looking at my father with such disgust as he was on his hands and knees, begging for another chance. "After that, she ended up telling me about his years of cheating and how she didn't accept a cent from him in child support after he left."

We round the corner of the last set of stairs in the parking garage and when I look at Blaire, there is such admiration in her eyes.

"Wow, your mom is such a strong woman. I can't imagine being a single mom and raising two kids on my own."

"Yeah, that's why I worked so hard to get this scholarship to Braxton. Soccer got me into college, and even if I'm not able to make a career out of it like I want to, having my kinesiology degree opens enough doors for me to make some good money and take care of her."

Ever since learning my mom has been doing everything on her own and not taking any money from my sorry excuse of a father, I went into overdrive and made sure I would get into college and get a good job to make something of myself so she can retire early, or at least cut back to one job. Now that it's just her and Trazia at home and my scholarship allows me enough for living expenses, she doesn't work three jobs like she used to and works one full-time and another every other weekend. To me, it is still too much, but she swears she likes the hard work.

As we approach the front of the building and the line to wait and buy our tickets, Blaire looks over at me. Her eyes are soft and her body leans into mine, close but not touching it. "I think you're going to do amazing things with your life, Camden. I can tell by the way you talk about it, you're deter-mined. Whether it's soccer or something else, you'll achieve it."

Having Blaire say what she said means more to me than I think she will know. For years I have pushed myself at prac-tices when my body screamed at me to stop and would end up going home to sit in an ice bath and study. My life revolved around soccer and having a good enough GPA to get into college, plus some extracurricular activities on the side to relieve the stress.

Instead of responding to her, I reach down and give her hand a tight squeeze. As I pull it away, the teller at the counter calls us over to purchase the tickets.

Once inside the aquarium, Blaire's eyes go wide, and her mouth hangs open as she takes everything in. "Wow, they just have fish swimming all around us like that. I feel like I'm in a submarine in the ocean or something."

Watching her take in everything around us reminds me of my excitement the first time I came here. When you walk into the entryway of the aquarium, the wall on the left side is stretched to the second floor with glass, and behind it are fish of every color and size. Blaire is right, it does make you feel like you are in a submarine. In front of us, there's a set of wide stairs that leads you to the second floor, and that has an outdoor area with some land animals. To the left is where you start your walkthrough with a dark tunnel that brings you to the shark exhibit and other creatures that live in the deep parts of the ocean.

I grab Blaire's hand and bring her that way. She makes a *huff* sound but doesn't break our connection. "Come on, there's a lot to see, so let's get started.

CHAPTER THIRTEEN

BLAIRE

This has got to be the best date in the history of dates. Although I really don't have anything to compare it to, I can't imagine anything being better.

Camden has blown away any expectations I had for today. I would have been happy to just spend time with him talking but can't deny that this is pretty great. The aquarium is filled with many colorful sea creatures I never even knew existed. The shark exhibit housed over ten different types of sharks. Some of them I recognized, like the hammerhead, but others were gross-looking and a bit scary.

As we walked through the dark section, Camden's hand never left mine. He told me about growing up in Tampa and how he got into soccer. Although he wanted to know about my life back in Texas, he caught on that it is something I did not want to talk about and instead changed the subject to my first two years at Braxton.

On the first floor and outside, we were able to see more types of fish than I have ever before, touched and got splashed on by stingrays, and were able to feed some dolphins and watch them perform tricks instructed by the handlers. One dolphin didn't have a tail and the handler explained to us that they believe she may have been in a fight and some fishermen found her, then the aquarium was able to rehabilitate her and even attach a prosthetic to assist her with swimming. Today she wasn't wearing it but seemed to be getting by perfectly fine.

Now we are walking through the second floor in an area that reminds me of a swamp. The tanks start at the floor and end around our chest area and are filled with water and tree roots that large fish are swimming through. Some of the tanks have ducks sitting above the water or relaxing on rocks.

Camden's hand has been clasped in mine as we stroll through the walkway between the many tanks. I'm less nervous around him. He has not tried anything besides holding my hand. Every few minutes, he will give it a squeeze and I think that is his way of reassuring me.

"You hungry?" he asks me as I am leaning over, looking down into the area filled with alligators. We have been at the aquarium for almost two hours. The time seems to escape me when we're together.

As if it wanted to respond for me, my stomach grumbles. Camden laughs. "I'm going to take that sound as a yes. You want to head to the café? We could grab a bite and something to drink."

"That sounds good," I tell him.

When we arrive at the café, it is set up more like a cafeteria. The smell of fried food and coffee hits me as we walk in. To the left, there is a station to pick up hot meals and across from it is a row of refrigerators with sandwiches and bottles of drinks.

"What are you in the mood for?" Camden asks me.

I'm tempted to do the typical girl thing and get a boring salad, but I spotted chicken fingers and those are a weakness of mine. "Chicken fingers sound really good," I tell him. My mouth is watering just thinking about them. "What about you?"

He guides me over to the hot food section before saying,

"Their cheeseburgers are surprisingly good here." Camden hadn't told me he comes here often, but by the way he navigates through the aquarium and knows about all the exhibits, I take it this is a special place to him.

After we grab our food, we head over to the drink section, and I pick a Sprite Zero while Camden gets a Gatorade. He pays, much to my argument that I can pay for our food since he paid for the tickets here.

Once we are seated, I pop off the top of the ranch I got and dunk one of my chicken tenders in it, then take a bite. I moan, closing my eyes and taking in the delicious taste. I hadn't realized how hungry I was, but I did skip breakfast this morning. The mixture of a crispy tender and the savory flavor of ranch hits the spot.

When I open my eyes, Camden has a handful of fries halted in the air close to his mouth. He brings his arm down and sets the fries in the basket. "Listen, I think you're extremely hot, Blaire, and I can sense what you need is slow, and I can do that because I really like you, but if you make noises like that, slow is going to be the last thing on my mind."

My eyes widen at his statement. There is an intensity in how he says it, but it doesn't scare me. "Noises like what?" I ask.

"Sex noises."

My jaw drops open.

"Yes, baby. Now pick that jaw back up and let's enjoy a moan-free lunch," he jokes with a knowing smile on his face.

As I eat my food, we take in the kids running around in the water park area and I become self-conscious of any noises I make while eating. Camden is laughing and pointing out a kid who is going around with a cup and pelting other kids in the face with water.

"That was basically me when I was younger. Always being a little shit." He laughs.

The kid is about seven or eight and having the time of his life, of course at the expense of a few other kids, but they seem to move on soon after the face full of water and continue playing.

"Did you spend a lot of time here when you were a kid?" I ask.

"Yeah," Camden tells me. "After my dad left, my mom had to work so many jobs. It was just me and my sister alone a lot of the time. We got discounted yearly tickets here and my mom thought it was cheaper than paying for any kind of camp to keep us entertained and out of trouble." Camden pops the last bit of his burger in his mouth, wiping his face with a napkin. "Trazia and I would come here most weekends and multiple times during the week over the summer," he says after finishing his bite.

My chicken tenders have long since been finished and I have been nursing my soda, playing with the green lid. "You speak fondly of your sister. Have you both always been close?"

A bright smile lights up his face when I ask about Trazia. "She's the greatest. Traz is a spitfire, always saying whatever's on her mind. When my dad left, she was so young, and I knew losing him would be hard on her and my mom." There is sadness in his eyes when he talks about his dad leaving their family. "Walking out on your family is fucked up and my mom was crushed and Traz was so young and innocent. I couldn't help but become protective of them."

Reaching across the table, I cover his hand with my own. "That's amazing, Camden. You have a big heart," I tell him honestly. He threads our fingers together and squeezes my hand. "I hate that your dad left, because I can't imagine ever walking out on someone as great as you, but I am glad your mom and sister have a son and brother like you with them."

Camden startles me by lifting our joined hands and placing a hard kiss on the back of my palm, his eyes never leaving my own. His lips are warm and soft against my skin, and I can't help but wonder what they would feel like against my own.

"As much as I wish I could kiss you right now, I feel like it's too soon for you, but I couldn't not have my lips on you for another second," he tells me as he drops our hands back to the table. "Thank you for saying that. I hate that he left, but we were better off without him if he could leave his family so easily."

I can't help but think of myself and my own family. Leaving my parents was easier than one would have thought, especially when you grow up in a cold household and have parents who do not support you in the worst time of your life.

"Enough with the depressing family shit." Camden breaks the window of silence. "Let's talk about our first date. How did I do? Good enough to get me a second one?" The hopeful gleam in his eyes makes me smile.

"It was okay, I suppose." Trying to hide my laugh is harder than I thought, and I almost break when his jaw drops.

"You're joking with me. This is top ten date material. You can't seriously sit there and tell me you didn't have a damn good time."

I break. The small laugh comes out. "Camden, I couldn't have imagined today being better than it was. You really blew me away with our first date," I tell him honestly.

A smirk appears on his face. "First date, huh? So, what you're saying is there's going to be a second one." He says it more as a statement.

"I suppose," I answer anyway. "Although I don't see how any date could get better than this."

"You're going to have to let me work my magic, baby." He releases my hand and spreads his arms out, leaning them against the chairs beside him. "I'm the king of perfect dates, Blaire."

I can't stop the eye roll. "Okay, I take it back. Date ruined by your ego," I say with a smile on my face.

He laughs and places his hands on top of the table, pushing himself to stand. Camden collects our empty food bins and discards them into the nearest trash can. When he comes over to me, he reaches for my hand. "Come on. Let's make another stop at the sharks on our way out. I know how much you love that snaggle tooth one that looks over a hundred years old."

Grabbing his hand, I let him pull me up and we head toward the creepy sharks.

MAKING a detour toward the sharks on the way out had been a great idea because it was feeding time and witnessing thousand-pound animals with sharp, jagged teeth shred apart other fish was an experience. Some of them fought over the dead fish they were fed, and it turned into a frenzy of who can get the most pieces of fish flesh.

As we walk back toward his car, I can't help but notice how right this feels. Camden makes me smile and laugh, and when he looks at me, I get these butterflies in my stomach I have never felt before. It sounds cheesy, like some Hallmark Christmas movie, but I can't help but feel that way around him.

The simple act of trusting someone should be easy. Trust is gained through gestures and words, all of which Camden has provided. He is slowly breaking down my walls and earning the trust I desperately want to give him.

We approach his Jeep and a small part of me is excited that it is so lifted he has to help me inside. Having his hands at my waist feels nice.

I secure my purse strap on my shoulder and open the door.

He is right behind me, looking a little too eager to lift me into the car. He raises his eyebrow as if to ask if I'm ready and I nod in response. The heat from his hands burns through my dress once again as he places me in the seat.

Just as I'm seated, my purse slips off my shoulder and falls to the ground. After making sure I'm fully inside, he bends down to pick it up.

"Jesus, Blaire, you carrying around a paperweight or something? Why is this so heavy?"

I blush and grab for the bag. "No, jerk, there isn't any paperweight in there. I just have my phone, house keys, wallet, and a book."

He reaches for the bag again. "A book? Seriously? You thought our date was going to be that bad?" he jokes. "For real, though, this weighs, like, ten pounds. How are you not walking around with a limp after carrying this?"

I roll my eyes at him but don't reach for the purse again. "You're being dramatic. If that's heavy to you, you need to hit the weights, mister."

"Yeah, yeah," he says. Camden opens the flap of my purse and looks at me, silently asking for permission to go inside. I nod, giving it to him. "All right, let's see what kind of book is worthy of first date material."

He pulls out my copy of *The Confidence of Wildflowers* by Micalea Smeltzer. I fell in love with the cover after walking past it in Target one day. Since starting it two days ago, I haven't been able to put it down and am almost finished. I had planned to go to the store after our date and get the next book in the duet. Salem and Thayer's love story has kept me on the edge of my seat, and I am going to need that second book before finishing the first.

He grabs the paperback and flips the back over, reading the description. "Damn, Blaire, an age gap like that? I know it's fiction and all, but I'd kill a dude in his thirties if he tried getting with my eighteen-year-old sister."

"Oh my gosh." I grab for my book, clutching it to my chest. "Yes, it is fiction, but you just don't get it. Their love is beautiful, and their age means nothing when they are soulmates." I never thought age gap books would be something I would be into, but recently they have grabbed my attention. I think it's the forbidden aspect that they shouldn't be doing what they're doing, but their love is so strong they can't not be together. I could only hope for a love that strong.

Camden leans forward, resting his forearm on the doorframe. "Aw, baby, are you one of those hopeless romantics who falls in love with book boyfriends?"

His face is so close I can smell the piece of gum he has been chewing since we left the aquarium. "Maybe," I say quietly.

"Trazia is into that shit too. Huge bookworm. I feel like you two will hit it off when you meet." He hands me back my purse and I sit there frozen as the door shuts. Meeting his sister? After just one date? Okay, I feel like there will be more seeing Camden, but meeting someone so important to him terrifies me, because what if she sees I'm not good enough for him?

As we drive back to my apartment, Harry Styles's "As It Was" fills the silence around us. Since Camden's Jeep is a stick shift, he has to change gears every so often and when he does, the back of his hand grazes my bare thigh. I don't know if he does it on purpose, but each time goose bumps scatter across my skin where he leaves a trail.

My body's reaction to him is something I have never experienced before and I like it. I like his soft touches and the way he looks at me as if he wants to grab me and protect me from the world. I don't know if it is just in Camden's nature to be a protector after his father left and he took over as the male figure in the household, but it makes me feel like I am safe around him.

Camden speeds up some and shifts into a higher gear as we get onto the highway. His hand grazes my thigh again and I clutch my handbag, waiting for the goose bumps to appear. This time, he doesn't move away. The backs of his fingers move up and down my leg, and I suck in a breath. He flips his hand over and lazily lays it on my thigh, just above my knee. When he doesn't go to move any higher, I release the breath.

"Is this okay?" he whispers.

It is okay. Surprisingly, I'm more comfortable with his hand there. The heat from his palm feels nice.

Releasing the grip on my purse, I place my hand on top of his and run my thumb along the smooth skin. "Yeah. It's okay," I tell him.

We sit in silence most of the way to my place, enjoying the variety of music the radio is providing us and the sunshine coming in from the open windows. My hair is for sure going to be one giant knot when I get out, but I'm too happy to care. Camden makes me feel good and relaxed and as I lean back into the seat, I can't help but look to my left at him driving and take in his features. The scruff along his chin and cheek from not shaving for a few days, the slope of his slim nose, his thick eyebrows that match the brown color of his hair, and his full lips. The freckles on his face seem to have grown, and maybe he has been spending more time in the sun the last week because his skin looks to have a fresh glow from a tan.

He's beautiful. I am sure he would scoff at me if I told him that, but it is true. Camden Collins is a beautiful man and I can't seem to take my eyes off him.

Camden's hand squeezes my knee, and I am jerked out of my gawking. "You keep looking at me like that and I'm going to forget I'm trying to be a gentleman, Blaire." He looks over and smirks. The one look tells me he would not do something I am not comfortable with.

"Hey, where does it say in the dating rule book that I can't admire how good-looking my date is?" I ask him jokingly.

He laughs. "You can stare at me all you want, Gray Eyes. Even touching's allowed. Here, go ahead, want me to take off my shirt for easier access?" He removes his hand from the steering wheel but keeps the car under control with his knee and reaches for the bottom of his shirt.

I cover my face with my hands, hiding my laugh. "Oh my gosh, could you not? You're going to cause an accident." Part of me is sad we are in a moving vehicle because I want him to take his shirt off so I can admire what's underneath too.

His shirt falls back into place once he releases it, but not before I catch a glimpse of his tanned and toned stomach, and he places his hand back on the steering wheel. His other hand never left my thigh, but he does give me another tight squeeze.

We pull into my apartment a few minutes later. It was much quicker coming home than going to the aquarium since he didn't take any of the backroads this time. Once the car is parked and he cuts the engine, we both take off our seat belts and make no effort to get out of the Jeep.

"I had a really nice time, Camden," I tell him. Reaching forward, I interlock our fingers and rest our joined hands on my thigh.

His thumb rubs back and forth against the side of my hand. "Does this mean you'll let me take you on another date?" he asks hopefully. There is a slight worry in his eyes, and I think a part of him is afraid I'll say no.

"Did you think this would be a one-and-done date? Come on, it was perfect," I tell him honestly.

That bright smile appears, and it warms my heart. "I mean, it could have been bad if you were afraid of fish or something," he jokes. "But seeing as your face lit up the entire time we were there, I'm going to go with yes, you'll let me take you out again?"

Feeling bold, I reach both my hands forward and place them on either side of his face. His eyes widen. "Camden," I say slowly while staring into his eyes, "I would love nothing more than for us to go out again. And maybe even another time after that." I have a feeling there may be many more after today.

After releasing his face, I go to place my hands back in my lap, but Camden has other ideas. Reaching for my left hand, he grabs it and brings me closer, slightly leaning over the center console. His face is close to mine and he keeps looking between my lips and my eyes. I know he is going to kiss me, and the thought scares me. What if it makes me think of the last time I was kissed and I freak out? What if I like it but am bad at it?

As if he can sense my worry, Camden places his large, warm hand against my neck. "I'm not going to kiss you until you ask me. I can see the tennis match going on inside your mind of should we or shouldn't we." He smiles and that simple act makes me melt. "I don't know what happened in your past for you to feel like you can't trust me, but I will do anything to gain just an ounce of it, Blaire. I won't push you. Everything is at your pace," he tells me, his breath ghosting across my lips with the closeness.

"I'm trying," I tell him as I lean into his hand resting against my neck.

He brushes his thumb across my cheek. "That's more than I can ask for." Ever so slowly, Camden leans forward and places a soft kiss on my cheek.

I can still feel his lips there after he walks me to my door.

CHAPTER FOURTEEN

BLAIRE

Safely in my apartment, I lean against the front door, clutching my purse to my chest and dropping my head back. Camden walked me to the door and left with a promise that he will see me again soon and to get ready for date number two. Even though I just left him after spending several hours together, I can't wait to see him again.

"Bitch, you better get in here and tell me everything!" Emree yells from the living room.

After dropping my bag on the entryway table and kicking my shoes off, I head toward her. She is sitting on the love seat, her legs under her and a textbook on her lap. She shuts the book and tosses it on the cushion beside her.

"All right, first off, cutest outfit, B. Your legs look long and sexy in that," she tells me. I look down and worry the dress is too short. "Don't do that. It is still modest compared to what some girls on campus wear."

"I know, I just worry it is too much for me. But Camden didn't tell me where we were going today and only said to wear something casual and comfortable." I take a seat on the sofa across from her, the very one Camden and I sat on together last week. I can't believe it was only a week ago I met and talked to him and now we are sort of dating, I guess. At least I think we're dating.

"Enough talk of the cute outfit," she says with excitement in her eyes. "Where did he take you? How did you feel about it? What did you eat? Did he kiss you at all? Did you want him to kiss you?" Something crosses her mind, and her eyebrows pinch together. "If he tried kissing you and you weren't ready, I will kick his balls in."

"Okay, easy there, tiger." I hold my hands up, hoping to help calm her down. "First off, no, he did not try anything with me. He was perfectly sweet." I can't help but smile at what he said at the end of our date about not kissing me until I ask him to. "And how about one question at a time, okay?"

For the next hour, we dive into all the details of the date. Emree swoons at the location and says the aquarium is an underrated date spot. I would have to agree with her there. She asks even more questions after I answer the ones she threw at me when I first walked in, and it seems like she is satisfied with each of my responses.

Even though Emree and I haven't been lifelong friends or anything, after she was witness to one of my few night terrors, I ended up telling her about what happened with Harvey when I was sixteen. She never looked at me with pity like I worry most people would. Instead, she hugged me fiercely and told me how brave I am.

Emree confessed to me that her mother was raped in college, resulting in her getting pregnant. Her mother never resented her and has always been open with Emree about what happened. She wanted her daughter to know that horrible things can happen in this world, and while people all over handle those situations differently, she felt she was strong enough to be the mother she knew her daughter would need. Emree and her mom are extremely close, and I feel like what happened to her mom formed a bond between the two like no other.

After I have answered all of Emree's twenty questions, she gets up to grab us each our favorite ice creams. Hers is rocky road and mine is Ben & Jerry's Americone Dream. As we fill ourselves with creamy goodness, Emree asks, "So when are you seeing him again?" around a mouthful of ice cream.

I scoop out a piece of broken ice cream cone and pop it into my mouth. "Well, I guess I'll see him in class Monday, but no idea about a second date. He did make sure I know that he intends to take me out again, though." Just talking about it gets me excited.

Emree sets her ice cream down and comes to sit beside me, putting her slender arms around my shoulders. "I know taking this step has been hard, but I need you to know how unbelievably proud of you I am." She squeezes my shoulders. "You probably don't see it like I do, but you have come such a long way even from last year, Blaire. You rarely have any nightmares now, you're opening yourself up to more people, you're *dating*. This is going to be a good year. I can already feel it."

She goes back to where she was sitting, and we finish off our ice creams, talking about her night staying with Conrad and how much she likes him. I notice that she hasn't mentioned him asking her out or saying they're together. They have been sleeping together since the party at the house he shares with Camden, but other than hooking up, it doesn't seem like there is more to it. I can tell by how Emree talks about Conrad that she likes him a lot and I worry it is going to be more for her than it is for him.

It's late by the time we are done talking and I'm exhausted from the long day out. After tossing out my ice cream carton, I head to bed and leave Emree on the couch to continue her studying.

Once I'm changed into my sleep shorts and tank top, I

snuggle into bed with the book I brought on my date and can't help but think of Camden and our day together. As I drift to sleep, I think of his breath against my face, his face coming close to mine, and him planting his lips on my cheek.

THE MONDAY MORNING following my date with Camden, I put a little more effort into how I look. It is an early class and I usually wear my staple outfit of jeans and a T-shirt, much like many of my other classmates. Today I'm wearing a loose pair of jeans with shredded holes strategically placed in them and a loose-fitted light pink blouse tucked into the front of my pants. I paired it with my Nike white sneakers. I have even applied some lip gloss and mascara.

Camden and I texted back and forth a little yesterday, but no mention of when we would go out again. We talked on the phone last night and he asked me about my favorite foods, movies, and TV shows. It was nice simply talking to each other about everything and nothing. He told me his favorite food was a cheeseburger and fries (specifically Checkers fries) and chicken and waffles. His favorite movie is *The Dark Night*, but that is the only DC Comic movie he enjoys, and his favorite TV show is *Sons of Anarchy*.

As I walk into class, I smile when I see Camden sitting at our table. He is usually walking in just as class is starting, but now he is about ten minutes early. Two cups of coffee from the café on campus sit in front of him and as I approach, I take in the strong smell.

"Good morning," he says as I take my seat. "I got you a caramel macchiato with a shot of espresso."

After taking my seat, I reach for the cup and breathe in the delicious smell. "You remembered my order." Taking notes on something simple like how I take my coffee warms my heart.

"Of course I did." He takes a sip from his own cup and reaches forward to grasp my hand. He brings it to his mouth, leaving a lingering kiss on the back of my hand. "How was your night? Had any naughty dreams about me?" he jokes.

I roll my eyes and remove my hand from his hold and shove his shoulder. "Oh my gosh, sweet moment over. You're ridiculous." I'm laughing along with him because the joking question caught me off guard.

"Aw, baby," he whispers, "I know I live free in your thoughts and dreams. There's no need to get shy about it." He throws his arm over my shoulders and places a kiss to the side of my head.

I shrug him off just as our professor comes in. He looks between Camden and me and raises an eyebrow. Professor Darfman turns away and tells us we are having a pop quiz. Everyone groans, including the man sitting beside me.

As he passes out our quizzes, the sound of punching calculators and pencils scribbling against paper fills the room. Camden takes a large gulp of his coffee after the paper is dropped on the table and he stares down at it like it has offended him.

Even though math is my strongest subject, I would have to say this pop quiz has got to be one of the more difficult ones I have taken. After answering the first two of fifteen questions, I feel something gliding along my knee and look down to see Camden's hand resting there. When I look up at him, he is completely focused on the test in front of him and not paying attention to what his hand is doing to me.

After answering two more questions, the hand on my knee becomes too much as he slowly rubs his thumb in one of the holes exposing my skin. It's warm and if we were anywhere but in our classroom taking a quiz, I may enjoy his light touches. "You're distracting me," I whisper to him.

In my peripheral, I can see him smile, but he doesn't say anything. The thumb continues to move back and forth, back and forth, until I reach down and slap my hand on top of his. "Stop." There isn't much fight in how I say it because I like his hand being there, but I need to focus on my test.

Professor Darfman's head shoots up. "No talking," he says with a stern look across the classroom. Camden reluctantly removes his hand and I now have a clear mind to ace this quiz, although I do somewhat miss him there.

Ten minutes go by, and our professor announces that once we are finished with our quizzes, we can turn them in to him and are excused from class. As I'm answering question after question, I get more confident with my answers.

Thirty minutes later and after reviewing my answers, I get up from the seat with my backpack strapped to my shoulder. Professor Darfman barely acknowledges me as I drop my test off and head out of the classroom.

Since class ended early and I don't have another one for a couple of hours, I sit on the bench outside the door to wait for Camden. With my copy of *The Confidence of Wildflowers* in hand, I sit back and get comfortable while I wait.

It isn't long before a large body drops itself beside me. "I think he enjoys our torture," Camden tells me, letting out an exaggerated breath.

"Aw, it wasn't so bad," I say, reassuring him with a pat on his thigh. "He is only preparing us for the final exam, which you know will be ten times worse."

"Ugh, don't remind me. It's months away and I'm already dreading it." Camden rubs his palms along his thighs and stands. "When's your next class? Want to grab some breakfast?"

After tucking my paperback into my backpack, I stand beside him, and he takes my hand. "Sure, I have a couple hours." And we head out the door toward the café.

CHAPTER FIFTEEN

CAMDEN

On Wednesday afternoon, I'm sitting outside of Blaire's last class of the day with some weird pink drink from Starbucks she said is one of her favorites from there. I felt embarrassed ordering it, and even more so as I walked across campus from the parking lot with it in my hand.

The class is released, and students file out one by one. Blaire is among them, and I wait for her to notice me standing on the opposite wall, but she looks too lost in thought to pay attention to anyone around her.

"Gray Eyes!" I call out and her head pops up. She smiles when she sees me and begins walking my way.

When she approaches, I hand her the bright-colored beverage.

"Wow, thank you," she says before taking a sip. "What are you doing here?"

I reach for her hand and direct us toward the double doors leading to the parking lot. "Since we're both done with classes and you said you aren't working tonight, I figured we could hang out."

"Like another date? Should I go home and change?" She

looks down at her loose jeans, fitted cropped tank top, cardigan, and some brown Jesus-looking sandals.

"You look perfect," I tell her, leaning forward to kiss the side of her head. Her hair smells like lavender and I smile, remembering my mom and sister.

We approach my Jeep, and I toss both our book bags in the back and head over to help Blaire in the passenger seat. She stands there, waiting for me after opening the door.

"Should I bother asking where we're going or is it another surprise?" she asks as I lift her inside.

Gripping the doorframe, I lean in so we're a few inches apart. "I would tell you, but I think you love the anticipation of where I'm taking you too much." I wink and shut the door.

As we drive the short distance, I rest my hand in Blaire's as it lies on her thigh.

"How is it coming along with *The Great Gatsby*?" she asks me.

Monday while we had breakfast, I told her I started the book the day before and she had been right, it had kept my interest. "I have to say, Gray Eyes, you picked a pretty good book for me."

She smiles. "I'm so glad you like it. That will make writing the essay much easier."

"I still think watching the movie could have been just as helpful."

Blaire huffs. "The movie adaptations of books are complete crap. They change so much, and how can you fit an entire novel into a two-hour movie? You can't. A book has far too much plot and detail that a movie could never handle."

"I can sense you're very passionate about this," I tell her.

Blaire's eyes go wide, and she leans forward in her seat as we pull into the parking lot of our destination. "Are you taking me to…a bookstore?"

After finding out she is a book lover like my sister, I figured what better way to spend an afternoon than to shop up and down the book aisles?

"Are you not happy about this? We can always go do something else," I say, putting the Jeep in reverse and pretending to back out of the parking spot we are in.

Blaire reaches for my hand on the gearshift. "Don't you dare. But this is dangerous, you know? I could spend hours in here and never feel satisfied."

"I have all the time in the world, baby." I grab her hand and kiss the back of it before getting out of the car.

Together we make our way toward Barnes & Noble. Once inside, the smell of fresh books hits us, and Blaire closes her eyes, taking in the earthy scent.

"This is heaven," she says with a wide grin on her face as she looks over at me. Blaire takes off, grabbing and dragging me by the hand toward the back of the store. By the way she maneuvers through the aisles of books, I can only assume she has been here a time or two.

We approach the paranormal romance selection and Blaire plucks a book off the shelf. "Ah, I've been waiting for them to get the third book in," she says, the excitement in her voice making it rise a few notches. "You have no idea how hard it is to finish a book in a series and not know what happens next."

"I can imagine." But really, I can't. Reading for fun has never been my thing. Trazia tried to get me into it when she started *Harry Potter*, but I much prefer the movies.

Blaire clutches the book to her chest, and I take it from her so that she can pick up more and read the back of them. Watching her be open and carefree about something she loves makes me happy, and I know I could spend forever in here just being with her.

TWO HOURS. Two *fucking* hours. That is how long this woman keeps me here. I am a prisoner among the stacks. She barely notices me, but after I took the third book from her that she decided to get, she began automatically handing them to me. I am now dragging along six books, two of which are twice the size of the rest of the others, in my arms.

We're in the romance section now and I fear I may lose my man card if I spend another second here. Each book she has read, she goes into detail to me about the characters and their love for each other, and I'm afraid if we spend any more time here, I may pass out from hunger. "Blaire, baby, I know you're having the time of your life, but if I don't eat something soon, I'm going to make your books my dinner."

She looks up from the orange book with cartoon-looking characters on the front and regards me as if I haven't been her pack mule for the last couple hours. "Oh no," she says as she puts the book down. She said it was one she already read on her Kindle but does not have the physical copy of. "I'm so sorry. We can go. I got way more than I can afford anyway."

"I'm not trying to rush you. I just haven't eaten since before practice and it's almost seven."

Her eyes widen when I tell her the time.

"Seven? I can get lost in here for hours. I told you this was dangerous." She reaches for some of the books in my hand, but I shrug her off. I can carry my woman's books.

We begin our walk to the checkout. "Next time I'll bring a granola bar or something." I'll need to come prepared if two hours seems like ten minutes in here to her.

As we take our turn in line, Blaire faces me. She's chewing on her bottom lip. "I'm genuinely surprised you would want to

THE ACT OF TRUSTING

come back here with me. Emree banned me from ever taking her here or going to the book section in Target when we do our shopping because of how long I can take," she says. "Which doesn't seem fair because when we go to the craft and fabric stores, I let her have her time with little complaint, but whatever." She shrugs.

We're called up next and I dump the large collection of books onto the counter. As the cashier rings up the books, I try not to gawk at the price. All that for some words on paper? I refrain from saying my thoughts out loud in a bookstore because I feel like it's cursing in church. Forbidden.

Before Blaire can hand the cashier her card, I beat her to it and pay for the mountain of books. She tries to grab the card and give them hers, but it is too late.

"I could have paid for my books myself."

I smile down at her pouty face. "Yeah, well, I like getting you something you wanted, so let me do that and enjoy them."

She sighs, but there is a small smile on her face. "Thank you, Camden."

We walk hand in hand out of the bookstore with me carrying the two heavy bags. The sun has gone down some and there is a faint amount of light lingering in the sky as we approach my Jeep. Once we're both buckled and ready, I start driving.

We decide to grab some fast food since it's quick and easy. After ordering, I pull into a spot in the parking lot so we can eat. Blaire unbuckles her seat belt and turns to me, leaning her back against the door and lifting her left leg onto the seat.

"You know, if you keep spoiling me like this, you'll never get rid of me," she jokes with a smile on her face.

"Maybe that was my plan all along," I counter.

She laughs and I hand her the chicken nuggets she ordered with ranch. We begin digging into our food, leaving little room for talking as we're both hungry.

Once I finish my burger and fries, I drain my Coke to wash away the taste. Blaire is finishing her last nugget and watches me as she sips on her lemonade. I take in her eyes as she watches my movements through her lashes. Her lips wrapped around the straw. Her cheeks are a light tint of red and I wonder what she is thinking as she looks at me.

I want to kiss her. Badly. But I told her I would wait. She has to set the pace of this relationship and I am not going to push her. She needs to know I would never do anything she's not comfortable with.

"Camden?" she whispers so softly I almost don't hear her.

"Yes?"

She puts her drink down, ever so slowly leaning toward the center console. "C-can you kiss me?"

Reaching forward, I cup the side of her face and bring her closer to me. Our breaths mingle together between us, hers slightly louder as if she is nervous. "I've been waiting for you to ask, baby."

Before she can respond, I brush my lips lightly against hers, just feeling them. They're soft and slightly wet from the drink she had taken a sip of. Her breath hitches when our lips connect and I fear she is going to pull away, but she doesn't. She shuts her eyes and leans into me. I take that as an invitation and kiss her for real. My lips pressing into hers, claiming her.

Although I have kissed many girls in my years, none of them have left a spark like Blaire is. Her lips fit perfectly against mine. As I move my hand from her cheek, I glide it down, my palm resting on her waist. My tongue darts out, silently asking for permission, and Blaire allows it, opening for me. We explore each other and I'm lost in her. Her smell. Her taste. The feel of her body in my hands. Blaire lets out a moan and her hands clutch the front of my shirt. I know this needs to end before I pull her into my lap. She isn't ready for that, as much as I would like it to happen.

As I break apart our kiss, she looks at me with wanting eyes. Her face is flushed, lips slightly swollen, and her shirt has risen to expose her stomach where I was gripping her. I run my hand along the smooth skin there before bringing it back down into place.

"Why did you stop?" she asks, slightly breathless.

Running my hand up her side, I rest it against her face and my thumb glides along her cheekbone. "Trust me, I'm thinking I made a mistake on that."

She bites her lip and I slide my thumb across it, releasing the grip her teeth are holding.

Blaire grabs my hand and brings my palm in front of her, kissing the center. She leans forward and places her lips softly on mine, lingering. She smiles against my mouth and her eyes open slowly. "Thank you for letting me set the pace," she whispers against my lips.

"I want you to want to be with me, Blaire. To kiss and touch me. To spend time with me. You need that, I can tell."

She smiles and presses her lips to mine once more before pulling back. "Thank you for another great day."

"Get used to them, Gray Eyes," I tell her. "I want to make all our days together great."

CHAPTER SIXTEEN

BLAIRE

As I lie in bed, my mind is filled with thoughts of Camden. I have only seen him once since our first kiss and that makes me long to be near him. This feeling is new and strange to me. Being around Camden, I feel cherished and safe. This is something I was afraid would never happen after my assault because Harvey had my trust and took what I gave him, stomping it into the ground.

I haven't told Camden about what happened to me when I was sixteen, and it terrifies me what his reaction could be. The only other person here who knows about it is Emree. Every time I think about telling him, bile rises. The worry of what he will think of me after he finds out keeps me up some nights. If he looked at me with pity, I would hate it. And if he looked at me with disgust, I don't think I would be able to handle that kind of heartbreak.

Emree comes bursting into my bedroom, where she finds me snuggled under my comforter up to my chin. "Hey, cutie, you have any plans for today?" Emree asks as she plops down beside me.

"Well, Garrett gave us this weekend off, so I planned on relaxing and lounging around reading."

She clutches a pillow to her chest as she turns to lie on her side, facing me. "How about we make tomorrow a boring reading day and this beautiful afternoon we spend it poolside getting nice and tan with the guys we're seeing?"

"What are you talking about?"

"Conrad texted me. They're having a little pool party, but nowhere near the size of the last one. Just the guys who live there, Mateo's best friend, Jules, and us. I mean, if you want to go." This is the first time I'm hearing about this, and I wonder why Camden didn't tell me himself.

As I reach for my phone, I say, "One second," to Emree. Unlocking it, I see a text message from Camden sent half an hour ago telling me about the get-together and how he wants me to go.

"Sure. If you say it will be small, I'll go." I reply to Camden after giving Emree my answer.

"Awesome." She jumps from the bed and tosses the pillow at me. "I'm going to shower and start getting ready. Want to be sure I'm smooth in all the right places." She winks as she heads toward the door.

"Ew, so not what I needed to hear," I tell her, grossed out by her comment.

"You mind if we take your car? I'm packing a bag and will probably stay with Conrad tonight." She lifts her eyebrow at me. "Unless you think you may want to join in on the sleepover too?"

The thought alone makes me nervous. "I think it's far too soon for that."

I had told Emree about Camden's and my kiss in his car the moment I got inside after he walked me to the door, planting another longing kiss on my lips. She screamed and dragged me onto the couch to give her every detail and forbade me to leave anything out. It was the first time I did that girl bonding thing over a guy one of us is seeing and it was something I never knew I needed. We giggled, which I don't think I had ever done before, and I told Emree I was getting closer and closer to trusting Camden.

Since the moment we met, he has been kind, considerate, and sweet with me. Camden continuously assures me that the pace of our relationship is up to me, and he has never pushed for anything more. When we get to class, he greets me with a cup of my favorite coffee and a bright smile. Both of which I am happy with and welcome. He even surprised me before his practice on Thursday when I was in the library tutoring to say he missed me and was thinking about me. And before leaving, he kissed me so hard I felt lightheaded for the rest of my shift.

I'm falling for this man, and it is much easier than I thought it would be.

As Emree vacates my room to shower and get ready, I check my phone to see if Camden replied.

CAMDEN

Can't wait. Bring a swimsuit, baby ;)

I blush, thinking of him seeing me in something as revealing as my bathing suit.

BLAIRE

See you soon.

BY TWO, Emree and I are showered, shaved, hair styled to perfection, and dressed in cut-off shorts and T-shirts that cover our bikinis beneath. Emree had tried to get me to wear one of her string bikinis that leave little to the imagination, but I drew a line there. No way could I wear that, even in private by myself.

As we drive to the boys' house, my nerves begin to grow with the anticipation of seeing Camden. He gives me butterflies with every look, every small touch, and every sweet word that comes out of his beautiful mouth. In the short time I have known him, he has broken down so many walls I have kept up for years.

The guys' house isn't too far, and we make it in less than twenty minutes. There are a few cars parked outside, but nothing close to how crazy it was the first party before school. The one where Camden entered my life in the most awkward of ways.

I think back to that interaction and how if I had taken the front door out of the house like a normal person and not the side gate in an attempt to avoid the people inside, I never would have come across Camden. Our first time coming into contact may not be traditional, but it sure is memorable.

As we exit my Toyota Camry, the beat of the music drifts from behind the two-story house Camden shares with four of his roommates. He has told me the school has provided the house because of the number of donors there are for the sports teams. A few of the guys are here, some in the dorms, more are in fraternities, and there are two more houses near campus where some of the players live. For the soccer team, upperclassmen get the pick of the three houses while freshmen and sophomores are restricted to the dorms unless they pay to live off-campus or join a frat. The football coach made the same decision for their players.

Bypassing ringing the doorbell, Emree opens the door as if she has done this a million times. Trying not to be bad guests, we picked up some ice and a variety of chips at the grocery store on the way. Conrad greets us in the kitchen and takes the ice from Emree, wrapping his free arm around her waist and pulling her in for a kiss.

"How'd you know we were out of ice?" he asks against her lips.

She smiles. "Never been to a party where they didn't run out."

He kisses her once more before grabbing her hand and dragging her outside. She drops her overnight bag on the couch on the way out.

Alone in the kitchen, I go in search of some bowls for the chips we bought. Coming up empty after closing the third cabinet, I hear the sliding door behind me open. As I turn to ask whoever came in where I can find some bowls, a body encloses behind me and I freeze, unable to breathe or move. Before I go into full panic attack mode, the familiar scent of spice and sunscreen that has invaded my senses the last couple weeks is there. My body relaxes knowing it's Camden behind me and he wouldn't do anything against my will.

"I missed you, baby," he whispers. His breath tickles my ear. As he pushes my long hair aside, he places a kiss on my neck.

I sink into him, loving the feel of the sweetest man I have ever met wanting me. "I saw you a few days ago."

He's placing wet kisses along my neck, and I tilt to the right, giving him more access. His hands glide along my waist, resting against my stomach.

"Too long without seeing you," he says against my skin. Camden turns me around so that I'm facing him, my back pressing into the counter. "This okay?" he asks, his lips a hair's breadth away from touching mine. I nod, a little too fast, and my lips brush against his.

He grips my waist, bringing his body flush against mine as he crashes our lips together. I sigh at the contact, having missed him as much as he missed me. My hands have a mind of their own as they make their way up his forearms, his biceps, resting on either side of his face. I brush my thumbs along the stubble of his jaw and he moans, amplifying the kiss.

Camden's tongue runs along the seam of my lips, asking for access, and I grant it to him, opening to allow his tongue inside. It mingles with mine and I taste the faint hint of beer and mint on him. My hands move to his hair, threading the wavy strands between my fingers, pulling him tighter against me. Wanting him closer, I bite his lip in frustration.

"Fuck," Camden groans against my lips, breaking our kiss.

Camden lifts me and the next thing I know, my butt meets the countertop. He scoots me forward, my center molding to his front. The contact is foreign to me, but I welcome it. His lips part from mine and begin their descent, gliding across my cheek, my jaw, and landing on the base of my throat. I lean my head back against the cabinet, giving him more access.

A featherlight touch ghosts along my hips, under my shirt, and moves up and up to land on my ribs, just below my breasts. Camden's lips on my neck stop their exploring and he pulls his hands away from my body. He doesn't step back but leans far enough away to look into my eyes.

"Hey, what happened there?" he asks me. There is worry in his eyes and it's hard for me to keep his gaze.

I hadn't even noticed, but my hands are balled into fists at my sides and my body is frozen. "I-I'm sorry." Ducking my head, I avoid looking into his eyes. "I think it just became too much for me."

A soft touch is at my chin, lifting my head up to meet his eyes. "We kind of got carried away there, huh?" He smiles, and it is so sweet and beautiful that it helps me unclench my fists and relax. "I told you we're going at your pace, remember? Anything that becomes too much, you let me know. My feelings aren't hurt."

"I'm sure you're used to girls who are ready and sleep with you right away." The thought of Camden with other women makes my stomach tighten, but I try not to let it show on my face.

He runs his fingers along my jaw. "I'm not going to lie to you. Yes, I've been with other women, and yes, most of them aren't the type to take it slow." Bile begins to rise hearing him admit it. "But, Blaire, I've never wanted to go slow with a girl before. I don't know what it is about you, but from the moment I saw you in my backyard at that party, I haven't been able to get you off my mind. There's something here, baby, and I'm more than happy waiting for you to be ready." His words are sincere, and my heart grows fonder of him at his honesty.

Reaching forward, I grasp his face between my hands, running my thumb along his bottom lip. "I like you. A lot. I've never felt this for another man before and it scares me." I take a deep breath. "This is all new to me. The dating, the touching... the kissing. I have some things I'm working through, and I have issues trusting other people, but you've been breaking down the wall I put up so long ago little by little."

He smiles and kisses my finger that is tracing his lips. "Well, dating is kind of new for me also, so how about we explore this together? I will never push you, but I do want you to know you can trust me. I would never do anything to hurt you, Blaire."

Leaning forward, I place a gentle kiss to his lips. "I'm truly starting to feel that."

CHAPTER SEVENTEEN

CAMDEN

Smoke from the grill is making me sweat and the Florida heat in August isn't much help either. Somehow, I <u>was put</u> on grilling duty when usually it's Mateo's job, but he vouched out of it because standing over a hot open flame in this weather is not desirable. I had ditched my tank I had been wearing and even with just swimming trunks on, I'm sweating nonstop.

From the corner of my eye, I see Blaire sitting on one of the loungers, talking with her roommate, who is stretched out, soaking in the sun in her bathing suit. My girl hasn't taken her T-shirt and shorts off and I'm partially glad because I don't want the guys looking at her and yet I wouldn't mind seeing her in a bikini.

After what happened in the kitchen, I wanted to give her space. If I couldn't already tell she had very little experience before, her confession only made my assumptions true. I didn't lie to her when I said I'm happy to wait until she's ready, but I feel like there is more to just her inexperience and she isn't telling me what. Blaire said I was breaking down her walls and hopefully, I can become someone she can trust. Someone who she felt comfortable enough to give herself to. Mind and body.

"Food is ready," I call out as I scrape the last burger off the grill. We kept it simple with burgers, hot dogs, and the chips the girls brought.

There are far fewer of us here than at our usual parties. It's only my roommates: Maddox, Mateo, Conrad, and Levi. Blaire, Emree, and Mateo's childhood friend, Jules, are the only women here. We also invited our teammates Drew and Jax. It's a more chill evening, except for the fact that Maddox is drinking himself away and stumbling as he walks over to the patio table we set up with all the food.

"You're such a good provider, Cammy," Maddox slurs as he grabs a plate and burger bun, lifting a hot patty with his fingers.

I eye him, worried he is going to do something stupid tonight. "You okay, man?"

He takes another swig of his beer, leveling me a look over the bottle as he tips it back. "You know I'm good, baby." He is definitely not good.

Choosing to ignore him, I focus on the beautiful brunette who walked up to my side. I hand her a plate and plant a kiss on her cheek. "Hey. What are you in the mood for?"

She looks between the cheeseburgers, hamburgers, and hot dogs, trying to decide. "It all smells amazing. I think I'll get a cheeseburger." She reaches for a bun while I use the spatula to get her a patty.

We all sit around the table, talking about practice, classes, jobs, and our upcoming game. Blaire sits beside me, smiling as Mateo tells the girls about how well our practice was this morning. The team has been more in sync this last week and it gives me hope for our first game a week from today.

Reaching over, I rest my hand on her thigh, giving it a squeeze. She looks over and gives me a shy smile.

"You going to come cheer me on at the game, baby?"

Reaching down, she puts her hand on top of mine. "As long

as you promise to win. Can't be walking out of there with shame from cheering on a losing team," she jokes.

Conrad bursts into laughter across from us. "Oh, we'll be taking that W. Nobody can beat our defense. Plus, Camden and Maddox are faster than any of the players on the Cornwall team. Those sorry fucks won't be able to catch them."

Conrad and Mateo are some of the best defensemen in the state and Levi is a damn good goalie. His height and hand size give him an advantage and he blocks far more balls from entering the net than any goalie I have been on a team with before.

"Well, I know I'll be there to cheer on my man," Emree says, wrapping her arm around Conrad and kissing his cheek. He smiles, but it doesn't reach his eyes. I can tell this girl is falling for Conrad, but he has never been serious about anyone he's been with and doesn't make it clear that what they have is only casual.

Blaire laughs, not noticing Conrad's uncomfortable expression. "If you're really that good, then I guess I can make it."

"I'll leave you both some tickets. I always get some for my mom and sister, but they rarely make it out," I tell her.

After the guys and I finish off the last of the food, we start cleaning up the table. Blaire, Emree, and Jules have long since left us after finishing their one serving of burgers and hot dogs. I'm finally full after three burgers and a hot dog. Being an athlete means burning a ridiculous amount of calories and constantly being hungry.

After tossing all the trash out, I make my way over to Blaire. She has been lounging on one of the lawn chairs along with Emree and Jules, chatting away. She has since lost her T-shirt that was covering her black bikini top, and it takes everything in my power not to ogle her tits that are spilling out.

"Hey, Gray Eyes," I greet her, bending down and kissing the top of her head.

She smiles and tilts her head back, looking up at me through her sunglasses. "Hi," she says quietly.

"Shots!" someone yells from the other side of the lawn. Maddox is over there, holding a bottle of tequila and a stack of plastic shot glasses.

"Is he okay?" Emree asks as she looks over at him with worry on her face.

Honestly, I don't know. Since before classes started, Maddox has been on a drinking rampage. He acted funny the weekend my sister and mom came to visit, but I figured something happened with his parents after he spent a week with them. We had a great summer. It was just the two of us at the house and we were working for his uncle's construction company, me trying to save up as much money as I could to not work this semester. Though he isn't close with them, his parents requested he join them at a beach house in North Carolina they had bought as a second summer home.

"He's been weird since school started. I don't think he's been sober a single weekend." Even though we didn't have a party last weekend, Maddox got trashed at Whiskey Joe's Friday night, and then Saturday he ended up passed out on the lawn at a fraternity house. One of our teammates helped get him home and he spent the night on the couch.

Mateo heads over, grabbing a shot Maddox offers him.

"Oh no, he and tequila don't mix well," Jules says, getting up and going toward her best friend.

Maddox's eyes light up when she gets to them and he grabs her around the waist, lifting her into the air. Mateo's face goes from laughing to serious as he jerks Jules away from Maddox's grip, causing him to stumble back in his drunken state.

A hand glides up my arm and grips my bicep. "He's going to end up hurting himself if he keeps drinking like that," Blaire says from beside me.

"I know, baby." I sigh, not wanting to have to deal with this tonight. I was hoping for an enjoyable time with my girl and our friends. "I'm going to grab him a bottle of water and try to pry the bottle of liquor from his hands."

Before heading inside, I kiss Blaire on the cheek and leave her standing beside the chairs and pool. I grab a bottle of water from the fridge, hoping Maddox doesn't start shit tonight and decides to sober up. It's getting late and I know Blaire isn't staying the night like Emree is, so I want to spend more time with her before she leaves.

A scream comes from the patio and before I register who it was, I'm outside the door. Maddox has Blaire pinned to his front, both his hands shackling her wrists, and there is a look of fear on her face. He swings her body, pretending like he is going to throw her in the pool, and she screams again, trying to get her hands free.

"What the fuck!" I scream, seeing red at the scared look on her face. He laughs, clearly thinking my anger is funny.

Before I can get to them, Maddox stumbles after pretending to throw Blaire into the pool again, causing the both of them to fall into the pool before I can get to her. Maddox's body fell on top of Blaire's and he's the first to break out of the water.

Bypassing the stairs, I dive into the pool and reach for Blaire's body underwater. As she comes up, she gasps for air and begins pushing me away. "Get off of me!" she yells.

"Baby, baby, it's me. I got you." One arm is around her waist, dragging her from the deep end, while the other is fighting her off as she is pushing against my chest.

When she realizes it's me and not Maddox, she relaxes. I get her to the shallow end where there is a bench underwater and sit, holding her in my lap. "You're okay. I got you. Are you hurt anywhere?"

She has calmed down and touches the back of her head, wincing. "I think I hit my head when we fell into the pool."

When she brings her hand back in front of us, there's blood on it.

"Fuck," I whisper. "Let me get you out of here and look at it."

Helping Blaire out of the pool, I carry her into the house and we pass Maddox sitting on a lounger, passed out. Half his body is falling onto the ground and Mateo is trying to lift his legs up to get him fully on it.

"Leave him like that. He deserves to wake up in pain," I grumble out. Blaire squeezes my shoulder, making me look away from my so-called best friend.

"I can walk," Blaire says to me. I grip her harder in my arms, bringing her closer to my chest.

"Not happening, baby. I'm taking care of you."

Her eyes soften at my words, and she relaxes into my hold.

Taking the stairs two at a time, I bring Blaire into my bedroom and drop her on my desk chair to go to my closet and get some towels, then wrap one around her to help dry her off and run one over my body. The blood is dripping from her head and down her back. I use one of the towels to stop the flow of blood from traveling any farther and apply it to her head. She whimpers and I feel like a son of a bitch for causing her more pain.

"I'm sorry, baby, but I need to apply pressure to stop the bleeding. Head injuries bleed more, but from what I see, it isn't too bad. You won't need stitches or anything." If Maddox wasn't passed out right now, I would storm downstairs and kick his ass.

Blaire brings her hand to rest against mine that is gripping the back of the chair. "I know. Thank you for taking care of me and please try not to be so mad at Maddox. He was so out of it and didn't mean for us to fall into the pool."

She's too good of a person. Any other woman would be pissed at Maddox for acting like an idiot. "Blaire, baby, he shouldn't have gotten that drunk and he should have never touched you. I saw how scared you were before he fell into the pool with you. That's not okay, and him being drunk isn't an excuse for how he acted."

As she bites her bottom lip, I can see she's fighting with herself on being upset with Maddox. "What he did was stupid, but being mad at him isn't going to change what happened."

"Let's not talk about him right now and let me clean up your head." I pull the towel away from her head and see that the pressure I have been applying has helped to stop the flow of blood coming out. "How about you take a quick shower to get the chlorine off of you and I'll get the first aid kit to clean up your head when you're done?"

Blaire looks down at her wet clothes. "How about I just head home. I don't have a change of clothes and I can clean my head up and everything there."

As she goes to stand, she stumbles, and I catch her before she falls forward. "As much as I believe you can handle all that at your place, I don't think you should be driving right now, and it would give me peace of mind if I can watch over you tonight."

A look of worry comes across her face. "I can't stay the night here," she says, looking around the room like she is trying to find an escape.

I bend down so that she and I are at eye level. "Blaire, you hit your head and I don't think you should be by yourself tonight. It would make me feel better if you stayed here. I will sleep on the couch downstairs, but I want to be able to check on you every few hours. Emree can even sleep in here with you if that will make you feel better, but you'll have to put up a fight with Conrad." I smile at her, and she laughs a little.

"Okay," she whispers, "but I don't have anything to wear." She looks down at her soaked clothes.

Standing, I give her a quick kiss and head for my dresser.

She's quiet behind me as I pull out a pair of clean boxers and a T-shirt and bring them over to her. "Here, these are clean but will probably be a little big on you."

She clutches them to her chest. "Thank you," she says, barely above a whisper.

I show Blaire to the bathroom across the hall from my bedroom and give her a fresh towel. She closes and locks the door and once I hear the water running, I head downstairs. Emree and Jules are in the kitchen doing the dishes and when Emree sees me, she drops the rag she was using to dry the plates.

"Where is Blaire? Is she okay?" Emree asks with slight panic in her voice.

"She's fine," I tell her. "Her head was bleeding from when she hit it at the bottom of the pool, but I got it to stop, and she is taking a shower now so I can clean the wound."

Emree's shoulders relax. "That's good. I would take her home, but I've had a few beers and don't feel comfortable driving."

Conrad comes in shirtless and with a pissed-off look on his face. "That motherfucker puked on me," he seethes.

Emree lets out a laugh from beside me and slaps her hand over her face to cover it up. He glares at her and disappears upstairs without another word to either of us.

The back door opens again and Levi and Mateo are carrying in a passed-out Maddox, who is covered in his own vomit. Seeing him after knowing how reckless he was with Blaire makes me furious. She should have never been put in that position, especially by any of the guys in this house. When he's sober, I'm giving Maddox hell for what he did tonight. He needs to get his shit together.

As I watch the guys drag Maddox upstairs, I can't help but wonder what the hell is going on with him.

CHAPTER EIGHTEEN

BLAIRE

I'm naked. In a boy's house. I have never been naked in a boy's house.

The hot water cascading down my body helps to relieve my nerves. Camden's friends are nice, but tonight terrified me. When Maddox grabbed me by my wrists, my body reacted the same way it did when Harvey held me in that same position. This time, though, I fought. Though it was ultimately useless, it was the biggest difference between what happened tonight and what went down four years ago.

I didn't fight Harvey off. To this day, I still don't know why. I begged him to stop more times than I can remember, but he never listened. He told me I would enjoy it, that all the girls enjoyed it with him.

He was wrong.

With what happened to me, I never thought I would enjoy affection or kissing. Never thought I would come close to thinking about having sex with someone. Having someone use you and violate you in the worst way possible changes you a lot. When I was younger, I was excited about dating. My father was strict and told me I had to wait until I was sixteen before I could date, which was a couple years later than when most my friends started. After being raped by Harvey, the thought of dating or being touched made my skin crawl.

Camden came in like a wrecking ball. I never expected someone like him, and especially never expected my reaction to his affection, his hands on me, or him kissing me. I like it all and none of it reminds me of that horrible night. Camden is gentle and patient and senses my need for taking this slowly. I'm grateful to him for that.

After washing the soap off my body, I rinse the conditioner out of my hair. I was surprised to see five men living in a house together have conditioner, but am assuming it's Levi's or Maddox's since the two of them have longer hair.

Once I'm thoroughly rinsed, I shut the water off and grab the towel Camden gave me. Staring at his clothes sitting on the sink, I wonder if I could convince him I'm fine to drive home. My head where I hit the bottom of the pool is still throbbing and there is a lingering headache, but I don't feel as dizzy as I did when I was in his room and the hot shower has helped.

Thinking it would be a useless fight, I grab his clothes and begin putting them on. He was right. They're way too big. I'm not a short girl, coming in around five-six, but his T-shirt still comes down mid-thigh. The boxers he gave me are those brief types with the elastic band and they slide off my hips a little, but they will have to do. Spotting some toothpaste on the counter, I apply a dab to my finger and begin brushing my teeth to the best of my ability.

I bundle my wet clothes in the towel I used and head toward Camden's bedroom. Before I can get through the threshold, someone wraps their arms around me.

"Oh my gosh, I was worried you had fallen or something while you were in there," Emree says, her words slightly muffled since her head is tucked into my shoulder. She pulls back and comes to stand in front of me, her hands on my shoulders. "How are you? How is your head? I can't believe that asshat threw you in the pool like that."

"I'm fine," I assure her. "And I don't think he really meant for us to go into the pool. He stumbled and we kind of...ended up in there."

She waves her hand through the air. "Doesn't matter. What he did was stupid, and you both could have been really hurt. He's lucky you don't have a brain injury or something. I'll kick his ass after Camden's finished with him. I have moves. I watched *The Karate Kid*."

Emree is one of the greatest friends. She is there to make you always laugh. "Easy there, killer, there's no need to whip out those moves," I tell her. "Speaking of, have you seen Camden?"

"He and Mateo were trying to find the first aid kit. Apparently, one of the guys used it and didn't put it where they usually keep it in the downstairs bathroom." She rolls her eyes. "Men, I swear they can't keep anything organized."

"Do you think you could find Conrad and see if he has anything to help with my headache?" Talking is making it worse and all I really want to do right now is go to bed. I don't even know what time it is, but the sun has long since gone down and it's been an exhausting day.

She smiles and rubs my arm. "Yeah, babe. Let me take your wet clothes too. Camden wanted me to throw them in their washer with his so you have something to wear tomorrow." She reaches forward and grabs my bundled-up clothes and towel.

"Thank you," I tell her. "If you see him, could you let him know I'll be in his room?"

"Of course." She heads toward the stairs and disappears as she makes her way down.

As I go into Camden's room, I notice the scattered clothes and open books that were lying around are now put away and smile at the fact that he must have cleaned up. The bed is now made and it looks like he put fresh sheets on there as well. Deciding to take advantage of his absence, I look around. On his desk is a computer and an open math textbook with the chapter we're currently working on in class. A picture of him as a kid and who I assume is his mother sits on the corner of the desk. She looks to be in her early thirties and is beautiful. He got his dark hair and green eyes from her. I would assume Camden is around ten in the picture and I know that is after his father left. His mother's smile is bright, but there is worry in her eyes. I can't imagine being a single mom like she was. With two kids so close in age and being as young as she looks, it must have been hard on her.

Moving along, I take in his calendar hanging on the wall beside his closet. He has notes on days he has games, practices, tests, and assignments due. I would have assumed athletes were able to slack off, but it seems Camden works hard. He mentioned he was here on a soccer scholarship, and I wonder if he struggles to keep his grades up because of the risk of losing that.

I smile as I see the copy of *The Great Gatsby* on his bedside table. There is a bookmark stuck into the halfway spot of the book. Beside it is a pair of black-rimmed glasses.

"That's my nighttime enjoyment."

I jump at the sound of Camden's voice from the open door.

"Sorry, didn't mean to interrupt your snooping." He smiles and I'm happy to find he isn't mad about me looking around his room.

"Sorry, I was just looking at your pictures and stuff." Beside his copy of the book is a photo of him in a graduation cap and gown with a young, beautiful girl on his back. I can tell they were both laughing as the photo was taken. "Is this your sister?" I ask, hoping it is and not some ex-girlfriend.

He walks over and picks up the framed photo. "Yeah, that's

Trazia. This was at my high school graduation. She didn't think I would actually be making it to college and tackled me to see the diploma to make sure it was real." Camden smiles as he looks down at the photo before putting it back. "I brought you some Tylenol for the headache. Come sit at the desk and I'll clean the cut on your head."

I follow him over and take a seat. He moves my wet hair out of the way and inspects my head injury. "How bad does it look, doc?"

He chuckles. "Better than I thought now that all the blood is out of the way. You definitely don't need stitches, but I'm going to clean it and add some antibiotic ointment on it."

As he's applying stuff to my head from the first aid kit he brought in, I take the medicine and water bottle he set down beside me and swallow the pills. I try not to wince as he uses a cotton swab to apply some ointment, but it stings some. After he's finished, Camden puts everything back into the kit and closes it.

"Are you hungry or anything? Do you want something else to drink besides water?" He is standing in front of me awkwardly with his hands tucked into a pair of sweat shorts he changed into. He's shirtless and his tanned chest is on full display.

I smile up at him. "Honestly, I'm pretty tired. Today kind of wore me out."

He nods. "Okay. Well, I put some clean sheets on the bed, and I'll just let you get some sleep."

I stand and grab one of his hands before he heads out. "Thank you for today and for taking care of me."

Pulling my hand forward, my chest collides with his warm body. "Please don't thank me for something that should have never happened. I hate that you were hurt here. I want you to enjoy being at my house and around my friends."

"I do," I tell him honestly. "Your house is very homey and

165

other than the fact that there was a minor mishap with Maddox today, I had fun with your friends. I especially like Jules. Emree and I already made plans with her to meet up for your game next weekend."

He smiles. "I like the idea of you being there. My own good luck charm." Leaning forward, he places his lips softly against mine. Lifting my hand, I hold his head there, deepening the kiss. If anything, tonight has shown me how sweet and caring Camden can be and in his arms, I feel like everything will be okay.

He moans, pulling me closer by the waist. When his tongue comes out to run against the seam of my lips, I open, allowing him entrance. The grip on my waist tightens, almost painfully, when his tongue meets mine.

I don't think I will ever get tired of kissing this man.

Camden's hand begins sliding along my ribs as mine tangles into the hair on the back of his head. He tastes like mint and the flavor is so strong it burns a little. His hands stop just below my breasts and part of me wants to grab his hand and move it up.

I do.

Using my hand that isn't in his hair, I help him by grabbing onto one of his hands and bringing it to my breast. He stops kissing me and when I open my eyes, his are also open and looking at me.

"Are you sure?" he asks, not moving his hand.

I nod, giving him permission.

He bends down and resumes kissing me while his hand explores my chest. With my lack of extra clothes, I'm left without a bra and the heat from his hand is burning up my sensitive skin through the T-shirt he loaned me. When he rubs his thumb over my nipple, I let out a moan, tilting my head back, breaking our kiss.

Nothing has ever felt as good as Camden touching me in such an intimate way.

With a groan, Camden pulls away and leans his forehead against mine. My heavy breathing matches his as we stand there. The hand on my breast comes to wrap around my neck. "Baby, as much as I want to lay you down on my bed and continue this, you need rest after what happened tonight, and I don't want the first time I touch this beautiful body to be after my idiot friend hurt you and while you're injured."

With both my hands at his head now, I pull his hair slightly. "My head is clear," I tell him confidently, trying to bring his lips to mine again.

He stops me. Closing his eyes, he cranes his neck back, so he is looking up at the ceiling. "You're pushing me, woman."

I smile. Seeing the effect I have on him makes me feel sexy. Wanted. Something I have never felt before.

"You get into bed and I'm going to sleep on the couch." He pecks his lips against mine, grabs his glasses and charger from his nightstand, and then is out the door, shutting it behind him.

After getting into Camden's bed, I turn the lamp off on the bedside table and snuggle down deep. The sheets are cool and soft against my exposed skin and his bed is that kind of memory foam that has you sinking into it. I could live in the cocoon I've trapped myself in if it was socially acceptable to never leave your bed. But alas, I'm sure there would be worry from the people around me.

The walls around me cry out and I can hear the moving of water through them. Someone must be in the shower and I wonder if it's Camden. Naked. Across the hall. I try not to think too hard about the possibility of his wet, sun-kissed naked skin so close to mine and how it would feel to run my hands along his smooth chest.

Squeezing my eyes shut, I try to change my course of thought to something less...sexual. But that's hard when all these feelings are emerging and I don't know what to do about them. Feeling his mouth on me, his hands on my body, makes me warm all over and I want nothing more than to continue the kiss we had going on earlier.

Rolling over, I count my breaths and hope that sleep comes quickly.

CHAPTER NINETEEN

CAMDEN

Rubbing my face into my pillow, I groan at the light coming in through my window. It's too damn early and I want nothing more than to stay right where I am plastered against the warm body beside me. I duck my head, nuzzling farthing into the scent I have grown to know recently.

The body beside me stiffens and I flex my hips forward, bringing us closer together.

"Camden," a voice whispers from near me. I must still be dreaming because the warm body that angelic voice belongs to wasn't with me when I went to bed last night.

"Just a few more minutes," I tell myself, not wanting to wake up from the dream I must be in. My hand, which is against a warm stomach, travels up and I grab hold of a soft, full breast. My dream angel is Blaire. I would know the feel of her in my hands even when I'm sleeping.

There is a gasp from near me and the body plastered to me goes from still to stone. I peek one of my eyes open and see the back of a dark head of hair. Leaning forward, Blaire's face comes into view and her eyes are wide open.

It wasn't a dream. I was groping Blaire for real and pressing my morning wood against her back.

"Fuck!" I shout, ripping my hand out from under her shirt. I shoot away from her until my back is pressed against the headboard. "Blaire, baby, I am so sorry. I was asleep. I don't even remember coming in here."

"It's okay," she says softly, moving from where she is lying on her side and avoiding looking at me.

I run my hands through my hair, cursing myself for somehow coming into my room during the night. Last thing I remember was taking a cold shower, needing to cool down after the hot-as-hell kiss we shared, and changing into a pair of sweats before falling asleep on the couch last night. Not sure how between then and now I ended up in my bed with Blaire against me.

"It's not okay. I shouldn't have been in here. I definitely should not have been touching you like that." Fuck, I hope this doesn't scare her off.

Blaire scoots up on the bed, sitting beside me with her back to the headboard as well. "It's your room, Camden. I'm sure you came in here subconsciously. I must have forgotten to lock the door like I usually do." She's looking up at me now and I take in how beautiful she is in the morning. Her hair is a mess, going in all different directions. Her skin seems brighter and her eyes have a dreamy look in them.

"God, you're the most gorgeous woman I've ever seen," I say without thinking. She blushes and ducks her head. I reach forward and pull her face back up by the chin. "Don't do that. I wasn't done looking at you."

She smiles and leans forward, placing a soft kiss on my lips. "You're making it really difficult not to fall for you, Camden Collins."

I smile against her lips. "It's all part of my charm, baby."

Putting my hand on the back of her neck, I bring her

forward and deepen the kiss. Even though how I acted this morning would have had me thinking she would pull away, Blaire leans more into me, resting her hands against my bare chest. My other hand travels down her body, skimming the outside of her breast and resting on her hip. She pushes her body more into mine, so we are chest to chest now.

The angle is uncomfortable, but I want nothing more than to continue kissing and touching this beautiful woman in my bed. Without thinking, both hands grip her waist and I'm moving her to my lap, straddling me. She gasps, breaking the kiss and looking down at me.

"Slow. I promise," I tell her, giving her hips a little squeeze of reassurance.

She nods and bends down, crashing her lips down to mine again.

I've never considered making out that much of an enjoyment. It was more of something you needed to do to get to the good stuff: sex. But while I know sex with Blaire would be epic beyond my imagination, kissing her and having my hands on her sexy body makes me more than happy.

She shifts her hips and I groan. The movement brings her core directly into contact with my hard-as-a-rock dick. Her lips freeze against mine and she moves her hips again, torturing me. Her eyes close and she throws her head back, basking in the feel of me against her most sensitive area. I watch her as she shifts her hips back and forth, and back and forth, completely lost in the moment as she gets herself off on me. Seeing her like this is unbelievably sexy. It's as if she has let her guard down and allowed herself this enjoyment.

Part of me thinks she has completely forgotten I'm here, too focused on enjoying the feeling of her body against mine. I grip her hips, slowing her movements, and she latches onto my shoulders. Her body begins to shake, and her eyes widen as an orgasm takes over. I move her hips faster, hitting just the right spot, and she cries out my name, the sound more beautiful than anything I've heard before. The friction of her grinding against me has me coming right behind her, like a damn teenager, in my pants and holding tight to her waist, pushing her down and holding her to me.

Slumped against my chest, I feel her steady breaths against my neck. "Baby, you okay?"

She nods.

"Give me your eyes, beautiful."

Ever so slowly, she lifts herself so we're face to face. I take in the flushed but satisfied look.

"There you are." Leaning forward, I place a kiss on her nose, then her cheeks, and finally on her lips.

"I'm so sorry," she whispers against my mouth.

Pulling back, I study her. "What the hell for?"

She blushes. "For going crazy on you. I don't know what came over me."

This beautiful, sexy, smart woman has no idea how hot what she just did was. I'm beginning to think she's even more innocent than I thought. "Blaire, baby...have you never had an orgasm?"

Her eyes widen. "What? N-no."

I can see her brain going through the motions.

"I-is that what that was?" Her voice is barely above a whisper as she stutters her question. It's as if she's trying to make sure no one hears her, but it's only us in this room.

Tucking her mess of hair behind her ear, I caress her cheek. "Yeah, baby, that was an orgasm, and it was fucking incredible watching your body come apart on me like that."

She ducks her head again. "Oh my gosh." The words come out muffled by my chest.

There's a loud knock at my door before someone bursts inside. "Rise and shine, my dear best—" Emree cuts off when she sees Blaire and me in a very...intimate position.

"Oh no," she says, slapping her hands over her eyes. "I saw nothing. Nothing at all. Continue. I mean, not continue." She backs up, bumping into the doorframe. "Ouch. Okay, I'm just leaving. Blaire, I-I'll see you downstairs." With that parting, she shuts the door.

"That wasn't embarrassing," Blaire says sarcastically.

I chuckle, running my hands under her shirt and up her back. "Guessing in my sleep state last night I didn't lock the door either." Blaire shivers under my touch. "You cold?"

She shakes her head. Leaning her forehead against mine, she says, "I think we should probably go downstairs."

Groaning, I know she's right, but it's not what I want to do. What I want nothing more is to stay here and watch her come apart again. "Yeah. I'll make you some breakfast before you leave. You said you work this afternoon, right?"

"Yeah, at four."

Lifting her off me, I scoot to the end of the bed, trying to hide my half-mast erection from her. "Come on. I'm going to change real quick and we can head downstairs. I need to put our clothes in the dryer anyway."

"Change?" she asks.

Looking over at her with her legs curled into her chest and her arms wrapped around herself, I can't help but notice how tiny she looks in my bed. "Yeah, baby, you aren't the only one who got off on that hot session we had." With a wink, I grab some shorts and a T-shirt from my drawer, then head to the bathroom.

After changing and using the bathroom, I wash my hands and meet Blaire outside of my bedroom. She looks cute as fuck in my shorts and T-shirt with her hair now up in one of those messy buns girls wear around campus. Her face is naked of any makeup, not that she wears much anyway, and her eyes seem a brighter gray without it.

Grabbing her hand, she smiles up at me and I'm glad she

isn't hiding like she was earlier. Her getting off on me was hot as hell, but I could tell she was embarrassed. I want her to be comfortable around me, in and out of the bedroom, and having her wrap her arm around mine and lean into me like she is now makes me happy she isn't backing away from me.

Conrad, Mateo, Jules, Levi, and Emree are already in the kitchen. The girls are setting out bacon on a sheet pan while Conrad fixes two cups of coffee and Mateo is cracking eggs into a pan on the stove.

"Good morning, you sexy things," Emree says with a knowing smile on her face.

Tucking Blaire into my side, I kiss the top of her head before she goes off to help Emree and Jules with the bacon. Emree giggles and whispers something to Blaire, and she shushes her best friend.

Conrad hands me an empty coffee cup and I proceed to fill it with just enough room to leave a splash of creamer. "Noticed you weren't on the couch this morning," he states while stirring in his spoonfuls of sugar.

Smiling, I grab my mug and lean against the counter. "Must've sleepwalked into my room last night, but you won't hear me complaining about waking up next to the most beautiful woman."

He eyes me suspiciously. "I've never heard you talk like this, man. What is it about her?" Conrad has never been in a serious relationship and grew up with two parents who taught him everything about what a toxic couple is. While my last relationship was in high school, my mom taught me when you find a woman worth it, you treat her right or you'll lose her.

"Everything, man," I tell him honestly. "She's the sweetest, sexiest, smartest woman I've ever met. And the damn thing is, she has no idea how incredibly stunning she is or what she does to me."

He looks over at Blaire, who is carelessly laughing with her friends, and studies her. His eyes shift between Blaire and Emree, and I wonder what he's thinking. "Yeah, man. I wish it could be that easy." Grabbing his mug, he walks over to the bar and slumps down on one of the stools.

We all settle into our tasks. Me toasting and buttering the bread, Blaire, Emree, and Jules chopping fruit, Mateo scrambling the eggs, Levi getting some drinks out, and Conrad supervising, I guess. After some bitching from Mateo and me, Conrad sets the table with some paper plates and utensils before we bring the food over.

As we sit around the table eating, Maddox stumbles into the kitchen, bypassing all of us and heading for the fridge. Conversation stalls as we all watch him throw open the door, reach in, and grab the carton of orange juice, then take large gulps straight from it.

Levi clears his throat and Maddox brings his attention to us. He looks like hell. There's some dried vomit on the side of his face, his long hair is sticking up in every which direction, and his eyes are bloodshot.

"Fuck, nobody came to get me off the bathroom floor for some food." He comes over and grabs a handful of bacon, leaning onto Jules in the process.

Mateo jumps up, shoving him off her. "What the hell, dude, get off of her."

Maddox almost falls back but catches himself on the kitchen bar. "What's your problem, man?"

"Our problem is you coming in here acting like you weren't a complete ass last night for what you did to Blaire," says Levi.

My girl ducks her head and I clench my fists together. Being reminded of what an idiot he was last night and how he hurt her makes me want to jam my fist into his jaw.

His face goes pale as he looks between Blaire and me, then back at Levi. "Wh-what did I do?"

Nobody says a word.

"What the *fuck* did I do?" he asks again, urgency in his voice.

Jules chimes in. "You were plastered, Maddox." Her deep voice is stern. "While we were all hanging around the pool, you thought it would be funny to grab Blaire and pretend to throw her in, but you lost your balance and you both went in."

He runs his hands down his face, seeming upset at what she's told him so far.

"Blaire hit her head at the bottom of the pool and was bleeding pretty bad. Mateo and Levi had to go in after you. They were afraid you would drown, you were so far gone."

Maddox's eyes widen as he turns to Blaire. "No. Blaire, I am so sorry." His voice cracks at the end.

She looks up at him with forgiveness in her eyes. "It's okay, really. I know you didn't mean it and I'm all right."

Beside her, I'm steaming. "It's not *fucking* okay. He needs to get his shit together."

Maddox stares at me for many seconds before saying anything. "I know, man." He looks at Blaire. "I really am sorry. That should have never happened." He heads upstairs, leaving me with too many questions that I don't think I'll get answers to.

An awkward silence comes over us. Blaire reaches over and lays her hand against my thigh, and I didn't know until now that I was tensed up, but one touch from her relieves it.

"Well, this is awkward," Emree chimes in, chomping down on her bacon.

Everyone laughs. Mine is a little more forced, but Emree breaking the silence helps to relax me.

CHAPTER TWENTY

BLAIRE

I s this what love feels like? As I lie in my bed reflecting on the events that have gone on over the last few days since I left Camden's house, I can't help but wonder if this feeling I have for him is love.

No, that can't be. I cannot possibly be falling for someone in such a short amount of time. I have known this man for a few short weeks, and we have only had our first date last week. Yet I can't help but wonder. My pulse races with the anticipation of seeing him each day, my skin tingles anytime he touches me, and my heart feels like it will burst out of my chest whenever I'm around Camden or even thinking about him, like I am now.

I read about love in the hundreds of romance novels I own; the way I feel about Camden Collins is how the authors describe their characters' love.

Since I left his house Sunday, Camden has texted me every morning and night, and several of the hours in between. We saw each other in class on Monday and Wednesday, where he insists on distracting me with a gentle touch here and there. On the days we do not have class together, he makes sure to catch me before his practices if I'm in the library or between classes.

If I'm not in love yet, this beautiful man is making it damn hard not to fall for him.

It's Thursday and though I saw Camden for a quick moment before his practice, the promise he made to come by Whiskey Joe's tonight has me more excited about work than I have ever been.

"What are you thinking about so hard over there?" Emree questions from standing in my open doorway.

I'm curled under my covers and was hoping to get a quick nap before we had to be at work. "Have you ever been in love?"

Her eyes widen and she steps forward, taking a seat on the end of my bed. "Well, I can't say I have. In high school, I told the guy I was dating I loved him, but I now know that was nothing like what I imagine love to be like." She pauses for a second. Her brows are drawn together as she studies my face. "Blaire...do you love Camden?"

Pulling the covers over my head, I hide. "I don't know." Every word comes out muffled from my heavy duvet.

She pulls them back, exposing my face. "You like him a lot, huh." It comes out as more of a statement than a question.

I nod.

"You know, I was honestly worried nobody would be able to gain your trust like you need. You have been so guarded for such a long time, and for good reasons, but I think Camden is your game changer. I see the way he looks at you, like he wants to protect you from everything bad in the world, and you look at him like he's something out of a dream." She has never been honest like this about the two of us. Sure, she says she likes him, and he is sweet and good for me, but this is deeper. "Don't get me wrong, it's sickening how cute you two are, and what I walked in on last weekend required some bleaching of my brain, but I'm happy for you. More than happy. I see how much you have changed in these last few weeks."

Leaning forward, I reach for my best friend and pull her into a bone-crushing hug. "You know I love you, right?"

She hugs me back just as fiercely. "Of course you do. I'm awesome." Emree flips her hair and jumps up from the bed. "Now you better start getting ready or we're going to be late for work and Garrett's fine ass will lecture us."

Looking at the clock, I see I have half an hour until our shift starts. "Crap."

WE MAKE it to Whiskey Joe's with a few minutes to spare, but not without a warning look from our lovely manager. We head to the back, where we have an employee area, to store our belongings in the lockers. After putting our bags away, we grab our name tags and aprons to get ready for the next five hours. Luckily, it's a short night and Thursdays aren't too bad, as long as there isn't a game playing.

Emree adjusts her bra and shirt to give her the most cleavage without showing too much. She's dressed the opposite of me in a pair of short jean shorts, red tank top, and her blonde hair is perfectly curled. I'm wearing a pair of my favorite jeans with the holes strategically cut out and a black cropped T-shirt, although my stomach isn't showing since my jeans are the high-rise type.

"Conrad stopping by tonight with Camden?" I ask her.

She's fluffing her hair in the mirror and adding some clear lip gloss that makes her already plump lips look bigger. "Wouldn't know. That asshole hasn't texted me since Monday."

"What? I thought you two made plans this week?" Since

they met, she's been staying over at his house every few nights, but now that I think about it, she has been home every night this week.

"Yeah, so did I. It's whatever. He wants to act like that, then I'll find someone else and stop wasting my time with him." Although her words don't match the hurt I can see on her face.

The next three hours of bussing tables, getting refill after refill, and almost slipping on mushed French fries someone dropped exhaust me. Camden isn't here yet and not seeing him is making this night drag on.

As I'm bringing another round of beers (their sixth already) to a table of men in their late twenties, I spot him from the corner of my eye at a table in my section. After placing the drinks in front of the guys at the table, with one giving me a look that makes my skin crawl, I turn toward Camden's table and the instant smile on his face at seeing me makes me want to run and jump into his arms. I don't, worried about what Garrett would say if I were fraternizing with a customer.

He's here with Mateo, Levi, and Maddox, and I can't help but notice Conrad's absence. When I reach their table, his arms engulf me, and he places a toe-curling kiss on my lips. Garrett be damned.

"There's my girl," he says against my lips.

His girl. I shouldn't like that as much as I do, but when he says it, it feels like dozens of butterflies are floating in my gut.

"Hi." From his angle on the high-top stool, we're face to face, and it is nice not having to crane my neck to look into his captivating green eyes. "You just made my night much less boring." He gives me a crooked smile and plants one more kiss against my lips before releasing me.

"Evening, boys," I greet the rest of the table. "I see we're missing one."

There is an awkward look exchanged between the four of them before anyone says anything.

"Uh, yeah, Conrad has some big test coming up, so he needed to stay home and study," Mateo says. Although I can read straight through that lie, I don't question it and take down their drink orders.

As I'm walking away, Camden brushes his hand down my arm and gives my hand a squeeze before letting me go. Walking away from him is harder than I thought because all I want to do is sit beside him and be in his presence all night. But I have another two hours of my shift and customers who need drinks and greasy bar food to fuel them while watching whatever game is on the TV they are near.

After getting the guys their drinks, I make my rounds to my other tables and end up helping Emree with one of hers. It's a usual group of white-collar men who come here after work once a week. They're polite, which is nice, but there are a lot of them, and she was struggling to carry all their drinks on one tray.

Camden and the guys opt for no food since they want to continue eating clean this week before their game. They all have given themselves a two-drink maximum for tonight, even Maddox, who keeps looking at me with remorse. I make sure to give him a reassuring smile. My head is completely fine after what happened last week and I want to tell him to stop worrying, but I know he feels guilty about it. Camden told me last night that his best friend hasn't had a drop of alcohol since Saturday.

"Hey, Em, I'm going to run to the restroom real quick. Could you look out for my tables, please?" I shout to Emree, the noise from the TVs making it hard to hear near the bar.

She nods and goes back to putting her order in with Garrett.

Unfortunately, we don't have an employee bathroom, so I'm stuck walking down the creepy hall past the utility closet and beer kegs along the wall. It's quiet back here and it's nice being able to hear my own thoughts.

After finishing my business and washing my hands, I step out of the bathroom and am immediately pushed against the closed door. Fear overcomes me as the smell of beer and BO invades my senses.

"Fuck, you are the hottest thing I have ever seen," a drunken voice says from above me.

He's tall. Too tall, and the way he's pressed against me makes it so I can't lift my head. His entire front is touching mine, making it hard to breathe or move.

"P-please don't d-do this," I stutter, afraid because there is no one else back here.

The stranger runs his mouth along the side of my face and down my neck and I want to vomit. Not only from his smell, but because I know what he plans to do, and I can't relive this again.

His lips are at my ear and the touch burns. "Don't be like that, sweetheart. I'll make it good for you."

Those are similar to the words Harvey said to me the night he took me against my will.

His hand runs down my body and I freeze. I should push him. I should fight back. I did against Maddox when he grabbed me, but why can't I now? Why won't my arms move?

Move, dammit. Defend yourself.

His hand reaches the button of my jeans and I whimper. Before I have a chance to beg him to stop again, his body is ripped from me and I cry out, gasping for air. My face is wet with tears I didn't know were there.

"Back the *fuck* off, man," Camden roars in front of me, shoving the guy against a row of kegs. The man is the same one who gave me a look that creeped me out when I brought his table their drinks.

Another sob escapes me as Camden slams his fist into the drunken man's face, causing him to stumble back.

"You." Another blow. "Don't." Hit number three. *"Fucking."* The guy isn't even blocking the hits. "Touch her." Camden isn't stopping and I'm afraid he is going to do a lot of damage to this guy.

I curl into myself against the wall, the tears not stopping as I watch him drill his fist over and over into the man's face, stomach, his ribs. Anywhere he can hit. The guy isn't fighting back, not like he could in his drunken state.

"Ca-Camden," I try to say over my cries, but my voice is low.

Arms circle around me and I jump back, screaming. "Shh, it's okay. It's just me, Blaire. I swear I won't hurt you," Maddox says with a soft voice. He takes in my face and the fear I'm sure is evident on it. "I need to get you away from this, okay?"

I look back at Camden and see Levi and Mateo pulling him off the now passed-out guy. He's fighting them, trying to continue what he started.

Looking over at Maddox, I nod. He puts his arms around me, keeping his body from touching mine. Emree is at the end of the hall next to a worried Garrett, and I run into her arms, sinking as I put my weight into her and let out another round of sobs.

"Get her to my car. It's parked right out front," Maddox says. The sound of keys being exchanged comes from somewhere beside me.

"You two head home. I'll take care of this," Garrett tells her.

Going through the bar is a blur as Emree ushers me toward the exit. I can't seem to stop the flow of tears. When we make it outside, I take my first breath of fresh air, although it is not as fresh as I would have hoped for with the smokers' area not too far away.

After clicking some buttons on the keys Maddox gave her,

LEXI BISSEN

Emree leads us toward a very large black truck. As she opens the back door, I'm grateful Maddox's car has a step to get in, unlike Camden's.

Once inside the safety of his truck, I break away from Emree. There is worry all over her face as she takes me in. I'm sure I look like a mess with my tearstained face, red eyes, and since I didn't use waterproof mascara today, I can imagine there are black smudges along my eyes.

"Blaire, sweetie, I need you to tell me what happened," Emree whispers. "You're really worrying me."

Trying to control my cries, I take a deep breath in and let it out slowly. "H-he pinned m-me." A sob comes out. "Emree," I cry out, lunging forward and wrapping my arms around her shoulders. She cradles me in her arms, slightly rocking back and forth.

"Shh, it's going to be okay. You're here with me, not there." Her words do little to soothe me because I *was* there. Again.

It almost happened again.

CHAPTER TWENTY-ONE

CAMDEN

I saw red. That motherfucker had Blaire pinned against the wall. He was touching her. The fear in her eyes tore at me and I could have killed the scumbag if it wasn't for Levi and Mateo pulling me off him. Currently, the lowlife, whose name we learned from his friends is Mark, is in the corner of the hallway being examined by Garrett and one of his friends.

My knuckles are still bleeding after running them under water and I don't even care about the split skin. I would go after Mark again if it wasn't for the people around us.

Garrett gets up and heads my way. Maddox, Levi, and Mateo are sitting by me on a few kegs. "His friends aren't going to call the police as long as Blaire agrees not to," Garrett says, looking as pissed as I feel.

I'm on my feet. "Fuck that, let them call the police. He was assaulting her." Saying the words out loud makes bile rise in my throat.

He drops his head. "I know, man. We both know what would have happened if you weren't here, but that doesn't mean shit. Police aren't going to charge him for groping, but they sure as hell will arrest your ass for assault."

Everything he's saying is true, and I know it, but I still want to see this piece of shit behind bars for what he did to my girl. "Fine," I say through clenched teeth.

"I'll go talk to Emree," Mateo says, leaving us to head out the emergency exit on the side.

While we wait for Mateo to come back, I don't take my eyes away from Mark. My blood boils seeing him as he comes to. His nose is bleeding, eye swollen, and his lip is busted up. I wish I had done more damage because he deserves it. Anyone who touches a woman like he was deserves worse.

A figure approaches from down the hallway and Mateo comes into view. His shirt is damp now and he shakes off some water from his hair. It must be raining out now. I want nothing more than to go out to Maddox's truck and get my girl and take her home and away from everything that just happened.

Mateo looks at me. "Emree says she just wants to leave. She's really shaken up, man."

Walking over to Mark, who is still waking up after passing out, and his friends, it takes everything in me not to go after him again. "You're a piece of shit human and I hope you rot in hell. All of you."

My teammates follow me out to the truck. The rain pouring down on us barely registers to me as I try to get to Blaire as fast as I can. Not wanting to scare her, I slowly open the door to the back seat. She's lying there with her head in Emree's lap, soft sniffles coming from her.

Emree turns to me but remains running her fingers through Blaire's hair. "Hey."

I muster up a smile, words seeming to be lost on me at the moment.

"I need to go inside and get our stuff." She looks down at Blaire. "You okay if I leave Camden here with you?"

I hold my breath, waiting for any kind of response from her.

After a few seconds, she nods.

Lifting herself up, Blaire sits in the seat and pulls her legs up to her chest, wrapping her arms around them. Emree exits the truck and I take her place, not sure if pulling Blaire to me is a good idea or not. Before shutting the door, I hear Emree talking to the guys about Garrett telling them she's good to leave early.

I fidget with my fingers in my lap, avoiding the spots on my right hand with open wounds. "Blaire, baby, I don't know whether it would help to hold you or make it worse, but I really want to pull you to me right now."

With sad eyes, she looks up at me. Even with her black mascara smeared and her eyes red and puffy from crying, she is the most beautiful woman I have laid eyes on. She reaches forward and in the next second I have her in my lap, clutching her to me so tight I'm afraid I'll hurt her.

"I'm so sorry I wasn't there sooner, baby," I whisper into her ear. She shivers and her hold around my neck tightens.

Hearing the soft cries and feeling her shaking body against mine makes me want to go back in there and beat the shit out of Mark some more. It's not like he wouldn't deserve it. Men like that are scum and the world would be a better place without them. I think of my mom and sister and how if anyone touched them, I would end up in jail for murder. Maybe it's because I grew up in a house of only women most of my life, but I have this fierceness to protect them. Like Blaire. I've never treated a woman like trash, maybe sometimes a little harsh if they come on a little too strong or annoy me, but scaring or forcing myself on someone like Mark was doing tonight is never okay.

The driver's side door opens, causing Blaire to stiffen and clutch my T-shirt tighter. I run a soothing hand down her back. Maddox comes in holding Blaire's purse, setting it down on the passenger seat.

"Mateo and Levi are going to ride with Emree. We heading toward the house or her apartment?"

Lifting Blaire's face from where she has it nestled in my neck, I look into her eyes. "Blaire, baby, I don't want you alone tonight. Can I take you back to my house? You can shower and I'll make you something warm to drink. Hot chocolate or tea?"

Many seconds go by as she stares at me. The tears have subsided, but her eyes are still puffy and red. She nods and tucks her head back to where it was before. Wrapping my arms around her back, I hold her to me tightly, thankful she said yes because I don't think I would have been able to handle being away from her right now.

Nobody says a word as we drive the fifteen minutes to the house. Some eighties rock music plays softly in the background, but I don't think Maddox is even paying attention since this isn't something he usually listens to.

Emree's blue Honda Civic is parked on the street and she is waiting outside with Mateo. Conrad's car is gone and I'm cursing inside because I don't want the drama I know will unfold when he comes home. My idiot roommate went on a date tonight and none of us had the heart to tell Blaire when she asked us where he was. Whatever is going on with Emree and Conrad will need to wait because my priority is Blaire.

After Maddox parks in the driveway and gets out with Blaire's purse, handing it to Emree, I rub Blaire's back. "Baby, we're here. Do you want me to carry you in?"

She shakes her head against my chest. "No, I can walk."

After she detangles herself from me, we both exit the truck. Blaire's hand never leaves mine and when I step down, she wraps both her arms around mine, holding herself close. I kiss the side of her head, reassuring her I'm here.

As we pass our friends, Blaire keeps her head down. There is sadness and sympathy written all over their faces and I'm glad she isn't seeing that because I feel like it would make her feel even worse.

After kicking our shoes off at the front door, we enter my room, and she takes a seat on the end of my bed and stares down at her hands in her lap. "I can feel his hands on me," she whispers.

My fists clench at my sides and I try not to let her see the anger in me. Taking a deep breath, I walk over and squat down so we are at eye level. "Why don't you take a shower and I'll get you something to sleep in?"

She nods.

After grabbing a T-shirt, boxers, and a fresh towel, we head to the bathroom where I set everything down on the counter for her. I pull out a new toothbrush I got for her the other day and lay it on top of the clothes. Leaning into her, I kiss her forehead. "I'll wait right outside the door for you."

As I turn to leave, she grabs my shirt. "Please don't leave me," she pleads. There is fear in her eyes and I wrap my arms around her.

"I'll wait right here."

We embrace for long minutes before Blaire breaks it, heading toward the shower and turning the water on. She plays with the hem of her shirt for a few seconds, avoiding eye contact. Reaching forward, I grab the bottom of her shirt and bring it up over her head, my eyes never leaving hers. Though the thought of seeing Blaire naked has excited me since the moment I saw her, right now isn't about that. She needs to know I'm here for her, no matter what and not just for her body.

Reaching for the button of her jeans, I stop before releasing it. "Is this okay?" The image of that piece of shit with his hands on her jeans flashes through my mind and I temper down my anger.

She covers my hands with hers and nods, helping me

unbutton her jeans. Slowly, I bring them down her legs until I'm crouched down, helping her lift each leg out of them, her hands on my shoulders. After removing her jeans, I take each of her socks off and toss them to the growing pile of clothes.

She stands in front of me in nothing but a black bra and matching underwear and fuck, she is more beautiful than I could have ever imagined. I brush some of her long, dark hair over her shoulder and kiss the smooth, pale skin there. She shudders, reaching for my hips to help her stand.

The water is hot by now with how much steam has engulfed us. Ever so slowly, I reach behind her back and unhook her bra, keeping eye contact with my beautiful girl the entire time. She lowers her arms as the straps come down and it falls to the floor. It takes everything in me not to look down at her full breasts, but I want her to know I'm here for her. I need Blaire to see me as someone she can trust in times that she is hurt, sad, angry, or happy.

She hooks her fingers into the sides of her underwear and removes the last article of clothing covering her body. My beautiful girl is standing in front of me naked and all I want to do more than anything is wrap her in my arms and protect her from the world.

Before going into the shower, she leans forward and softly places a kiss on my lips. As she walks away, I get a view of the most perfect ass and I have to think of anything besides the naked woman in my shower to tame my growing erection.

As I stand in the bathroom, thoughts of anything but her in that shower cross my mind. Our game we have coming up in two days. My grandma Jane and the giant muumuus she used to wear no matter what company she had at her house. How painful practice was this afternoon and how sore my legs are going to be tomorrow.

A sob comes from the shower and without thinking I'm across the room, ripping the shower curtain open. Blaire is sitting on the tub floor, her arms wrapped around herself and a washcloth scrubbing at the skin on her arm.

"I can't get him off," she cries.

Still wearing all my clothing, I go in and scoop her up. Grabbing the washcloth, I begin gently running it over her body as she cries in my lap and the water is running down on us.

"Baby, I would do anything to erase what you went through tonight. He should have never touched you like that. *No man* should ever touch a woman the way he did."

She clings to my neck and every cry that comes out of her breaks my heart.

We sit in silence, her soft cries and the sound of the water cascading around us the only noise. After washing her body, I use some shampoo and conditioner in her hair, making sure to rinse it all out. After the water starts to run cold, I know we need to get out.

Standing with Blaire cradled in my arms, I turn the water off and reach for the towel to wrap it around her. "I need you to stand here while I get my jeans and shirt off, okay?"

She nods, not taking her eyes off me.

I lift my wet shirt off me, struggling because it is clinging to my body. Blaire watches my movements. As I reach for my jeans, she follows my hands to the button at my waist. Luckily, the cold water helped some with the hard-on I was having issues with. After I'm in nothing but my black boxers, I grab my towel from the rack and wrap it around me, pulling my wet boxers down while keeping myself covered. I help Blaire get changed into the clothes I brought in, and we brush our teeth side by side before exiting and going to my bedroom.

While she gets settled in the bed, I grab a pair of sleep pants, slipping them on under the towel before discarding it on the floor.

Once changed, I pull the comforter back on my side and

scoot in, bringing Blaire over to me so I can hold her. She sighs and nestles her head against my chest. I'm sure she is exhausted after the night she has had, and I hope sleep comes quickly for her.

"Sleep, baby," I whisper into her hair. "I'll be right here all night. Nothing will happen to you." With that, she closes her eyes, and her body becomes heavy as her breathing steadies, and she drifts to sleep.

CHAPTER TWENTY-TWO

BLAIRE

Light filters in through the cracks of the blinds, leaving the room slightly lit. Beside me, Camden is still sleeping, snoring ever so lightly, which is kind of cute. He's on his back, one arm wrapped around me and the other stretched out above his head. His chest is exposed with the blanket resting near his hips, leaving his beautiful, tanned skin on display. He truly is a work of art. Even in a relaxed state, you can see the definition of the muscles on his arms and abs. I can't help but run my hand along his stomach, marveling at how stunning this man is and how he is *mine*.

Last night flashes back to me and my hand on his stomach freezes. Camden was there for me. He saw me at my worst, after almost experiencing something again that nearly killed me the first time it happened. Part of me can't believe he would defend me in such a way and then be there soothing me the next. His right hand that is wrapped around me has open wounds on the knuckles. That makes me feel guilty. He saved me, defended me, and I want to run my fingers along his hand, but I'm worried it would hurt him.

When I was raped at sixteen years old, I had no one. Not my

parents, not my so-called friends, and not any teachers for support. I felt like everybody saw me as a whore who lied because she slept with a guy she wasn't dating.

This time, it was different. Not only did I have Camden, but Emree was there alongside Camden's roommates and my manager, Garrett. I have people who genuinely care about me and realizing that opens a whole new set of floodgates. People I have known for such a short period of time seem to care more about me than my own family and the friends I had most of my life.

Camden stirs beside me, his arm wrapped around my shoulder flexing and pulling me closer. I relish in the fact that not too long ago contact like this would scare me, especially after what happened last night. But Camden feels like safety to me. He has never once made me uncomfortable and has shown me nothing but love and care.

Turning his head, he opens his eyes, and looking into those bright, green eyes makes everything feel like it will all be okay. "Morning, beautiful." Leaning forward, he kisses me, and morning breath be damned, I kiss him back. Wrapping my arm around his waist, I lift myself up some to deepen the kiss.

He breaks away. "I know it's a stupid question, but how are you?"

Smiling up at him, I lay my head back onto my pillow and rest my hand against his chest. "I need to tell you something."

His body tenses.

"I just don't know how."

Rubbing my arm, he looks at me, worried. "Okay. Why don't you take it one sentence at a time and tell me what you can."

I think his patience with me is the first thing I fell in love with, and for good reason. Camden doesn't push me as I lie here and think about how to tell him something I have only ever told one other person in the last four years.

Taking a deep breath, I go for it. "Last night wasn't the first time." The words come out hushed and when he doesn't respond, I'm afraid he didn't hear me.

After more than a minute goes by, he says something. "I'm sorry. First and foremost, I'm sorry it happened last night and I'm sorry for what happened in the past. No one should have to experience something like that."

His words warm my heart because I know Camden is nothing like Harvey or the guy from last night. He would never hurt me, or any woman. While he has admitted to sleeping around, I can't judge him for that when he was honest with the women he was with about the arrangement they had.

"When I was sixteen, I was r-raped." Saying that word out loud is harder than I thought it would be. Even when I told Emree about it, I would always say 'attacked' or 'assaulted.' They sounded less...real. But I need Camden to know what I experienced to the full extent.

"*Fuck*," he growls. His body beside mine tenses and the hand around me grips my shoulder almost painfully. I let the honest bomb that I just dropped on him sink in. Hearing the girl he's seeing say she was raped, especially after what happened last night, I'm sure causes a range of emotions in him.

Camden shoots up from the bed, leaving me cold without his body heat against me. He's pacing at the foot of my bed, his hands clamped behind his neck. I'm not sure what to say right now and he hasn't said anything besides whispering curse words. Maybe it was too much, too soon. We only just started seeing each other and something like this could change his mind about dating me.

Deciding it's best to leave him to process this news, I climb out of the bed. "I'm sorry. I'll just leave."

Before I can make it to the door, Camden is in front of me. "Don't. Do not ever say you're sorry. Not for this." He wraps his arms around me and pulls me into a tight embrace. "I'm trying not to throw my fists into the walls right now and scare you," he says against my ear. "Hearing my girlfriend was...raped, it makes me want to find the motherfucker and kill him, Blaire."

To be honest, I have contemplated Harvey's death in my head a time or two. "I thought you would see me differently. Not want to be with me after finding that out."

Pulling back, he grasps my face in his large hands. "God, no. Never. Blaire, you are perfect. This doesn't change how I feel about you or how I see you." He kisses my forehead, my cheeks, my nose, and finally my lips. I feel cherished by him.

"I hated myself for so long after it happened. Like I did something wrong. It made me feel dirty and used," I tell him honestly. Recalling how I felt walking home from that party, my dress ripped, my makeup smeared, my hair a nest of knots, and my eyes bloodshot from having cried so much. When my mother saw me, she was worried, but it all changed when I told her what happened. *Who* it happened with.

Sitting on the bed, Camden brings me to stand between his legs and rests his head against my stomach. "I hate this for you. The thought that you went through this, at such a young age. Baby, what happened has no reflection on you. The guy who did it, he's the one who is dirty. I hope he is rotting in prison right now."

This is the hard part. When I told Emree that Harvey saw no jail time and wasn't even served, she threw a pillow from our couch in anger and considered driving to Texas to find him.

"Unfortunately, no."

His hands on the backs of my thighs freeze.

"His father is the police chief of our small town, and his mother is on the board of...well, everything there. His family runs that town, and my parents are close with them." The fact that my parents chose their friends over their own daughter still hurts me. "My mother said maybe I was confused because it was my first time and said it would only hurt me in the long run if I told the police."

Lifting his head, Camden looks into my eyes. "I hate your parents."

I can't help but let out a small laugh. "Yeah, I'm not too crazy about them either. I haven't spoken to my parents since I left for college." Leaning down, I kiss Camden softly on the lips. "I need you to not feel sorry for me. The last thing I want from anyone is pity, and that's why the only other person who knows is Emree, and it took me a while to tell her."

"Gray Eyes, I don't pity you. I think you're the strongest woman for going through what you went through and still being this beautiful, funny, smart person standing in front of me."

Smiling, I caress his face. "Don't think I was always those things. It took me a long time to overcome what I went through, and Emree has helped me so much this last year. I practically cut myself off from forming new friendships, any relationships, because of my trust issues. The guy who...raped me. He was a family friend. Someone I had known since we were kids. I trusted him and never thought he would do something like that to me, but he changed me that night."

Standing, Camden frames my face in his large hands again. "You have me. You have my trust. My heart. Everything. I would never do anything to hurt you, Blaire. I'm happy you found Emree and have been able to open up more. Getting to know you has been incredible and I'm glad you see me as someone you could give your trust to."

"You have it. Wholly."

He smiles, rubbing my cheeks with his thumbs. "Thank you, Gray Eyes."

Leaning down, he kisses me. Hard. As if he's afraid I'll disappear. My hands snake up his arms and grip his bare shoulders. One of his hands leaves my face and descends, tightening around my waist and pulling my body flush against his. He's not wearing a shirt and I can feel the heat from his body against mine through the thin shirt of his I wore to bed. He groans into my mouth, and his tongue glides across the seam of my lips, tangling with mine when they meet. I can feel him hardening against my stomach and while the thought of that alone would have scared me before, I know Camden wouldn't use sex forcefully with me. He cares about me, and I think sex with him would be like what I read about in my favorite romance novels. Magical.

There is one more thing I need to confess to him, something I'm embarrassed about, but I know Camden won't judge me for it or see me differently after he knows. At least I hope not.

Pulling away, I catch my breath. Looking into his eyes, they are brighter right now than I've ever seen them. Lust is evident on his face, and I smile at the fact that I do this to him. Me, the girl who has been too closed off to form any relationship with a guy for years. The girl who has no experience and, until meeting him, had only ever kissed two boys.

"I need to tell you one more thing." Worry crosses his face and I grip the back of his neck, reassuring him that I'm here. "I like you, like a lot. More than I thought I ever would. But I need you to know, I've never...had sex." I consider myself a virgin since my first time was stolen from me. While some may not come to that same conclusion, I don't care. I have never willingly had sex with a guy before.

Camden kisses me on the lips. "Did you think that would scare me off? Baby, finding out my girlfriend is a virgin only means it's going to be more special between us because you're choosing me for something important."

"*Girlfriend*," I squeak out. I vaguely remember him saying it earlier when he was angry over hearing what happened to me, but I didn't think anything of it. Hearing him say it again, my heart flutters.

"Yeah, Gray Eyes. Girlfriend." He laughs and I can feel it through my body with how close we still are. "I haven't done the whole 'girlfriend' thing in a long time, and even then, I don't think I was that great at it, but this feels right."

"Yeah," I tell him, squeezing around his waist and leaning my head against his chest. "This feels right."

"How about you let me take you out to breakfast? I have a team meeting this afternoon, but I'm yours all morning."

"That sounds perfect," I tell him. He kisses me on the forehead, and I get dressed in his bathroom in my clothes from last night while Camden gets ready in his room. The rest of his roommates must still be sleeping because the house is quiet as we leave. Emree's car is also gone now.

As we drive to a local breakfast spot he says is the best, I sit lost in thought. For so long I have worried about what would happen if I opened my heart like this and let people in. I have been scared that someone would hurt me again like Harvey did, like my parents and friends did. I now know I hadn't been living for myself. There will always be bad people in the world, but there are the good ones, like Camden and Emree, and even Camden's roommates, who make up for all the bad.

CHAPTER TWENTY-THREE

CAMDEN

B*laire was raped.*
The top of my foot connects with the soccer ball as I kick it into the goal.

My girlfriend was fucking raped.

Kicking another ball, it soars through the air and makes a *swish* sound when it lands on the back of the net.

I can't get the words out of my head. They're running through my mind over and over, and I thought coming out to the fields and letting off some steam after our meeting would help, but it is having the opposite effect.

Blaire was raped. At sixteen. A fucking child. She had no one, not even her parents, there for her. I can't imagine a tiny, scared Blaire going through that and having no one to turn to. While we were at breakfast, she told me some more about what happened after she was raped. How even her friends chose that douchebag's side because of his precious status in their small-ass town. Small towns suck for that reason alone. If you come from an important family, they don't give a shit what you do. Like rape innocent girls.

"*Fuck!*" I shout, landing another blow into the last soccer ball in front of me.

"Whoa, man, what did those balls ever do to you?" Maddox says from behind me. I thought he left with everyone else an hour ago after the meeting.

"Nothing," I grumble. He starts jogging over toward the goal.

After kicking back the balls that have been collecting in the net, he comes back over to me. "Want to tell me what has you taking your anger out on our equipment?"

Maddox is my closest friend, but I don't know about telling him what Blaire told me. Although I trust him, she confided in me when I knew it was harder than anything else. But I need to talk to someone about this.

"Blaire told me something from her past this morning that really makes me want to smash some stuff." That's the most I can tell him without breaking the trust she gave me.

My best friend studies me without saying a word. "She was assaulted before, wasn't she?"

"How—"

"Something I overheard her say to Emree last night when I went out to the truck. She kept repeating 'it almost happened again.'" Shaking his head, Maddox drops the back of his head. "Gotta tell you, man, I was really hoping I heard that wrong because fuck, someone as sweet as her shouldn't ever go through something like that. No woman should."

"She was raped. It happened four years ago. She was only sixteen, man." God, saying the words out loud hurts.

Maddox's eyes widen. "Shit, Camden, I hoped it wouldn't have been something like that."

"Yeah, it shocked me and all I want to do is drive to bumfuck nowhere Texas and beat the living shit out of the guy."

Running a hand through his hair, Maddox looks around at

the soccer balls at our feet. "Well, now I understand why you needed to blow off some steam like this. Can't blame you."

"Yeah," I say, kicking one of the balls into the net. Hard. "Blaire told me she trusts me, and she hasn't been able to do that since it happened. Shit went down and she basically lost everyone close to her after it happened."

"That's fucked up, man, but you know what, having someone like you there for her is good. You may have slept your way through most of this school the last two years, but you're a good dude. You're more sensitive to women shit since you have your mom and sister, ya know?"

I know what he means, but I can't help but think of what a dick I had been in the past to women. While I was never outright rude, I did sleep around and know that a lot of the girls had hopes of being more than one night with me, even after I told them I don't do relationships. Funny how things change when you meet *the girl*.

For the next hour and a half, Maddox and I kick the ball around, having a little lightweight practice of our own. Coach opts for meetings the day before we have a game rather than practice to make sure all the players are well-rested and not sore. Neither of us pushes ourselves and the little scrimmage we have helps clear my mind of everything that went down last night and this morning.

As we head back to our cars with our bags tossed over our shoulders, Maddox breaks the silence. "Hey, man, I know I've already said this before, but I really am sorry for what went down with Blaire in the pool last weekend. I've had a lot on my mind lately and drinking has helped, but I know I fucked up and hurting Blaire was the last thing I would ever want to do."

Since that night, Maddox hasn't gotten drunk and there have been multiple times I can see his regret when he looks at Blaire. "I know, Mad. What's going on anyway?"

He looks over at me and I can see the war going on in his

head on whether to tell me. "Nothing. Just some bullshit with my family. I can handle it, though, and I'll be better about my drinking. I can't let you all down this season."

I decide not to question him more on it, knowing him and his family issues and how much he has struggled with them in the past. We part ways and before getting in his truck, Maddox tells me Mateo is on dinner duty tonight. Nights before games, we decided to have a sort of 'family dinner' with just the five of us and rotate who cooks. Mateo is by far the best in the kitchen out of us and we all grimace anytime it's Maddox's night. His idea of a meal is anything he can cook out of a box with easy instructions, yet somehow it always comes out horrible.

Deciding to take the long way home, I clear my head some more as I drive the windy roads. Thinking about what Blaire went through makes me grip the steering wheel and I struggle to try and cool down again. She is an amazing woman for how she overcame not only her assault, but how she lost everyone close to her. People she should have been able to seek comfort in. I want to be that person for her. Someone she can go to anytime she needs a shoulder to cry on or wants to talk about anything and everything.

BACK AT THE HOUSE, I pass by Maddox and Conrad sitting on the couch watching some show on Netflix. I head up the stairs and to the bathroom to shower. As the steam fills up the room, I can't help but remember last night and taking care of Blaire in here. How she trusted me to protect and comfort her after what happened. Finding out about her assault when she was sixteen makes last night even more important to me because I know how hard it must be for her to let people in like she did.

She's never had anyone there for her until Emree, and now me.

Back downstairs, I grab a bottle of water from the fridge and join the guys in the living room. When I notice what they're watching on TV, I can't help but laugh.

"You idiots are seriously watching *Riverdale*?"

Maddox looks over at me while Conrad is trying to hide his smile. "You try starting this show and then stop watching it. It's addictive and ridiculous, but I can't go on without knowing what happens," Maddox defends himself.

"Well, what's your excuse?" I ask Conrad.

He shrugs. "He had the remote first."

Maddox whips his head over to our roommate. "Oh, don't even act like you haven't been asking me questions this entire time or that you don't think Betty is a complete babe. I saw you adjusting your junk when her stripper scene was on the other day."

"The fuck you looking at my junk for?"

Maddox rolls his eyes. "Not like someone can't notice when you're fidgeting all over the seat and making the couch move."

I can't help but laugh. These two act like an old married couple. "You both need couples therapy."

Laughing, Maddox leans toward Conrad and pinches his cheeks. "Aw, no, we don't, snookums. We love each other very much."

Conrad swats his hand away. "Fuck off."

We settle into a comfortable silence and watch the most insane show on television and although it makes no sense, the damn thing really keeps you hooked. Now the red-headed guy is on trial for murder and I'm still trying to figure out what this show is even about.

Mateo comes through the door with both arms full of groceries. "*Hola*, bitches," he greets us.

Without looking away from the TV, Conrad and Maddox

grunt out hellos. I get up to help Mateo with the groceries in his hands.

"Always the gentleman, Camden," Mateo jokes, glaring at the two of them still glued to the TV.

We unload cases of chicken breast, a variety of vegetables, the largest bag of brown rice sold at the store, and an assortment of spices.

"Damn, man, you making that blackened chicken again?" I ask after seeing the label of some of the seasonings.

He smiles, knowing how much we liked it. "Of course. After the meal Maddox made for us last week, we need something home cooked and good to cleanse our memories of his burned steaks."

"I heard that!" Maddox yells from the living room.

"You were supposed to!" Mateo responds.

At least we're honest with Maddox about his cooking skills, or lack of, and Mateo and Levi have even shown him a few things since they're the two most comfortable in the kitchen. Doesn't mean Maddox can now cook, but he at least knows how to make eggs and not burn bacon now.

Mateo starts getting everything prepped for dinner. He seasons the chicken and veggies and puts a pot of chicken stock on the stove to start boiling the rice. I sit on a stool at the bar, keeping him company and offering to help when needed.

"How's your girl doing?" he asks me while dusting the chicken with some delicious-smelling spice.

"She's going to be okay. We talked some this morning. I'm going to go to the bar on Sunday and see if I can catch Garrett to talk about maybe having someone escort the waitresses to the bathroom and to and from their cars. At least for now, after everything is so raw."

He nods. "They need to not have that goddamn bathroom at the end of the hallway like that. It's sketchy for anyone walking down there alone. No one can see you from the bar."

He's right. The setup of the bar is lacking with the bathrooms being right next to an emergency exit and at the end of a long, dark hallway that is secluded from the rest of the building.

"Maybe after telling his dad about what happened, they can figure out a way to make it safer. Not even just for the employees, but guests too."

Mateo nods in agreement.

After he's seasoned all the food and set the rice on simmer, I help him carry the trays of chicken and vegetables outside to the grill. Over the summer, we all decided to chip in and splurge on a grill one of the seniors was selling after he graduated. It's big and being able to cook large amounts of food for five athletes is a major help. Plus, who doesn't like grilled food anytime?

Once all the food is cooked, we call for the guys to come outside and Conrad brings the rice out. Levi got back a little while ago after checking in at work. He's the only one of us who works during the season, but he loves his job at the bookstore. Conrad is lucky enough to get an allowance from his parents each month that is far more than anything he would need. Maddox and I work for his uncle's construction company over the summer and that makes me more than enough for the semester until he needs us during winter break. Maddox doesn't need the money, but it is an excuse not to go home to his parents in Boston during the summer break. Mateo is like me and on a full-ride scholarship, with living and food expenses covered. Since he doesn't have any family to go to over the breaks, he lifeguards at the beach almost every day during the summer and in the winter break he takes odd handyman jobs here and there. We're lucky to have someone like him around because the guy can fix anything.

We sit together around the outdoor table, shooting the shit. Maddox and Conrad catch me up on what I missed in the episodes of the show while I was helping Mateo, and Levi laughs at the craziness that is *Riverdale*. He's more of a true crime binger or sticks to reading his books. We talk a little about the game tomorrow and how in sync the team is, especially after how our first few practices were complete shit. I feel more confident that we will win this first game and coming in strong from the beginning will help us the rest of the season.

"You guys hear the Macki kid broke his foot over the summer?" Levi asks us.

Macki is the goalie for the team we're playing against tomorrow, Cornwall University. He's ranked one of the best goalies in Georgia, but this news may knock him down some.

"No shit? What happened?" Maddox responds.

After swallowing a mouthful of chicken and rice, Levi answers. "One of the girls I work with has a boyfriend at Cornwall and said they've been trying to keep the injury hush-hush, but Macki got plastered at a party last weekend and blurted it out."

An evil smile comes over Maddox's face. "This is very useful knowledge for us. Tell the girl thanks." He looks over at me. "Now we just have to figure out which side is fucked up and make our shots there."

"We got this in the bag," I tell him, confidence radiating with each word.

CHAPTER TWENTY-FOUR

BLAIRE

It's official, sports and I do not get along. The stadium is loud, so loud I can barely hear my thoughts. It smells like fried food, sweat, and fresh-cut grass. We are surrounded by people wearing blue-and-gold jerseys with a variety of players' names and numbers on the back of them. Collins is by far the most popular name I have seen, as well as his number twelve.

This morning before he had to meet the team at school, he stopped by my apartment to give me my own jersey with his name and number, as well as a memorable kiss I can still feel on my lips all these hours later.

Emree is sitting next to me with a lap full of loaded nachos, a hot dog, and popcorn. Her slushy is resting in the cupholder in front of us. Our seats are close, right in the front row and not far from the benches the players will be sometime soon. My body tingles with excitement in anticipation of seeing Camden.

Since Braxton is not a large school, they convert the football stadium to a soccer field during home games.

"Can you believe your guy got tickets this close?" Emree says around a mouthful of popcorn.

I can't help but laugh at her and the smorgasbord she is balancing on her lap. "It is crazy. I can't believe how packed this place is."

Jules comes back down the stairs with a drink and burger in her hand, making her way through the row of people before taking the seat beside me. "The concession stand is nuts. I had to fight a guy who almost tried snatching my burger." She rips a bite off and begins chewing.

"I was just telling Em how insane it is with all these people. I never knew soccer was so popular."

"It's usually not." Jules laughs after finishing chewing. "It's one of the least popular sports in the country, but we have a football team that sucks, a nonexistent hockey team since it's Florida, and the baseball season isn't until later, so everyone needs something to cheer about and a reason to get drunk."

We laugh because she makes sense.

After the girls chow down on their food and I sip on my Coke, we wait for the game to begin. There are announcements here and there going off about a variety of things from where to buy clothing to support the team and other knickknacks to how much longer until the game begins.

When the announcer starts telling everyone to get on their feet to welcome the teams, the stadium gets louder, which I didn't think was possible. People are stomping their feet and shaking something that sounds like cowbells all around us. It is a madhouse.

The opposing team comes out from the locker room in a separate building and are greeted with a mixture of cheers and boos. More boos than cheers, I notice. In the stands across from where we're sitting are fewer people and they are wearing gray-and-red-colored clothing, matching the colors of their team's jerseys.

The stadium goes quiet as the opening to "Can't Stop" by Red Hot Chili Peppers comes over the speakers and I smile as the team comes walking out of the locker room, Camden leading in the front. He has a serious look on his face, and I know he is focused on getting into his game mode. The guys are all wearing blue jerseys with gold-colored letters and numbers and blue shorts. Aside from Levi, who is wearing the same shorts but a long-sleeved jersey that is bright yellow with his number and name in blue and a pair of oversized gloves on his hands that he is clapping together.

The team makes their way to their benches and Camden scans the stand before making eye contact with me. He gives me a wink before turning back to listen to their coach. That single gesture has those darn butterflies fluttering in my stomach again.

Beside me, I can tell Emree is hurt that Conrad didn't do the same for her by the sad look on her face. She shoves the hot dog into her mouth, taking a giant bite as she grumbles about 'stupid soccer players.' While I have not asked her what is going on with her and Conrad, I can tell there is something going on between them and hope it works out in the end. She seems to really like him and he is a nice guy.

Camden and Maddox head out onto the field at the same time two players from the opposing team do, and they all meet one of the referees in the middle. They flip a coin and Camden says something none of us can hear, and after the coin lands on the ground, Maddox pumps his fist. Guess they won the coin toss.

The players shake hands and return to their sides of the field. Braxton's coach calls the players into a huddle, giving some kind of pep talk, and before Camden takes the field again, he looks over at me and points, bringing two fingers to his mouth and kissing them. My cheeks redden at his gesture.

The start of the game is intense. Levi is jumping around as he stands in the goal, not taking his eyes off the ball from the beginning. Camden and Maddox work in sync and it's quite a show. They pass the ball so fast between the two of them, I'm not sure how the other team even has a chance to catch them to get it.

Maddox has the ball and is running toward the other team's goal, when another player slides in front of him, but Maddox jumps, missing the player and gaining control of the ball again. I'm on the edge of my seat as Maddox bypasses player after player, dribbling the ball closer to the goal. Camden is beside the goal, waiting for Maddox and being shoved left and right by two Cornwall players.

Just when I think Maddox is going to pass the ball to Camden, he fakes and kicks it straight into the goal. The Cornwall goalie misses it as he dives toward the right corner.

Our side of the stadium goes crazy, everyone standing, jumping, and cheering. Emree, Jules, and I are along with them, clapping with enthusiastic school spirit. Maddox and Camden high-five as they run back to the middle of the field to get back into the starting position.

The game goes by fast and before I know it, it's halftime. The score is now 2-1, with Braxton leading. Levi cursed up a storm when one of the Cornwall players got the ball past him but blocked the last three attempted shots.

The next half has me biting my nails. The teams have switched sides, making it harder to see Levi in the goal on my left. I can tell Camden is getting more exhausted because his movements are slower, but he is still dominating the field. His shorts and jersey are covered in grass stains and his hair is soaked from sweat.

Something wet hits me in the eye and I look up, feeling it again but on my forehead this time. Raindrops start coating my face as they fall from the sky. Within seconds, it is pouring and most of the people around us are groaning, grabbing their ponchos or umbrellas.

Jules pulls out her own poncho and looks over at Emree

and me, who are among the few without protection. "Erm, I'd share, but it's kind of a single-person use. We'll get some for you both before the next game," Jules says to us sympathetically while covering her head to protect her hair.

There should only be a few minutes left in the game, according to Jules, and Braxton is dominating with a lead of 4-1. Emree and I are soaked through our clothes and my hair is sticking to my face and neck. I can't help but laugh. We look like a couple of wet dogs.

The referee blows his whistle three times, signaling the end of the game and, while everyone jumps up to cheer, it is not as loud, and I think some people are happy it is over to get out of the rain. Camden and his teammates are jumping around in a mosh, celebrating their win. We make eye contact before he follows everyone else into the locker room after being lined up to slap hands with the other team and his smile makes me being soaked and now cold completely worth it.

Emree, Jules, and I wait under the covered awning near the locker rooms and each time that door opens, my heart rate speeds up thinking it is Camden. He is taking his sweet time, though, and with every passing minute, I am ready to go in there and find him myself.

Just when my patience is about to run out, the door swings open and there he is. Freshly showered wearing a pair of fitted, dark jeans that hang low on his waist, a white T-shirt that is a little tight around his biceps, and a pair of beat-up Vans. His roommates are around him, each of them carrying a bag over their shoulder, and Maddox is tossing a soccer ball up in the air, catching it when it comes back down.

Without thinking, I run toward him, leaving the safety of the awning. When he sees me coming toward him, his face lights up and just as I'm about to collide with him, he drops his bag, catching me effortlessly in his arms and lifting me. My legs automatically wrap around his waist and his hands go to my butt, holding me to him. Our lips clash as the rain pours over us and I can't help but moan at the feeling of having him against me. His lips on mine. His tongue seeking entrance into my mouth.

I allow him in, and our tongues mingle. He tastes like mint mixed with the Coke I drank. He squeezes by bottom and my hips grind involuntarily against him. One of his hands snakes up my side, tangling in my wet hair, pulling me closer to deepen the kiss.

Around us, through the sound of rain, I hear hooting and hollering. Pulling away from Camden's lips, I see his room-mates standing by Emree and Jules. Maddox is gripping the air, grinding his hips against the spot in front of him in a crude gesture. Mateo and Levi are cheering us on while Jules laughs beside them. Conrad and Emree are behind everyone, huddled and talking.

I can't help the blush that burns my face and duck my head into Camden's neck. "Oh my gosh."

He laughs and his grip on my butt tightens. "That was some greeting, Gray Eyes."

Slowly, he releases me, and my body slides down his, feeling every inch of his hard frame. The rain has slowed to a light drizzle, but we are both drenched now.

"I'm so happy for you," I tell him, smiling, thinking about how exciting his game was to watch.

He smiles proudly. "You have a good time?"

"Yes." I jump up, pecking him on the lips. "It was stressful but so much fun to watch. You're amazing, Camden."

He grabs me around the waist, pulling me to him. "Come home with me?" he whispers against my neck as he nuzzles his face.

My body feels like it's on fire at his question. I'm ready. I know I'm ready. I trust Camden, with my heart, my mind, and my body. He has shown me on more than one occasion that he is deserving of my trust, and I know going home with him right now means more than just going there to hang out.

Pulling him back with my hands in his hair, I bring him far enough away so I can look into his eyes. So he knows the meaning behind my answer. "Yes," I tell him.

His eyes widen in understanding. He leans forward and kisses every inch of my face before landing on my lips.

This is it. I'm willingly giving myself to a man I am falling hopelessly in love with. A man I get to choose to give myself to.

CHAPTER TWENTY-FIVE

BLAIRE

The drive to Camden's house is a blur. I'm nervous but excited. Worried it will hurt, but also happy to feel closer to this beautiful man beside me. He hasn't stopped touching me since coming out of the locker room. His hand roams from my thigh to my knee, and currently his fingers are tangled with mine and I am rubbing his forearm with my right hand.

Neither of us has said a word since walking away from our friends. I told Emree I was going to stay the night with Camden, and she gave me a knowing look. She said she and Conrad were going to our place, and she would text me in the morning, demanding details of everything.

When we pull into his driveway, the nerves resurface and my palms begin to sweat. Camden senses my hesitation and cups my face.

"Hey," he says softly. "I've always told you we're going at your pace. That will never change."

I've lost count of how many times he has told me this and I feel reassured. "I know," I whisper to him, turning his hand and kissing his palm.

As we head inside, I notice how dark and quiet the house is

without the rest of the guys here. Levi, Jules, Mateo, and Maddox went out to Whiskey Joe's with their other teammates to celebrate the win.

He slowly opens his bedroom door and I shiver, whether from my half-dried clothes or the anticipation of getting naked with Camden.

"Do you want to shower or something?" he asks me, still standing at the entrance of his room. He's trying to make me more comfortable, and I love him for that.

I nod and he goes over to his drawer to grab the usual T-shirt and his boxers. When he passes by his closet, he snags a fresh towel for me.

"I'm going to take a quick shower in Maddox's bathroom since we got rained on." He kisses me on the forehead after grabbing his own towel and a pair of sleep pants.

Once in the safety of the bathroom, I take a few deep breaths and try to calm my nerves. The hot water cascading down my naked body brings some relief, but then I remember Thursday night when Camden comforted me in here after what happened at work.

He saw me naked. He saw me naked and was a complete gentleman, focusing more on comforting me than taking advantage of my lack of clothing.

I'm getting too much in my head. I trust Camden and know he will cherish and love my body the entire time. After rinsing the conditioner out of my hair and making sure all the soap is off my body, I turn the water off and grab for my towel.

Brushing my teeth with the toothbrush Camden got for me, I stare at the clothes sitting on the counter. I want to give Camden a clear sign that I'm ready. That I want us to take that next step. That I'm not scared anymore.

After rinsing my mouth out, I tighten the towel around my chest and open the bathroom door, leaving the T-shirt and boxers behind.

When I enter his room, he is sitting against the headboard with his phone in his hand. One arm is tossed back behind his head, and I can't help but gawk at his tan chest and arms on display for me. When he looks up at me in the doorway in nothing but a towel, he drops his phone to the nightstand beside him and leans forward. His eyes darken and his mouth opens just slightly.

I close the door behind me, locking it for good measure, and approach him. My movements are slower, and he keeps his eyes connected to mine with every step, studying me. When I'm standing right in front of him, he doesn't reach for me. His hands clench beside him like he is restraining himself from touching me. I run my fingers through his wet hair, taking in his beautiful face and the clear lust in his darkened green eyes. The way he is looking at me is the way a man looks at a woman he wants and that gives me the confidence to drop the towel.

It lands in a pool at my feet and Camden's eyes don't stray from the hold I have on them. His nostrils flare. My grip on his hair tightens and I bring him forward to kiss me. He comes to me eagerly, and one of his hands grips my waist, not wandering. His naked chest is hot against mine and I relish in the feeling of him against me.

With the grip on my waist, Camden pulls me forward until there is nowhere else to go but on his lap. I'm straddling him, feeling very exposed given that I'm completely nude and he still has sleep pants on. He turns me so I'm lying flat on my back, with my head hitting the pillow, and he is hovering above me. He pulls back, staring into my eyes, and I run my hand down the side of his beautiful face.

"I think...I think I'm falling in love with you," I tell him.

He smiles down at me. "I don't think I'm falling in love with you, Gray Eyes. Pretty sure I damn near fell face-first the moment I met you."

I can't help but smile at his words and pull him down for a

searing kiss. He greedily claims my lips and amplifies the kiss. My head goes foggy as our tongues mingle together and I have to pull back to catch my breath. That doesn't stop Camden. His lips descend down my neck, sucking lightly at the exposed skin, then move lower until he's right at my chest, giving my breasts attention.

For years I always thought I would hate this. After what Harvey did, I never thought affection or sex was in the cards for me, but I can't deny that my body wants Camden. I want his mouth on mine and his hands admiring my body. In his hold, I feel cherished.

After nipping at my chest, he comes back up and stares into my eyes. "I'm gonna go slow, baby, but I need you to tell me if anything is too much. Can you do that for me?"

I nod.

He kisses my lips. "I need words, babe."

"Y-yes. I'm ready, Camden."

He smiles and kisses my lips again before moving his hand down the side of my body and settling between my legs. They fall open automatically with the anticipation of his touch. While still kissing me, his fingers slide against my center before he plunges one into me and I bite his lip at the intrusion. His lips move to my neck as he adds another, slowly moving them in and out. As his palm presses against my sensitive area, my body heats up with the beautiful feeling. Before I know it, I am exploding with my second orgasm thanks to this beautiful man above me.

"Fuck, you are so goddamn beautiful when you come," he groans.

Trying to catch my breath, I hear the drawer beside his bed open. He comes back and lays a foil package beside us. This is it. I'm about to have sex for the first time.

Nuzzling my neck, Camden pushes his sleep pants down and kicks them onto the floor, leaving him completely naked on top of me. "Since it's your first time, it's going to hurt. But, baby, I'll do everything I can to not make it too bad. I promise."

More than anything, I love that he sees this as my first time since my technical first time was taken from me. With both hands, I grasp his face and look into his eyes. "I trust you."

He kisses me hard, leaving me breathless as he pulls away to grab the foil. I watch, mesmerized, as he slides it over his length. He's big. Like, I'm afraid this is going to be extremely painful kind of big. I know he will fit, our bodies are made for this kind of stuff, but damn if I don't question it some.

Camden must sense my worry as I stare at him and he gives me a soft smile. "You trust me, right?"

I nod. "Wholly."

He comes back over me, settling between my thighs, and I feel him against me and my body tenses. He kisses my neck, whispering reassuring words into my ear, and I relax. With one hand braced, holding himself above me, he uses the other to guide his length into me. He goes slowly and the feeling of being stretched is scary and erotic at the same time.

Without breaking eye contact, he pushes himself in inch by inch. I wince at the pain, and he stops his movements. "Fuck, I'm sorry. I'm so sorry, baby."

I clutch his back and try to relax. "It's okay. Maybe just rip it off like a Band-Aid?"

He nods and stares into my eyes as he plunges into me, making me gasp. "God, baby, you feel so good," he groans into my ear.

He doesn't move for a while and the burning pain fades away, becoming tolerable. The room fills with a mixture of our panting and bodies fusing together as he slowly pulls out of me and then pushes back in a little faster. With every pump into me, I get lost in the sensation and feel my body building to release. Camden's movements become more forceful, and I know he is close too.

Within minutes, I'm clutching to him, riding the waves of my orgasm. He comes close behind me, shouting my name as he pushes into me deep and drops his head to the pillow beside mine.

We lie there for I don't even know how long. Camden's body weight is slightly crushing me as we try to catch our breaths, but I welcome having him so close. I feel happy. Happier than I have ever felt. I have a man who loves me and who I have fallen hopelessly in love with, who just made love to me. What more could a girl want?

After we are able to breathe without panting, Camden kisses me on the forehead and rolls to the other side of the bed. I hear him toss something into the trash and I assume he has removed the condom.

He rolls back over and wraps his arm around my waist, bringing me against his chest, my head tucked under his chin. "Thank you, Blaire."

I feel like I should be the one thanking him. "I've been so scared of this moment for years and I can't think of how it could have been better. It was always meant to be you, Camden." I snuggle into his chest as his arm around me tightens, and I can't help but feel safe as I admit something so vulnerable to him.

"It was perfect," he tells me. "How do you feel?"

I look up into his eyes because I want him to see the honesty in my words. "Amazing. Happy. Loved. Cherished. A little sore, but tingly all over."

He smiles and runs the backs of his fingers down my spine. I shiver at the feeling of his touch. "I'm sorry it hurt, but it'll get better each time. I promise."

"Better?" I laugh. "I can't think of how that could get any better."

He gives me an evil smile and rolls me until I'm on my back and he's half on me, hovering just an inch from my face. "Oh, baby, the things I can do to this beautiful body of yours." His hand slides from my hip to my stomach and stops to grab my breast. I moan. "Just you wait. I'll have you telling me I'm a sex god in no time with how I'm going to worship you."

I laugh and shove him away from me. "Oh my gosh, you did not just say you're a sex god."

"Nope, Gray Eyes, I said *you're* going to be telling me I am one. Just you wait." He gives me a knowing smile and pulls me back so my head is resting on his chest. My eyes drift closed as my body gets heavy and before sleep takes over, I faintly hear the words "I love you" being said in my ear.

CHAPTER TWENTY-SIX

CAMDEN

Life couldn't get much better than this. I have the most amazing girlfriend anyone could ask for. Our team has won all five games we have played this season already. My grades are better than they've ever been, with the help of said amazing girlfriend.

I'm happy. Genuinely happy.

The last four weeks have flown by. Blaire spends most nights at my house where we have mind-blowing sex, something she never thought she would enjoy, but I have been able to help her learn her own body each night. She knows what she wants, and my sexy girl has discovered a liking for my dick, my fingers, and my mouth.

Since the incident at Whiskey Joe's, Garrett convinced the owner to tear down the wall between the stage and the hallway leading to the bathroom, making it completely open. Blaire and the other waitresses have felt much safer with the renovation and there is a weight lifted off my shoulders since I can't be there every shift to look out for her.

Being in a relationship has been much easier than I thought it would be. I don't feel like Blaire is tying me down or I don't have the freedom to do what I want. She isn't the kind of girl to get mad when I don't text her throughout the day or have to cancel plans we made. She's easygoing, and I love her for that.

Although right now, she is anything but the chill girl I have grown fond of. Sitting beside me in my Jeep, Blaire can't seem to stop fidgeting. I place my hand on her bouncing leg and she turns her head from the window to look at me.

"I'm sorry," she says, biting her lip. "I'm just nervous."

"I told you they're going to love you."

"But it's *your mom*. And your sister. The two women in your life. What if they hate me? What if they don't think I'm good enough for you?"

Blaire has been worried about meeting my mom and Trazia since my mom asked us over for lunch a week ago. We finally had some time today since Blaire doesn't have to tutor or work at the bar and it's Friday, the day before a game, and there is no practice.

"They are *two* of the *three* women in my life, and my mom already likes you from everything I've told her. Trust me, she's just happy I found someone to date and I'm not sleeping around anymore." My girl makes a face of disgust and I know she hates the thought of my dating life before her.

"Gross. I can't believe you were whoring around and your mom knew."

I shrug. "What can I say, with a face as pretty as this, how can you expect ladies not to be attracted to me?"

Blaire rolls her eyes and pushes my hand off her thigh. "You're ridiculous."

Laughing, I shift down a gear as we get off the exit. "Yes, but I'm *your* ridiculous."

"That was too cheesy," she groans.

The house I grew up in isn't a far drive from where I live now. About an hour or so. One of the reasons I wanted to go to Braxton so badly was because I was still close to my mom and sister. My mom can't come to as many games as I would like, but on the weekends she doesn't have to work, she and Trazia drive out for them. She promised she'll be at the next game for sure.

We pull into the short driveway of my childhood home. While it is small, I can't imagine growing up anywhere else. It is a one-story, boho-style house. The exterior is a dark gray with an open porch in the front with two outdoor chairs and large, square pillars in the front supporting the roof of the porch. The house is open and filled with windows, but my mom finds it weird that people could be looking in at any time, so she put white curtains up years ago. The front door is solid wood and a dark green color with a gold knocker on it.

After helping Blaire out of the Jeep, I grab her slightly damp hand and give her a reassuring squeeze. She takes a deep breath, and we head up the driveway. Before we can make it to the door, my mom swings it open with her arms wide.

"You're here! Trazia, they're here!" she yells.

"I can see that," my sister responds from somewhere in the house.

Mom comes down the three steps from the porch and pulls me into a hug. "My baby. I've missed you so much. It's been forever."

"Hey, I thought I was the baby?" Trazia grumbles from the doorway. We can argue about this all day and night, but I'll forever be my mom's baby.

Without breaking the chokehold she has on my neck, my mom responds to her. "You're my baby girl. Cammy is my baby boy." Pulling back, she winks at me.

Yeah, forever a mama's boy.

While my mom is in her early forties, you wouldn't know it by looking at her. She is active and because of nursing, she needs to stay in good shape. She is lean but strong and she only started graying a couple years ago. Although she has Trazia color her hair on a regular basis. My mom's skin is a light olive tone, and her face is clear and bright. She has a faint hint of crow's feet along the side of her round eyes that are the same color as mine and Traz's. Her smile is wide and welcoming, helping her win over all her patients. My mother is a beautiful woman, and my sister and I are lucky to get the majority of our looks from her.

Turning to Blaire, my mom stretches her arms and pulls my girl into a hug. "It's great to finally meet you, Blaire. Cammy has told me so much about you, I feel like we already know each other." Leave it to my mom to embarrass me in front of my girlfriend by telling her how much I've talked to my mom about us.

Blaire smiles at me over my mom's shoulder and then back at my mom. "It's wonderful to meet you also, Ms. Collins."

My mom waves her off. "Oh, none of that. Call me Claire."

After my mom hugs Blaire again, we climb the stairs to the porch. "And this here is my brat of a little sister," I tell Blaire as I pull Trazia in for a hug, picking her up because I know how much she hates that.

Trazia and I have always looked scary alike that some people think we're twins at times, even though I'm three years older. The only difference is that she changes her hair every time I see her. Currently, it's a platinum blonde, so even with the same eyes and facial features, we look different enough.

Trazia pulls from my hold. "You're an ass."

"Language," my mom scolds. My sister and I laugh because my mom is the one who curses up a storm.

Trazia walks over to Blaire and gives her a gentle hug. "I don't know what you see in my brother, but you seem like a nice girl. It's not too late to run."

Pushing Trazia away, I wrap my arm around Blaire's waist. "Oh, fuck off, she's not going anywhere." I nuzzle my girl's neck and she tries to push me away, but my hold on her only tightens.

"Gross, get a room," Trazia says before following my mom back through the front door.

The house is an open floor plan and the first room you enter when coming inside is the living room. It's small, fitting a five-seat sectional, a stand with an old TV sitting on top of it, and a small, rectangle coffee table. My mom has made the most of the space we had, and it never felt like it wasn't enough. It's always felt homey to me.

With my hand on the small of her back, I guide Blaire toward the kitchen that is just off the living room. My mom made her famous lasagna that has won the hearts of all her coworkers and many patients at the hospital where she works as a labor and delivery nurse.

"Wow, it smells delicious," Blaire says, closing her eyes as she takes in the aroma of spices, tomatoes, and melted cheese.

Trazia is cutting a loaf of Italian bread and I sneak over, snagging a piece to dip it in the sauce that I know my mom made too much of.

I moan after taking a bite. "Baby, come over here. You're gonna die after you've had this."

Blaire joins me and after dipping a piece of the bread in the sauce, I lift my hand to her mouth. I try to ignore the look of her lips as she closes them around the tip of my finger, taking the soaked bread into her mouth. She moans and damn, I need to focus on not getting hard in front of my mom and sister. "That's the best sauce I've ever had," Blaire tells my mom.

My mom serves us all a piece of lasagna while I get everyone drinks and we gather around the four-person kitchen table. Blaire seems to have relaxed since we were in the car and is laughing at my mom's story of how I tried helping her make this same meal when I was eight and she ended up burning the sauce because she didn't realize I turned the stove temperature up to high.

"Blaire, tell us about yourself. Where are you from?" my mom asks.

Blaire stops her fork just before it reaches her mouth and freezes, then puts it back down on her plate. "Oh, um. I'm from a small town called Maskon in Texas." I know talking about her life there makes her uncomfortable. I haven't pushed her to tell me much, especially after hearing how horrible her friends and family were to her.

"Wow, you're a long way from home. Do you still visit your family? Your parents still live there, right?"

Just before I can change the subject, Blaire answers. "Well, yes, they still live there, but I haven't seen my parents since coming to Braxton. We had a bit of a falling-out."

"Oh no, I'm so sorry to hear about that." My mom seems to understand it is not something Blaire wants to talk about and doesn't ask any more questions about Texas or her family.

After a second serving of food, I'm ready to be rolled out of the house. We have covered every standard meet-the-parents conversation from what Blaire's major is, and my mom seemed genuinely interested in what Blaire said about her English degree, to more embarrassing stories of when I was a kid.

"May I use your restroom?" Blaire asks.

My mom is cutting some kind of apple cake she made. "Of course. Honey, why don't you go show her where it is."

I take Blaire's hand and she follows me down the short hallway off the side of the living room. The first door on the left is Trazia's bedroom and just a few steps down on the right in the bathroom we shared as kids, which she took full advantage of making it girly with pink decorations the moment I left.

She heads into the bathroom, and I lean against the wall outside to wait for her. When she comes out, I can't help but smile. I love having her here with my family and how right it feels. She approaches me and I pull her to me by her belt loops, bending down to kiss her.

"What was that for?" she asks after pulling away.

I kiss her again, never being able to get enough of her. "Just because. I like having you here with my family."

"I like them a lot. They're sweet and love you so much, Camden."

"They really like you too, you know. I keep catching my mom looking between us and smiling." She doesn't think I notice, but when my mom looks at Blaire and me, she gets this hopeful look and it makes me feel like shit that it has taken me this long to bring someone home to meet her, but I'm glad I waited for the perfect girl.

"How about you show me the bedroom of Mr. Ladies' Man Camden Collins," she says, biting her lip.

Pushing her so that she is walking backward toward my room at the end of the hall, I shut the door behind us once we enter and grab her by the back of her thighs and bring her legs around my waist. "You trying to get lucky in here, baby?"

She throws her head back and laughs. "Absolutely not."

"Damn shame," I say, nuzzling her neck. "Would make for some beautiful memories in here."

She swats my shoulder and wiggles until I release her. "You're insatiable."

Nothing in my room has changed in the two years since I left. There's a variety of trophies from different soccer tournaments I won from peewee to my senior year of high school. On my desk, there are schoolbooks lined up and some family photos of me with my sister, mom, and grandma. Blaire walks along, admiring the photos. She picks one up of me in the bathtub with a soccer ball.

"That was after the first game I ever won. My coach gave me the winning ball since it was my goal that got us there and I wouldn't let it go all night. I even slept with it." I can't help but laugh at the memory. Soccer was my obsession, even at a young age.

"That's so sweet, Camden. You can see how happy and proud you are in the photo." She sets it down and takes in the rest of my room.

On the wall, there are posters. Some of my favorite bands and some of famous Playboy Bunnies and football cheerleaders. Blaire raises her eyebrow and looks over at me when she stops at a poster of a Bunny wearing nothing but the tiniest bikini that is covering up some insanely oversized boobs. It's funny how that was something I drooled over as a horny teenage boy but now I can't stand the thought of fake breasts.

I shrug. "What can I say? I was a teenage boy."

Blaire rolls her eyes and moves on to my bed.

She sits down and lies back against the pillows. "Your room is very...you. Soccer, family, naked women. Pretty much sums you up." She's smiling and I know she's teasing me because if anything, she of all people has learned over the last two months together that I'm more than that.

Walking over, I climb on top of her and push her thighs open so I can settle between them. "Woman," I tell her.

"Huh?"

"Naked woman, not women. I only care about a naked woman."

"And who's that?" she teases, fighting a smile.

"Oh, it's going to be like that, baby?" I begin tickling her sides and she screeches, trying to push my hands away.

"No, please. I was kidding. Camden, I'm going to pee." Having mercy on her and her bladder, I stop.

As I roll to the other side of my full-sized bed, I bring her with me so she's lying half on top of my chest.

"Your mom is probably wondering if I fell into the toilet," Blaire says as she kisses my neck.

My hands drift down to her ass, and I squeeze it, pulling her closer to me. "Maybe we should go back out there then."

"Mhhmm," she moans against my neck as she sucks.

Not being able to take it anymore, I turn my head and capture her lips. She adjusts herself so she's straddling my waist and grinds against me. Fuck, I can't get enough of this girl. Just looking at her gets me hard, but when she pulls this shit, I can't see straight.

Flipping us over so I'm on top of her again, I press my pelvis into her core, and the loud moan she gives me as she throws her head back makes me smile. Blaire isn't afraid of making noise, and at this moment I'm happy my room is the farthest from the kitchen so my mom and sister can't hear.

"I need you naked. Like now," I say as I start to lift her shirt up.

She stops me and grabs my hands. "No, your mom is, like, right there."

"Don't fucking care," I say and bring my lips back down to hers.

"Cammy, Mom wants to know if you want ice cream with your ca—" The door swings open and Trazia screams and then covers her eyes. "Oh my God, no. No. No. No. I went my whole life not walking in on you doing that while you lived here, and you do it *now*." She turns and runs down the hallway.

Blaire's face is beet red, and I can't help but laugh. "Shut up, your mom is going to think I'm some kind of slut."

That makes me laugh harder. "Baby, I can guarantee you my mom thinks you are the furthest thing from a slut."

She pushes me off her and sits up, adjusting her light green blouse.

"Whatever. I can't believe your sister just walked in on us making out."

Linking my fingers behind my head, I lie back on my bed.

"It's a good thing you stopped me from getting that top off or she would've seen those great tits too."

She glares at me. "Could you not call them that? It's so… crude."

It also makes her blush, and that's why I like saying stuff like that, but I don't let her know.

After she has taken some calming breaths, we make our way out to my sister and mom. Trazia won't look at me and Blaire keeps pushing my hand away from her thigh. Mom is oblivious to everything going on. After she caught me having sex on the couch in high school, I think my mom is immune to my antics. In my defense, Trazia was staying at a friend's house, and I thought my mom was working a double that night.

The evening ends too soon, as it usually does when I visit my family. Eventually, Trazia forgets about walking in on Blaire and me because she is laughing at a story Blaire is telling them of when we came home from a date and Maddox had declared a Nerf war on the household and had already convinced Mateo, Conrad, and Levi to join in on the game. It ended with Blaire camping out in the bathtub the entire time and when it was only Maddox left, she took him by surprise when he went in there to take a leak.

As we say goodbye, my mom promises again that she will be at my game next weekend, and I tell her I will leave the tickets for her and Trazia at the entrance and they'll be sitting by Blaire, Emree, and Jules.

It's late by the time we get back to my house and Blaire had fallen asleep during the ride. I carry her up into the house and she stirs awake. "I can walk."

"Of course you can, but then I wouldn't be able to grab your ass while I'm holding you." I smile down at her and she rolls her eyes.

After we change and get into bed, I close my eyes with my

girl in my arms and my heart so happy that I feel like I have everything I could ever want.

CHAPTER TWENTY-SEVEN

BLAIRE

"Fuck, baby, just like that," Camden encourages me as he closes his eyes and leans back against my headboard.

We're in my room at my apartment where I'm currently straddling his lap with him inside me. It's a new position and my legs are getting tired, but the lost-in-lust face he is giving me makes it all worth it.

He grabs my hips and guides me up and down on him, and I can feel that welcoming build coming. I toss my head back and get lost in the feel. Camden wraps his arms around my waist and begins shooting his hips up, causing me to go off.

"Oh God, Camden," I moan, breathless as my orgasm takes over.

"Fuck yes," he groans, burrowing his face in my neck as he finds his own release.

He holds me there, his forehead against mine as our ragged breaths mingle in front of us.

"I could die in this moment and be the happiest man alive."

I can't help but laugh and the movement causes me to clench around him.

"Oh hell, don't do that," he groans.

Camden lifts me off him and takes care of the condom, throwing it away in the trash by my desk. After using the bathroom, I meet him in bed and cuddle up against his chest. He begins playing with my hair as we bask in the bliss of this post-sex feeling.

We're staying at my apartment tonight, something we rarely do, since the guys won their game today and were having an impromptu party, but neither of us was in the mood. I wasn't able to go to their game because of work, so Camden came by the bar and waited until my shift ended. I told him more than once to go and enjoy celebrating with his friends, but he said all he wanted to do was go to bed with me. Which we did the moment we got through the door of my apartment.

Being with Camden is unlike anything I imagined. I never knew sex could be like this and thought Emree was overreacting when she would tell me about her hookups over the last year. Turns out, I truly enjoy something I have been scared of for so long. Not sure if I would enjoy it if it wasn't for the man beside me.

Camden is gentle with me and admires my body each time we're together. And every time after we have sex, he cuddles me against his chest, where I get to hear his heartbeat as I fall asleep. I can't imagine it is always like this. He has told me sex for him was simple before. He never cuddled or even spent the night with the girls he was with, but with me he enjoys that part almost as much as the actual act. I think part of that has to do with our feelings for each other.

I haven't told him those three important words and he hasn't said them again since the first time we had sex. I think he is waiting for me to get to that point also, but the problem is I'm already there. I'm just afraid of giving him my entire heart and it being broken in the end.

"Hey, Camden?" I whisper.

"Yeah, baby."

Biting my lip, I go back and forth in my head if this is the moment I tell him. But I'm happy and I want to remember this feeling. "I love you."

"I know," he says simply.

I lift my head to look up at him and his eyes are closed, his arm resting behind his head. "You know?"

He peeks his eyes open. "Of course, Gray Eyes. I've known for a while. I'm glad you came to your senses and decided to tell me, though."

"If you've known, then why haven't you said it again?" I sit up but hold the sheet to my naked chest, needing the sense of security.

He sighs, but there is a smile on his face. "Baby, I told you we're going slow for you. Me? I'm pretty sure I fell in love with you the moment I looked into those beautiful eyes." He cups my cheek. "Blaire Wentworth, you are the most beautiful, smart, adorable, wildly sexy, and strongest woman I know. How could I not fall in love with you?"

A single tear falls from my eye, and he rubs it away with his thumb. "I never thought I'd find this. Someone to love," I whisper to him, trying to hold in the sob that wants to escape.

"I can't erase the fucked-up shit that happened to you in the past. If I could, you best believe I would. But, baby, you have this, for as long as you want it. I love you and that isn't going to change anytime soon."

Leaning forward, I stroke his lips with my own. "Please don't break my heart," I beg him. Camden Collins has the power to crush me. He has my heart, my trust, and my love; three things I have never given to another person. I learned at a young age that giving these things to people means they have enough power to destroy you.

His fingers tangle in my hair as he brings me closer and kisses me. Hard. I feel his promise in the way his lips move along mine and know he will protect me. As his tongue strokes mine, I can't stop the tears that are falling. He kisses them away and I laugh at the gesture because it's too sweet.

As we lay there, both naked under the covers in my bed, I jump when I hear the front door slam. A frustrated scream comes from the living room, and I get up, worried about my roommate.

Camden comes off the bed and tugs on his jeans as I pull my oversized T-shirt and sleep shorts on. After we both are clothed, we make our way out of the room.

Emree is sitting on the couch in the clothes she wore to work tonight with a tub of Neapolitan ice cream on her lap. She jams the spoon into the container, pulling out an oversized scoop that she then shoves into her mouth.

"Em…is everything okay?" I hesitatingly ask her. She said she was going to Conrad's after work since they made up last week after yet another fight, but I'm worried something happened between work and then.

"Oh nothing, just that men suck balls," she says, eyeing Camden, who is keeping a safe distance behind me.

I want to laugh at her statement but know now is not the time. "Care to elaborate?" I ask as I take the open seat beside her on the three-person sofa.

Instead of answering me, she turns her attention to my boyfriend. "Mr. Collins, is it fair to assume that if you are fucking a girl and invite said girl to your house party for the night, that you would not be making out with another girl in your living room when she gets there?" Emree asks sarcastically.

Camden drops his head. "Oh shit."

She points the spoon at him. "'Oh shit' is right. What a

lovely show I got of some ho straddling Conrad while another girl sitting beside him sucked on his neck. It really made me just so happy."

My heart hurts for my best friend because I know how much she likes Conrad, and he seems to like her but is making poor decisions left and right.

Camden slowly comes over, almost as if he is gauging Emree's level of men hatred right now. He sits on the love seat across from us. "Listen, what Conrad is doing is fucked up. Like really fucked up, and I'm sorry, Emree, I really am. He's not known for being a committed kind of guy, and that's not an excuse, but I know he likes you."

She rolls her eyes.

"I'm not saying what he's doing is right, because it is wrong on so many levels, but maybe next time when he comes groveling to you, make him tell you why he's doing this shit."

She groans and throws her head back on the couch. "Ugh, I just can't say no to him. He's going to come to my door tomorrow, looking beautiful as ever with that hair I love running my hands through and those bright blue eyes, and he says he wants me so much but makes mistakes and that he'll be better. Why? Why do I keep forgiving him? My heart freaking hurts every time, but my lady bits want him too bad."

Reaching over, I grab her hand, the one without the ice cream spoon. "Maybe that's the problem, hon. Give him an ultimatum. No more free sex. He wants to be with you, then he needs to make a choice. Date and be exclusive, or you move on and find someone who wants to be with you and only you."

Her eyes fill with tears, and she shovels more ice cream into her mouth to distract herself. "I really like him," she says softly while looking into the tub on her lap.

"Then tell him," Camden chimes in. "Nothing happened between Blaire and me until I admitted my feelings to her. Conrad has been more of a manwhore than me. Girls and feel-

251

ings don't mix well with him. He comes from a fucked-up family and closes himself off too much."

"What if he decides he doesn't want me anymore?"

"Then screw him," I tell her. "You're beautiful, smart, funny, have a wicked yet weird fashion style, and are an absolute sweetheart. If he can't grow a pair and realize that, then he isn't the one for you. There are tons of hot guys out there who would love nothing more than to date you."

"You noticing some hot guys, Gray Eyes?" Camden asks me, his eyebrow raised in question.

"Oh hush, I mean for her. But you have to admit, this campus has some good-looking people on it."

"You both are right." Emree sighs. She places the tub of ice cream on the coffee table and rubs her hands together, warming them up. "I'm looking for a relationship, not someone who wants to sleep with me and every other girl available. You know, he's never even taken me on a date."

Camden curses and I can see he's struggling between his loyalty to his friend and what he thinks is right.

"He tells me I'm the girl of his dreams and how much he likes me, but then goes out and hooks up with other women and can't even take me out to dinner? It's messed up when I think about it."

I scoot closer and wrap my arms around her. "You're worth more than that and if he can't see it, then he can watch you walk away and find someone worthy. He's out there, hon, and we'll find him."

"Yeah." She leans her head against my shoulder. "I guess you're right. But can you do me a favor and remind me of this in the morning before he comes here? I need that tough love speech you guys are good at."

Camden and I laugh and promise to remind her that she deserves better in the morning. After scooping out some ice cream into a bowl for Camden and myself and Emree showers and changes out of her work clothes, we settle on the couch and start the first season of Emree's and my favorite show, to which Camden groans because he thinks it's cheesy. I snuggle up to him and can't help but think of how grateful I am to have a guy who loves me, and I don't have to worry about him wanting other women.

CHAPTER TWENTY-EIGHT

CAMDEN

Halloween is quickly approaching, and my roommates and I have somehow gotten roped into hosting a party at our house. The holiday is on a Saturday this year, so everyone is pumped there is no game or classes the day after. Maddox decides to make it a mandatory costume party and currently we're all in Spirit Halloween, adding random decorations to the cart. Mateo picked out a spider he thinks will be funny to put at the front door because it has a motion sensor and jumps out when you walk in front of it.

The costume section is limited, but Levi finds an Elvis Presley suit while Mateo decided on a cop uniform. He said he plans to get laid that night and women love a man in uniform. Blaire told me she has to work but will be coming by when she gets off, and Emree is making them matching costumes but won't tell me what it is yet. Whatever Blaire wears, I hope it's sexy and easy to get her out of.

Conrad grabs a dinosaur costume and smiles. "How fucking awesome is this?"

I laugh. "Dude, if you wear that, you're going to pass out

before the night ends." Even though it's October, Florida has no fall and it's still in the eighties here.

He puts the costume back. "Well, what are you going to wear? The options here suck."

A bag catches the corner of my eye and I smile. "I know exactly what I'll wear." Blaire has made comments when she sees me in my glasses about how I look like Superman, and I can't think of a better costume.

Grabbing the bagged leotard, I make sure it's my size and toss it into the cart. "I'll wear my black trousers and white dress shirt over it and leave the middle buttons open. A little Clark Kent and Superman combo."

"Ah come on, man, that's too good of a costume," Conrad groans. "Find something for me. I can't think of shit."

Looking through the costumes, I try to find one that would work out. After pulling two out, Conrad decides on the gladiator one, saying he wants his muscles on display.

"Do you know what the girls are wearing?" I ask. The morning after the shit that went down with Emree and Conrad, he showed up at her apartment, like she said he would, and told her how sorry he was and how messed up he is, begging her to give him another chance. After an hour of yelling and crying, all while Blaire and I hid in her bedroom, Conrad promised to be better and take her on a real date. Since then, they have been inseparable, which shocks me because Conrad and monogamy have never mixed.

"No, Em is keeping it a secret. She said it's sexy as hell, which makes me want to know more and she knows that is torturing me."

Before I can respond, Maddox comes over. "You guys think if I put a mistletoe on my belt, girls will offer blow jobs?"

"Dude, it's not Christmas."

"So?" Maddox responds. "Who says mistletoes are strictly for Christmas? Maybe I'll start a new trend of Halloween mistletoe that has a happy ending." He tosses the fake plant into the cart and walks away toward the masks.

"Where did he even find that?" Conrad asks. "We're in a Halloween store."

"Nothing stops Maddox when it comes to ideas of how to get laid."

Our cart is filled with a variety of decorations and costumes. Levi decided on a lumberjack outfit rather than the Elvis Presley, and the guy fits the part perfectly, while Maddox found a fireman costume and said he is going to ask ladies to hold his hose. Really, he should come with a warning label.

We check out and of course Conrad insists on paying, saying that we can pay him back later. He does this almost every time we have a party. I'm positive when we make an alcohol run, he will be sure to pay for that too since out of the five of us, he and Mateo are the only ones who are twenty-one. At least for the next few months.

Back at the house, we begin setting up decorations. Since we live in a neighborhood with a few kids, we decided to get some candy to set up on the porch for anyone who comes by. When the house is halfway set up, Blaire and Emree show up. The moment I see my girl's car pull in, I'm off the chair and tell Levi I'll be back to help him finish putting the fake spiderwebs along the wall.

She smiles at me as she opens the door and I pick her up in a crushing hug. "What're you doing here, baby?"

She laughs as she tries to wiggle out of my hold, but it only makes me pull her tighter to me. "Emree texted Conrad to see if you guys needed help." Deciding to stop fighting me, she places both her hands on the sides of my face and kisses me. "You can let me down now."

Sliding my hands down, I grab onto her beautiful ass. "Not until you give me a proper kiss."

She rolls her eyes. "That was a perfectly fine kiss, Camden."

"Nuh-ah, baby, I need tongue."

She looks over at Maddox, who is on the roof setting up a bloody skeleton, and Conrad as he holds the ladder steady.

"They're not watching. I haven't seen you in three days. Kiss me like you mean it."

"Ugh, fine." She groans, but I know she wants me just as bad as I want her.

Like our kiss before, her hands frame my face, but instead of the quick peck she gave me, she presses her lips to mine, opening them just barely so I can stroke my tongue against hers. As I walk forward, her back meets the side of the car and I amplify the kiss, causing her to moan and slide her hands into my hair, gripping it tightly. Her long legs automatically wrap around my waist and the heat from between her legs is a major turn-on. My hands slide up the sides of her body, enjoying every delicious curve, until I stop just below her breasts.

"Oh, hell yeah, a free porno!" Maddox yells.

Blaire must not have heard him because she tightens her legs around me, pulling me closer to her. Ignoring my best friend behind us, I mold my body to hers and she whimpers, breaking the kiss and rolling her head back. Not wanting to break away from her, I begin kissing her neck as her hands get tangled in my hair.

"Give it to her, Camden!" Levi shouts, and I turn my head to look behind us. All my roommates and Emree are standing by the front door. Maddox is bent over, and Mateo is pretending to smack his ass. Emree looks mortified, while Levi and Conrad can't stop laughing.

Blaire ducks her head into my neck. "Oh no, please tell me none of this is happening."

I can feel how hot her face is against me and know she is several shades of red right now.

"That was one hell of a kiss, Gray Eyes." I chuckle.

She slaps my shoulder. "Don't you dare laugh, Camden Collins. This is embarrassing."

"Trust me, baby, I have seen these guys in more than one compromising situation in the two-plus years we've known each other." I shudder at the thought of some of the shit I've seen.

Releasing my grip, she slides down my body and the moment she steps away, I already miss her. Never would I have thought I'd be the guy who would be whipped like this. Missing my girl even when she's right by me sounds insane and I would get my ass kicked by the guys if they ever heard me say it out loud.

Blaire grabs my hand, and we head toward our friends. Maddox is smirking and I know he still has plans to embarrass Blaire more, but I give him a *shut the fuck up* look and he rolls his eyes and goes back to securing the skeleton to the roof.

Inside, Blaire and Emree help me with the rest of the cobwebs, and I'm glad Conrad took them up on that offer for help because the two of them blow our work away. By the time we're done, we have a good-looking setup for a spooky Halloween.

Maddox ordered pizzas and we set up a bunch of waters and sodas on the coffee table. It's Friday, the night before a game, so there is no alcohol for us, although pizza and beer are my favorite combo. Blaire is nuzzled beside me as we sit around talking. I kiss the side of her head and she smiles up at me.

Goddamn, what that smile does to me.

Maddox is going on about how boring the book he chose for American lit is and if he doesn't pass the class, he will be kicked off the team. He has never taken his classes seriously but got lucky with teachers who understand how important passing is for athletes. The only issue now is Professor Hebert doesn't care and will flunk our asses.

"I can help you if you want," Blaire offers.

His eyes widen and I know where his thoughts are going.

"She said help, not do the work for you. She isn't one of the ball chasers who'll do your assignments in exchange for sex."

Blaire's head whips around to me. "Ew, girls offer themselves to you guys if they do your work?"

I shrug my shoulders. "I mean, sometimes. Sleeping with an athlete is very desirable."

"Yes, sweetheart, you should be so lucky," Maddox chimes in and I wish he would just shut up. "I mean, your boy here being off the market has only helped me with the ladies, but that doesn't stop them from wanting him. Hell, just last week I heard Chloe and her friends talking about taking bets when he would be available again."

"Dude, shut the fuck up," I say through clenched teeth.

"Who's Chloe?" Blaire asks.

Before I can respond, Emree gets up and leaves the living room, walking outside through the back door.

Conrad throws his empty can at Maddox. "Thanks, dude. Can you not bring her up around Em?" He follows her outside and shuts the door.

Maddox looks confused until it clicks in his head. "Oh shit, she was part of the three-way Blondie walked in on, wasn't she?"

"Yeah, dipshit, and Conrad and Emree are still on thin ice," Levi answers.

Maddox brings his attention to Blaire, who has shifted just slightly away from me. "Dear Blaire, Chloe is what you would call a slut, and I know, I know, that is not a politically correct term, and I am a fellow feminist, but she is. That girl has slept her way through the soccer team since her freshman year, and I swear she is trying to trap one of us or something. It isn't even like she likes us, just wants us for our dicks and status."

Blaire's nose scrunches up in disgust. "So have you all...

slept with her?" She is avoiding looking at me, but I know who the question is mainly directed at.

"Hell no," Levi answers. His love life is a mystery to us since I have never seen him bring a girl home, so that answer doesn't really shock me.

Mateo rubs the back of his neck. "Um, yeah. Freshman year. I was too horny to know I was being used. She slept with my roommate the week after."

She looks at Maddox, who has a sheepish smile.

"Well, yes. A few times. It's an easy lay and I will not be ashamed for being a man with needs."

I can't help but roll my eyes because it's the dumbest excuse. He wanted a relationship with Chloe last year because he said she was the wildest sex he had ever had, but when he found out she was also sleeping with...well, everyone else, he wanted none of that anymore.

Ever so slowly, Blaire turns to me. Her beautiful gray eyes are filled with worry, and I hate myself for my past sex life, knowing it could hurt her. "No, Gray Eyes. I've never slept with her. Not that she hasn't tried, but I didn't want to be another checked-off guy from her list."

Relief washes over her face. "Well, that's good, I guess. Sounds like she just wants to use you guys."

"Ah, and use us she does. All night, in fact," Maddox says with a dreamy look on his face, I'm sure thinking back to one of the nights he spent with Chloe.

Deciding we need a subject change, I go back to Blaire's offer. "Anyway, man, you should really take her up on getting help with that class. She picked out a good book for me and I'm already almost done with the assignment."

She smiles proudly. "See, I told you it wouldn't be so bad."

"I may have to take you up on that, sweetheart. Getting booted from the team would pretty much leave me homeless

261

since I live in the athletic department's house and all." We all laugh, but in reality, he's right.

Together, we finish off four pizzas. Conrad and Emree come back inside after a while, and her hair looks like someone was running their fingers through it. Looks like they made up, although you can still sense some tension between them.

Blaire decides not to stay the night, much to my objection, since she has to work tomorrow, and I have a game a few hours away. I'm bummed she can't come to it, but my mom and sister promised to be in the stands, cheering me on.

After a mini make-out session by her car, she tells me she really has to go, and I reluctantly let her. It is getting harder and harder having this beautiful woman walk away from me, and I wonder if it'll always be like this. I feel like I can never get enough of her.

CHAPTER TWENTY-NINE

BLAIRE

O nly an hour into my shift and work is already dragging on. It's Halloween and Garrett encouraged us to wear costumes. Deciding not to wear the one I had planned for Camden's party, I'm wearing a simple pair of black leggings, a black T-shirt, and I bought a headband that looks like cat ears. Emree did my makeup to look like I have a cat nose and whiskers. She decided to dress up and is wearing a short Tinker Bell dress with wings and a pair of green heels. Her blonde hair is held up perfectly to look just like that character. When we walked into Whiskey Joe's for our shift, Garrett shook his head at us. I can't help but notice how good he looks in his Thor costume, and I guess he has heard us saying how much we think he looks like the actor and went with it. He even tied his long, blond hair back into a half up, half down man bun.

There are more people here than a usual Saturday night, and while the crowd is making me slightly nervous, I can't help but look at the open floor that used to be a long, dark hallway that led to the bathrooms. On top of the new renovation, Garrett also suggested to the owner that he hire someone for security on the weekends. Not only for the staff but any guests too. Silas has done a good job of making sure that no female staff walks to their car alone after a shift and keeps an eye on all areas inside and outside of the bar. We have all appreciated the care these guys have given after what happened to me last month.

Although I love my job and the people I work with, I wish I weren't here tonight. Missing Camden's game had bummed me out, but knowing he is drinking and having fun at his party is stressing me out. It's the first big party they have thrown at their house since before classes started, and while I don't particularly want to be there, I'm worried about the girls Maddox mentioned the other day. Especially this Chloe chick, who seems to have Camden in her line of sight.

I never thought I would be the jealous type, but hearing how girls throw themselves at these guys and thinking about how many Camden has slept with makes me upset. I can't be mad at him for what he did before we were together, but it doesn't stop my head from going there.

"Blaire, your drinks are ready," Garrett yells out, breaking me from my thoughts. I fill up my tray with a variety of mixed drinks a table of college girls ordered.

As I approach the table, all the girls start clapping and get excited about their drinks. I can't help but smile with them because they all look adorable in their matching cowgirl costumes, each sporting a bright pink hat.

A few of the bars in town are participating in a Halloween barhop and Garrett decided it would be good for business to join in. Each group that comes to the bars gets a round of shots on the house and a picture taken. At the end of the night, a winner will be chosen for best costumes and wins a one-hundred-dollar gift card to each bar. So far, with the turnout we have had, I would say it's working.

There are a few groups on the dance floor, but every table

THE ACT OF TRUSTING

in here is full. I'm used to it being busy on the weekends, with us being a popular college bar, but with the number of bodies here tonight, I'm worried we're going to exceed the max capacity for our building.

It's almost nine and I'm grateful to Garrett for giving Emree and me the early shift tonight because I don't think I could handle much more of this. The barhop started at six and as the hours passed, each group coming in was sloppier and sloppier with the amount of alcohol they had consumed.

Three of our coworkers walk through the front door, looking great in their sexy nurse, Batman, and Red Riding Hood costumes. They all look around the place with wide eyes before they disappear to the employee area.

Emree skips over to me with a wide smile on her face. "It's party tiiiimmmeeee," she sings.

I can't help but laugh. "If their party is anything like this place, I don't think I want to be there."

She rolls her eyes. "You know your sweet boyfriend will escape with you the moment he thinks you don't want to be there."

She is right. Camden has told me multiple times that we don't have to stay around everyone for too long. He even said he would much rather snuggle in his bed and watch a movie with me than be around everyone. I know that is partially true but also can tell he likes the college party and drinking life. I told him to have fun with his friends while I'm at work and will tell him if it becomes too much for me at any point.

Emree and I head over to the bar where Garrett is making some change in the register. "Howdy, boss man. You done with us since our replacements are here?" Emree asks.

After counting some dollars, he closes the register. "You sure you ladies don't want to stay and enjoy the life of *Girls Gone Wild*?"

We both laugh. "I've seen that show and this is far from that.

There are no girls flashing guys and you, sir, do not have T-shirts or hats to offer girls in exchange for seeing their tits."

"Em, how on earth have you seen that show? You're like twelve."

"I find your comment about my age insulting and I have seen basically every reality show known to man. Except *Naked and Afraid* because seeing that much of someone's butt in a one-hour show is too much."

Garrett and I look at her, and she shrugs her shoulders. Sometimes it amazes me the things that go on inside her head. "Well, tits and ass talk aside, you both are good to go. We can handle it until closing."

"Closing?" I ask. "Garrett, you got here when we did. You're going to work all night?"

He raises his shoulders. "Gotta do what you gotta do. Can't leave my employees to handle this mess." He waves his hand through the bar.

We say goodbye and he goes back to taking drink orders from guests and waitstaff. He hasn't stopped once tonight, and I wonder how he can do it. Garrett is here almost every day and since I have started, I haven't seen him take a vacation or even a weekend off.

Emree and I grab our bags and I stop by the bathroom to clean off the cat makeup before we head to my car in the parking lot. Silas offers to walk with us, but we tell him we're good since we are using the buddy system. When I look back, I see him watching us from the front of the building and smile. It's nice working with people you can trust.

Our costumes are tucked away in the back seat of my Toyota. Seeing the bags, I get giddy with the anticipation of Camden seeing me in the costume. Emree decided we couldn't go traditional with it since all the girls at the house will be a sexy version of something. Instead, she opted to make our costumes and boy did she deliver.

Grabbing my bag out of the back seat, I reach inside and pull out the articles of clothing. Inside is a pair of blue knee-high soccer socks, a black pair of Soffe shorts, a pair of Adidas indoor soccer shoes, and a blue-and-gold cropped jersey matching the one Camden wears with his number twelve and last name on the back.

Emree crawls into the back seat and begins taking her clothes off. I keep a lookout to make sure no one is walking by as she changes out of her work clothes and into the homemade costume. Her jersey is representing Conrad's number nineteen and last name, and she cut the neck of it low so that her boobs are on full display. She tried to do the same with me, stating I shouldn't cover up my 'perfect double Ds,' but I vetoed it and settled for a somewhat sexy, but still modest V-neck.

My best friend comes out and fluffs her hair up. "How do I look?" She does a little twirl.

"Perfection, darling."

"Good, now you get your pretty little ass in there and change so we can head on over."

I do as she says, but not before checking the parking lot. It's completely deserted, and I feel better about getting almost naked in the back seat of my car. Changing in the small area is harder than I thought, and I wonder how Em made it look so easy. I feel like our height difference would factor in. I struggle to get the tight top on and hit my head on the ceiling a couple times. After I tie both the laces of my shoes, I make sure that everything is in place and covering all the necessary parts before heading outside to join Emree.

"Girl, you are going to make that boy speechless," she tells me. "Seriously, your boobs are sitting perfectly in that top. I must say, I did well with our costume choices."

I can't help but laugh and feel somewhat self-conscious about her comment on my chest. Looking down, I make sure that both the girls are tucked away enough. Compared to the groups of women coming into the bar tonight, I have to say my costume is more modest. I don't usually show my stomach like this, but the Soffe shorts I have are high-waisted and Spandex, covering more than Emree is with her rolled up Soffe cotton shorts. I feel sexy and I know Camden is going to love the outfit, especially his name on my back.

Reaching back into the car, I stuff my work clothes into the bag my costume was in and hop into the driver's seat. Emree climbs into the passenger side. She reaches for the USB cord and plugs her phone in, connecting to my Apple CarPlay and blasting some Taylor Swift. I send Camden a text that we're on our way before pulling out of the parking spot.

At the top of our lungs, we sing about a love story, and I can't help but smile thinking about the guy I'm in love with. How funny it is how I relate to this song now after this new experience in my life. Camden is the Romeo to my Piper. My own prince. My love story.

CHAPTER THIRTY

CAMDEN

The house is shaking with the beat of some techno song coming from the surround sound speakers. Sweaty bodies are covering the living room, grinding against each other. Maddox had the idea to make that room a dance area and had us push the furniture against the walls. People seem to like it because it's the most packed room in the house.

Since one of the frat houses was shut down for hazing, there are more people here than we planned for and the house is littered all over with college kids. Luckily, Conrad always buys more alcohol than needed when we have parties, so there is not any worry of running out. Downside is that this place is going to be trashed and filled with passed-out drunk people in the morning.

As I try to squeeze through the crowd of people, someone snakes their arms around my waist, resting at my belt. Jumping away from the unwanted touch, I turn to see Chloe practically naked in only a purple seashell top and green miniskirt. She's dyed her blonde hair red or is wearing a damn good wig and is in platform green heels. Her full lips are coated in red gloss, and she lifts the corners of them as she saunters over to me.

"Dance with me, baby," she purrs. Her hands make their way back onto me and I swat her away.

"I've told you repeatedly, it is not happening. I have a girl-friend, Chloe." I'm tired of her not taking no for an answer.

She rolls her eyes. "That virgin? I know she can't satisfy a man like you, Cam. You need a real woman. One who knows what to do with a body like yours."

Too fast for me to stop her, Chloe reaches down and palms my dick through my pants. My nostrils flare and before I can shove her off me, Maddox is there, coming between us. "What do we have going on here? Chloe, baby, do you need some dick? You know I'm always here for you." He wraps his arm around her waist and runs his hands up her body, pulling her to him and off me.

I try to calm down and take controlled breaths. I'm sick of this girl and worried she is going to do something to fuck with Blaire. Chloe keeps looking at me from the corner of her eye as Maddox pulls her to the dance floor and I make my escape to the kitchen.

Conrad and Mateo picked up a keg after our winning game to save on money and trash. We still have a few coolers with more girly drinks for people who don't like beer, and Conrad keeps a pack of his fancy IPA in the back of the fridge so no one touches it. He also adds a note that he will hunt down anyone who touches them.

Levi and Mateo are playing a game of flip cup on our dining room table with Jules on their team yelling at them to hurry up. I can't help but laugh because who would have thought this sweet, quiet girl would be that competitive inside.

We didn't anticipate this many people coming tonight and only set up two tables of beer pong outside, so there are a lot of stragglers waiting around for their turn. Some are in the pool playing chicken with bikini-clad girls on their shoulders.

Others are chilling on some of the loungers and beach chairs we set up.

Looking around, I can't help but feel like this is the last place I want to be. Especially without Blaire here with me. For the last two years, soccer and partying have been two activities I looked forward to the most. I'm not even twenty-one yet and getting drunk doesn't appeal to me right now. I would much rather be on the couch with Blaire curled up in my arms and watching a chick flick. Well, I don't particularly like watching them, but watching her watch them makes me happy. She gets this sappy look in her eyes anytime we watch a romance movie or she's reading one of her books in bed.

Fuck, this girl has got me by the balls.

I'm twenty years old, twenty-one in a month, and I should be enjoying college life. Partying, sports, and girls. But that's not what I want. I want one girl. Blaire. And her being somewhere else is making me not want to be here. I promised her I would enjoy the party until she got here and make the decision if we would leave or stay. As of right now, the moment she walks through those doors, we're getting the hell out of here and into her bed. It's been a whole day since I've seen her, and I need to be with my girl.

After throwing back the rest of my beer, I head over to the keg to refill my cup. I told myself I'd keep my alcohol consumption to a minimum tonight since we're in the middle of our season and I plan to head home with Blaire later, but I'm not sure what else to do besides drink. So far I'm only on my third cup and not feeling anything, so I tell myself the moment my head starts to feel that familiar alcohol fog, I'll stop.

As I sip on my drink, I head outside to watch the games of beer pong, hoping that will help pass the time. It's still light outside and Blaire doesn't get off until nine. It is taking everything in me not to head over to Whiskey Joe's and wait for her.

The two tables are surrounded by people cheering on all the

teams. The tables are wet with spilled beer and the ground is littered with the typical red disposable cups. A college party must-have. I can already tell the cleanup tomorrow is going to be a bitch and I know the guys will try to get out of it, claiming their hangover is too much.

Time passes faster as I watch different teams take the beer pong table. A few people have asked me to be their partner, but I declined since I don't want to get shit-faced tonight. I'm nursing my sixth beer when someone comes up beside me, slipping their hands into my button-up dress shirt that is open in the middle to show off the Superman costume underneath. Before I can step away this time, Chloe grabs me by my belt with her other hand and pulls me to her. She smells like cheap perfume and desperation.

"Just fuck me already, team captain. I'm tired of this game you're playing," she begs.

Grabbing the wrist of her hand in my shirt, I pull it away and squeeze a little too tight. Her eyes widen as I lean in close. "I don't know what the fuck is wrong with you and maybe Daddy never had the heart to say no to his precious little girl growing up, but if you don't get the hell away from me, I will make sure none of the guys on the team touch you again. It will be a dry two more years for you, Chloe." I stare into her eyes as I apply more pressure to her wrist as I make sure she hears each word I say.

She pulls her arm free and shoves at my chest. "You're an asshole. I'm just trying to give you a good time and you act like you're not even attracted to all this." She runs her hands down her body.

"I'm not." After downing the rest of my beer, I toss the cup to the growing pile on the ground.

Chloe smirks and I instantly freeze. Nothing good can come out of a look like that from a woman like her. "You will be," she tells me before walking away.

A woman like Chloe is dangerous. She is determined when she sets her sights on something, or someone, and unfortunately it seems like I'm the current target. Many of the guys would feel honored to have Chloe's attention, but I want nothing more than for her to leave me alone.

With her being gone, I feel more comfortable. As I continue to watch the beer pong matches, I start to feel lightheaded, and I wonder if that last beer I downed was too much. I go to the cooler and snag a water bottle and a handful of chips out of the bags scattered on the patio table. Maybe these will help me sober up before Blaire gets here.

"Hey, man, you okay? You don't look so good," one of our freshman teammates asks me.

Standing starts to become difficult and I lean on one of the chairs around the table for support. "Yeah, just think I had too much to drink."

He laughs and Maddox comes up behind him. "Aw, did our captain have a little too much to drink tonight?" He laughs.

I try to muster up a laugh with him, but the movement makes my head feel like there is a blown-up balloon inside of it. "Must be, man. Hey, I'm going to head upstairs for a little. Will you send Blaire my way when she gets here?" Fuck, my head is killing me.

Maddox gives me a concerned look. "Yeah, of course. You sure you're good, dude? You're looking kind of pale now."

"I'll be fine," I tell him as I focus on my feet as I walk into the house.

The music sounds far away as I walk through the kitchen and into the living room. The bodies have seemed to multiply, if that's even possible, and it takes me longer than it should to get to the bottom of the stairs. As I look up at the second floor, everything becomes dizzy. Someone comes beside me and puts my arm around their shoulder.

"Come on," the person says. "I got you, stud."

On autopilot, I let the person guide me to my room, where I collapse onto my bed. The room is spinning, and everything is blurry. The door shuts, closing me off from the party and the music. My head is still pounding, but losing the beat outside may help.

I shut my eyes, hoping whatever this feeling is will go away with some sleep. Never has alcohol hit me this hard and I am starting to wonder if I drank more than the six cups of beer I remember having. Six beers have never done this to me before, so it must be something else.

As I start to drift off, I feel the bed move. My head hurts so bad that I can't open my eyes, but I feel someone crawling closer to me across the mattress.

"You—" I try to finish my sentence, but the words are lost on me as the balloon feeling in my head increases.

As the person comes closer, I want nothing more than to push them away, whoever they are. I feel hands on my chest and a weight on my lap. I try to swat them away, but my arms are too heavy to lift. Nails scrape down my chest and rest on my belt before releasing it.

The last thought I have before blacking out is of Blaire and how I hope to fuck she comes and gets whoever is in my room out.

CHAPTER THIRTY-ONE

BLAIRE

People are overflowing out of the guys' house, and I can hear the music from down the street. The road is filled with cars, and I struggle to find a spot. There are a few older kids in costumes walking around the neighborhood, but it seems the trick-or-treaters have called it a night.

Unless I want to block someone's driveway, I have to drive at least ten houses down to find a place to park on the street. This party is crazier than any I have seen, and I'm worried about going into the house. While I have made more progress the last year, especially the last couple months, with the issues I have struggled with since my assault, a party like this is not something I would have prepared for.

As Emree and I exit the car, I take a deep breath to mentally prepare myself to go in there. Camden promised me that the moment I was ready to leave, he would be right there with me, and I have to hold on to that. I have a boyfriend who is amazing and will be there for me when I need him. I trust him, more than he knows.

Arm in arm, Emree and I walk along the sidewalk toward the house with the much-too-loud music. "I'm surprised their neighbors haven't called the police with a noise complaint at this point. The cars are practically bouncing." She isn't wrong. If I lived by them, this kind of party would annoy me.

"Maybe with it being a holiday, everyone is letting it slide. Or they could be out themselves." Many of the houses around us are dark inside.

"True."

Much like at Whiskey Joe's, there are girls surrounding the house in every version of jobs and characters, but of course the sexy kind. There are a few dressed like police and some in schoolgirl outfits. The guys are dressed in a variety of costumes from superheroes to funny ones like Twister and Ricky Bobby. There are a few people masked up in scary outfits, and I'm thankful they are in the minority because, while I love Halloween, I don't enjoy the scary aspect of it. Haunted houses and I do not go well together.

As we walk up the driveway, Emree squeezes my arm. "You going to be okay?"

I love my best friend. Instead of running inside to find Conrad, she is right by my side because she knows how difficult parties have been for me. "Yeah. Camden kept reassuring me that we can leave anytime I want to."

"Good," she says. "I'll head home with you if you want to. This party is even more wild than I like."

As we walk through the front door, my eyes widen. Bodies are covering every area from the entryway to the living room and into the kitchen. The guys' house isn't small, but it isn't that large either. It's a standard two-story suburban house. They have used the limited space well and turned the living room into a makeshift dance floor with bodies bumping and grinding on each other. The stairs have people lingering around and talking with drinks in their hands and there are a few I can see upstairs.

As Emree and I walk farther into the house, I can't help but cover my nose at the smell of liquor and a mixture of cologne and perfume and BO. Not the most appealing of smells, considering everything hits you at once.

A guy dressed in a Where's Waldo costume cuts us off as we walk through the house and spills his beer all over Emree and me. "Oops," he says with a smile on his face. "You ladies should really get out of those wet clothes." He saunters up to Emree and rubs his body against hers.

Before she can say anything, the creepy guy is pulled away by the back of his shirt. "I swear to God, Jensen, if you touch these girls, I will tell Coach you got hammered at the strip club and he'll bench you for the next game," Conrad says through clenched teeth.

He still has his teammate by the back of his shirt and the guy's eyes widen at Conrad's threat. "Y-yeah, man. I was just messing." After he is released, the guy moves away, leaving Emree and me covered in his spilled beer.

"This is just great. I made us these fabulous costumes and that idiot had to go and ruin them the moment we walk through the door," she complains.

"Aw," Conrad says as he grabs Emree around the waist and pulls her to him. "You still look hot. If I turn you around right now, will my name be on you?"

She flashes him a knowing smile. "Maybe." She kisses him on the cheek and steps back to look at his outfit. "My man looks sexy in this gladiator costume. Make sure you keep this on all night."

He bends down and takes her lips in a crushing kiss. I look away and try to find Camden among the crowd of people. He didn't tell me what he was wearing tonight, so for all I know he could be one of the masked scary characters.

"Looking for your boy?" Conrad asks. He has Emree tucked into his side now.

"Yeah, have you seen him? There's a crazy amount of people here."

"He was outside watching the beer pong games last I saw him." He nods toward the back door. "Let's head that way. It's less crowded outside anyway."

Still crushed to Conrad's side, Emree reaches for my hand as he guides us through the crowd of people. It seems the partiers move out of his way more easily than they did ours as we head through the living room and into the kitchen and out the back door. Not sure if it has to do with his large size or status, but the fact that we did not have to fight our way through the house anymore makes me happy.

Conrad was right, out back is much less crowded. There are still a lot of people, but they are more scattered between the pool, beer pong tables, and outdoor loungers and chairs. As I scan the area, I'm still not seeing Conrad, but do find a couple of his other roommates. When Mateo, Levi, and Jules spot us, they head our way.

"Wow, you ladies look sexy," Jules says.

"Us? I'm pretty sure you're every guy's wet dream in that Princess Leia gold bikini costume. Girl, your stomach is crazy toned," Emree says with admiration. She isn't wrong, though. Jules is incredibly fit, with lean, muscular arms, a toned stomach, and strong legs.

"Oh stop," Jules says with a blush creeping on her cheeks. "It's the Pilates. I'm telling you, you should both come with me. It's fun and a great workout."

"If it means I can look like that," Emree says, waving toward Jules's body, "then I am down for it anytime."

"Same. She's right, you look incredible."

"Enough about me. You made these, didn't you, Em? The costumes are super cute and look amazing."

Emree does a little twirl, showing off every part of the costume. "I must say, I have outdone myself. We sure do look cute in our boys' numbers." She giggles as she reaches up and kisses Conrad on the cheek.

"Speaking of boys, where's yours, Blaire? I can't imagine him not pouncing on you the moment you pulled up," Jules says.

Looking around the backyard, my shoulders sag as I realize he isn't out here either. "Not sure. I texted him when we left the bar but never got a response. He wasn't in the kitchen or living room either." I look over at Mateo and Levi. Both are hot as ever in their cop and lumberjack costumes. "Have either of you seen him?"

They shake their heads and I'm starting to get worried. "We've been playing rounds of pong for a while. This is the first time I've really talked to anyone away from the table," Levi says, a slight slur in his words.

"My ladies!" someone shouts from behind me, and I turn to see Maddox in a fireman uniform. He comes up between Emree and me and drapes his arms over our shoulders. "I must say, seeing you both looking as sexy as ever is doing things to me. You know, in the downstairs area. Any chance either of you beauties plans on dumping your boys tonight and giving me a chance?"

We both laugh, but Conrad is giving his friend the death glare. "Fuck off, Mad," he says through clenched teeth and pulls Emree out of Maddox's arm.

He takes the opportunity and wraps both his arms around me. "What do you say, Blaire baby? Ditch the captain and help a sexy fireman with his hose tonight?"

I can't help but smell the beer coming off Maddox's breath. He's a little more than tipsy, but I know everything he says is in good fun. Ever since the incident that happened in the pool, Maddox and I have become somewhat friends and he has shown me he isn't someone to be nervous around.

Patting his arms that are lying across my chest, I laugh at his ridiculousness. "You and your hose are going to need to stay away from me, Maddy."

"You wound me." He clutches at his heart and comes to stand next to me. "What are we all doing? Forming some kind of super-secret club away from all our guests? I must say, I agree with this formation because the amount of people here is starting to make me want to leave my own house." He shudders as he looks around. "Although I do appreciate the lovely ladies and their lack of clothing in these sexy costumes, there is only so much of me to go around."

"It would be a great secret club, but we are missing a member. Have you seen Camden at all tonight?" Mateo asks.

Maddox taps his finger along his chin. "Hmm, our Cammy boy? He's missing. Ah, that makes sense why I was able to get away with asking Blaire to touch my hose." He winks at me. "Haven't seen him in a while. He looked a little drunk earlier and said he was going to bed, but I'm not sure if he came back down."

"That's not like him to get bombed at a party during the season," Levi says with concern, and I start to worry as well.

"You didn't go check on him at all?" I ask Maddox.

He stares at me. "Did you not hear me say there is only so much of me that can go around? There are women practically naked here, Blaire baby. Many of them have daddy issues and left their morals at the door. You can't expect me to play babysitter tonight."

Rolling my eyes, I shove his shoulder. "You're ridiculous. What if he's sick?"

"Oh, he's a big boy. I'm sure he's up there crying because he had to try and enjoy the night without you here. The moment he sees you, he will be back to his lovey-dovey self."

"Come on." Jules grabs my arm. "We'll head up there with you."

Mateo nods in agreement.

Emree gives Conrad a look with a silent question in it. He smiles and grabs her hand. "We'll come too. I need to show Em something in my room." I'm sure that's exactly what he needs to do.

As we walk away, Maddox shouts to me, "Blaire baby, if our boy is down for the night, me and my hose will be more than happy to invite you to our room!"

I roll my eyes as we make our way through the back door and into the crowded bodies. As I try to avoid sweaty people dancing, people try to pull us into a few group dances, and I want nothing more than to get away from this. This party only solidifies my dislike for these kinds of events. I would much rather enjoy a night snuggled on the couch watching a movie or reading a book, or even a BBQ like we have done a few times here since Camden and I got together. Those nights at the house are fun and relaxing, and I have been able to get to know Camden's roommates and a few of their other team-mates better.

Mateo continues to take the lead as we make our way up the stairs. Much like when we walked through the house with Conrad, people see the over-six-foot soccer player and move out of his way. The upstairs is much less crowded but still has a few people hanging around, talking, and sipping on their drinks. Camden had told me all the guys lock their bedroom doors anytime they throw a party, so less people want to be up here since they don't have a room to hook up in.

Camden's room is the farthest down the hall. Conrad and Emree pop into his room on the right after unlocking it the door and wave to us as they close it. When I get to Camden's room, I knock before checking if it is locked and then slowly open it.

Of all the things I imagined seeing tonight, this is not even close to being one of them. Sitting on the bed, the side I have slept on multiple nights, is Chloe. Her seashell top is barely covering her large breasts as she slips it up her arms and clips it in the back. Her hair is a tangled mess, and she pulls her skirt down, adjusting it, as she stands up.

All the air leaves my body as I look at Camden lying beside her. His glasses that he wears at night after he takes his contacts out are crooked on his head. The white button-up shirt is pulled out of his pants and wrinkled. Underneath he is wearing a tight Superman shirt. His belt is undone and his zipper...his zipper is pulled down, and his pants are down enough to expose the front of his white boxer briefs.

Chloe must sense someone at the door and when she turns to me, there is an evil smile on her face. Her red lipstick is faded and smeared and when I look back at Camden, I can see the faded red coating his lips. He is lying there with his eyes still closed, not even realizing I'm standing here, witnessing what I can only describe as my worst nightmare.

"Oops," Chloe says. "Sorry you had to find us like this. Your boy here just needed a real woman for the night, and I couldn't say no to that handsome face and incredible body." She leans over on the bed and kisses him hard against the lips. Barely opening his eyes, Camden moans and kisses her back.

My heart feels as if it was just shattered into a million pieces. I clench my stomach and drop to my knees. Somewhere I hear a scream. *Was that me?*

I'm being lifted into the air and arms are wrapped around my body. I want to fight them. I want to kick and scream and run into that room and confront the man who told me he loved me. The man I gave myself to. The man I trusted more than anyone in this world.

Something comes over me and I scramble to get out of the hold someone has on me. I fall to the ground and land on the grass. *When did I get outside?*

The hands reach for me again and I fight them off. "No! No!

Why? Why would he do this?" Something wet is covering my face and I didn't even realize I started crying.

"Blaire, I need to get you away from here," Mateo says.

Jules comes in front of me and blocks my view of the house while Mateo has his arms around my waist, keeping me from running back inside. "Sweetie, I need you to breathe. You have to try and calm down."

"Blaire!" Emree runs out of the house with Conrad behind her. "Blaire, what happened?"

"H-he." I sob and dive into my best friend's arms. She holds me as I cry into her shoulder. "Please take me home. I need to get away from here."

As she cradles my head, I feel her body go rigid. I can't bring myself to say the words out loud. Though the image of what I saw in that bedroom keeps replaying in my head, I want nothing more than to get it out. My stomach clenches as I remember Chloe putting her top back on and adjusting her skirt. Before I can stop myself, I'm out of Emree's arms and vomiting into the grass beside us. Everyone jumps back to avoid getting splashed as my best friend comes behind me and pulls my hair back as I empty my stomach right there in front of our friends and strangers.

After my stomach has nothing left to bring up, I sink to the ground and cover my face with my hands. Emree is rubbing my back in a soothing way, but it is doing nothing to help. I just want to get away from here. Away from his friends, his house, his party. Him.

"Please take me home. I can't be here anymore," I whisper to her. I'm afraid to look up and see the faces of the people who have grown to become my friends in the last few weeks. Afraid to see the pity on their faces as they look at me, a sobbing, vomiting mess on the ground.

"I got you, Blaire," Emree says as she wraps her arms around me.

I avoid looking at anyone as we walk to the car. I know Conrad is behind us, though, and hear Emree and him exchange words here and there on the way, but I tune them out. I don't want to think about what just happened. I don't want to see his friends or him or anyone who reminds me of the man I love. The man who broke me in a matter of seconds. The man who made me think I could trust him with all my heart.

In one night, he broke my trust. Something that has taken me years to give to someone was destroyed in a matter of seconds. I hate him. I hate him for making me love him. I hate him for making me think he loved me back. I hate him for ruining everything I have worked so hard to overcome.

But most importantly, I hate him because I still love him.

CHAPTER THIRTY-TWO

CAMDEN

I'm dead. This is what death must feel like. Never in my life has my head felt this foggy or been pounding this hard. Throughout college and even high school, I have been drunk on several occasions, but alcohol never did this to me. It hurts to even move.

As I try to open my eyes, I snap them shut. The sun is coming in through the window beside my bed and the bright light is making the headache worse.

"We know you're awake, so get over whatever the fuck hangover you have going on because we need to talk to you," Conrad says from somewhere in my room.

"Fuck, what time is it?" My throat is dry, and the words sound scratchy as they come out.

No one answers me and after rubbing my eyes, I open them to see four angry faces in my room. Conrad is standing at the end of my bed with his arms crossed. Mateo and Levi are leaning against the wall beside the door. Maddox is sitting at my desk with the chair backward and his arms leaning against the back of it.

"It's almost noon, fuckface," Maddox says.

I look at him and my usual fun-loving and joking friend is serious and means business. "What's up with you all? You look like I ran over someone's dog or something." I sit up and the movement causes my stomach to roll. If there was anything in it, it would be coming up at this moment.

"Were you seriously that wasted last night?" Conrad asks.

I grab my head. "I guess so. I only remember drinking six beers, but hell, maybe it was more. I don't know. I've never been this drunk before."

"You don't remember anything last night, do you?" Levi raises an eyebrow.

Closing my eyes, I try to think back to last night. I remember getting ready for the party, the people showing up and filling our house, Chloe being a bitch and not leaving me alone, and going outside to watch the games of beer pong. That's where my memory ends. I try, but nothing is coming back to me.

"The last thing I remember is watching some games of beer pong. Chloe was being a bitch and not leaving me alone, but you got her away from me." I point to Maddox. His jaw twitches.

"Apparently, my efforts weren't good enough," he says through clenched teeth.

Ignoring what he said because I don't want Chloe to take up any space in my head, I look at Conrad. "What happened? Did the girls ever show up? And how did I even get to my room?"

"You're a goddamn idiot. You got wasted and really fucked up your girl."

My body goes cold. "What *the fuck* are you talking about?"

All my roommates look at each other, silently communicating who is going to tell me what they're talking about. They look at Levi, our unofficial dad of the group, and he sighs. "Dude, you got wasted and, well, you fucked Chloe."

This time, I do lose the contents of my stomach.

It takes a while for me to get it together enough to process what they tell me. Blaire walked in and found Chloe in my bed putting her clothes back on. I was on the bed, my shirt rumpled and pants undone. I try to remember any of it, but I can't. I wouldn't have believed them if my clothes weren't exactly like how they said they were last night.

There is no way I would have fucked Chloe. Even in my drunken state, I wouldn't go that far. Or would I? I can't imagine I would. She repulses me with her desperation and clinginess. But maybe I did? Could I have really done that?

"It couldn't have been what it looked like," I whisper to no one in particular. My head is resting in my hands as I sit on my bed, willing my brain to remember what happened, but nothing comes back to me.

"I was there, man. Jules and I both were. It was exactly how it looked, and I gotta say, it looked bad. I've also never seen someone scream like your girl did. Don't even think she realized she was too," Mateo tells me.

Blaire. I don't even want to imagine what she is thinking right now. If I were in her position, I would be on a murdering rampage, finding whatever guy touched her. Never would I intentionally hurt her, but fuck, I'm questioning everything with not being able to remember what even happened.

"I can't remember. I can't fucking remember, and my head is killing me. How the fuck did I get so drunk that I can't remember touching a girl I have wanted nothing to do with and can't stand?"

"Dude, you need to figure out what happened last night because you lost that girl. I've never seen someone so heartbroken. She couldn't even look at us." You can clearly see the sympathy in Conrad's eyes. "She was like a robot walking to the car. Em says she hasn't even come out of her room since last night."

My heart breaks even more knowing she is hurting. I want nothing more than to go to her, but I can't without knowing what actually happened last night. If I did fuck up, and I truly hope I didn't, I can't hurt her. I wouldn't be able to stand it if I did this to her.

"I need to talk to Chloe."

"Fuck that. She's the reason this shit happened," Maddox says as he stands.

Rubbing my temples, I try to rid myself of the headache that is still lingering. "She's the only other one who was there and can tell me what the hell happened. I need answers before I talk to Blaire. There's no way I fucked Chloe. It couldn't have happened. I wouldn't do that to Blaire." The more I say it, the more I keep trying to make myself believe that I would never do this to the woman I love.

Maddox claps his hands together. "Okay, first things first, you need to shower because the smell of you is making me sick." He looks at Conrad. "Second, you take care of that nastiness. He missed most of the trash can and you know I have a weak stomach."

Conrad peers down at the mess on the floor where I did, in fact, miss a lot of the trash can. "Why the hell do I have to clean that up? And who made you in charge?"

"I did, duh. As Cammy's bestie, I'm in charge of Operation Get His Girl Back. You think you can do a better job?" Maddox raises his eyebrows. "You're barely holding on to your girl by a thread."

Conrad rolls his eyes and exits the room without responding.

Maddox claps his hands together twice, making me want to strangle him for what that does to my head. "Chop, chop. Get that butt in the shower and freshen yourself up. We have a ho to find."

Getting up is easier than I thought it would be after having enough time to control my throbbing head. After grabbing a towel and steading myself as I leave the room, I focus on getting into the shower and cleaning myself up.

As I stand under the hot stream of water, I close my eyes and try to come up with any memory from last night. Every time I get somewhere, it stops when I was out back. With the shampoo being washed out of my hair, Chloe being outside with me flashes through my head. Her hands on my chest and her body pressing against me. The memory ends and I try to get it back. No way would I entertain her enough to think she can feel me up like that. I had to have pushed her away.

After rinsing off and getting changed, I head to my bedroom and see Conrad on the floor, cleaning up the puke. "Hey, man, sorry about that. I can clean it up."

"It's whatever," he grumbles. "Levi brought up some Advil and a water bottle for you. Take it and let's get out of here."

Once I've swallowed the pills and downed the water, Conrad and I make our way downstairs to meet the rest of the guys. My head feels less foggy after the shower, but the slight pounding is still lingering.

Levi throws me a piece of buttered toast when I enter the kitchen. "Here. Get something in your stomach. I'm not so forgiving if you puke in my car."

I eat the offered food and let it settle in my stomach before saying anything. "Thanks. I think I'm good, though."

"All right," Mateo calls our attention. "Anyone know where this bitch lives?"

We all look at Maddox, and he raises his eyebrows. "What? Do not look at me like that."

"Dude, you're the only one here who consistently boned her. Safe to assume you did it at her place," Mateo answers.

Maddox looks offended. "Our boy Conrad here was all up in that just as much as I was."

Conrad laughs. "Twice, man, and I never chased her and pounded on her door on my hands and knees to get her to let me in and fuck me."

"I told you that in confidence!"

"Can we end this arguing? Mad, we obviously know you've been to the she-witch's house. We will never let you live it down how you practically begged her for sex, so just get in the car and lead us to her." I want to get this over with and need answers as to what happened last night.

"Fine," he grumbles. "Let's go."

We all follow Levi out the door and into his SUV. My palms begin to sweat as we get closer to the girl who may or may not have destroyed my relationship. As we drive, I try not to think of Blaire and what I imagine is running through her head right now. I want nothing more than to go to her and wrap my arms around her in bed. The only thing stopping me is I know I am the last person she wants near her right now. I'm the one who caused this, and I can't be the one to comfort her, even though everything in me screams that this is wrong.

I need answers, no matter what those answers are. Whatever I find out, I need to figure out a way to fix this. I need Blaire. I need her love, her trust, and her heart. This can't be what ruins us.

CHAPTER THIRTY-THREE

BLAIRE

My tears are dried up and I have nothing left in my eyes to come out. I haven't left my bed since yesterday. My body hurts, but not as bad as my heart. I have never known pain like this before. Even when my friends and family betrayed me, it didn't hurt as bad as the man I gave my heart to breaking me the way he did. The worst part? I still freaking love him no matter how much I will myself not to.

The sun rose hours ago, but I have no idea what time it is. Emree has come to my door several times to check on me, but I don't answer her. I can't. My throat burns from the night of crying and I know if I try to say anything, no words will come out. It's not like I want to answer her anyway, so the fact that my body is linked with my mind and heart works in my favor.

Luckily, I don't have work today, so there is no need to worry about smiling and faking it in front of customers. I can't imagine mustering up enough energy to get ready and go there anyway. I can barely even roll myself over to the other side of the bed.

All night the image of Chloe and Camden ran through my head. I would squeeze my eyes shut, hoping anything else would come to mind other than that visual, but I couldn't escape it. It replays over and over and each time, I crumble a little more. Sleep never came to me last night and part of me wonders if I could pass out. Maybe then I could escape the nightmare that is my life.

I trusted this man. The first man I let into my body, mind, and heart. He had all of me in the short amount of time we knew each other, and I am left broken at the end of it. I should have continued the way I had been living for the last four years. Letting people in only leads to getting hurt in the end and I'm tired of this happening to me. I'm tired of feeling like this.

More time goes by, and my bladder decides it has had enough and I get up to relieve it. As I sit up, my head feels dizzy, and I steady myself before standing. My body feels drained as I walk to the door. While I open it, I peek outside and check for Emree. I don't see her and take the three steps to the bathroom across the hall quickly. After emptying my bladder, I wash my hands and sneak back into my room and lock myself in it again.

As I lean against the door, I can't help but stare at the bed in the middle of my room. Two months ago, this was a normal queen-sized bed that I used to sleep, read, or do homework in. Now? Well, now it holds far too many memories. When I look at this bed and its white comforter with flowers coming up from the bottom, all I can think about are the nights Camden held me. The nights we made love, and he had my body feeling more alive than I could ever imagine. Then there are the nights we would lie there, me on his chest and his arm around my shoulders, watching some comedy he would pick or a romance movie of my choice. Those nights were a personal favorite of mine. Or even the ones where I would be reading a book of mine and Camden would be studying his soccer notes from his coach. On those nights, he would idly be touching me. It didn't matter that we were doing two different things. He would blindly find my hand and link our fingers or run his fingertips up and down my back. It would be as if he couldn't not touch me if we were that close.

Just when I thought there were no more tears left in me, a few escape as I'm reminded of perfect nights we spent together. Each day with him I fell more in love. He made it so easy with his sweet words, kind gestures, and the way he made me feel safe and loved.

Deciding to avoid the area that holds far too many memories, I go to my desk and take a seat in the chair. Opening the drawer, I pull out the box of tissues in there and blow my nose and dry my face.

Just before closing the drawer, something catches my eye and I stop. The letters. The letters from another person who had broken me, but in a different way. I haven't gotten a new one since before classes started and have completely forgotten about them. Reaching inside, I grab the stack of letters and close the drawer. Maybe it's my weakened heart or maybe I'm a glutton for punishment, but something inside tells me to open them.

Not here, though. Not in a room that haunts me with memories of a man I love far too much, yet want to forget about. I need to get away from here. Away from anything that reminds me of Camden Collins.

After changing into a pair of jean shorts and a long-sleeved shirt, I grab the stack of letters and dump them into my purse. Cracking the door open again, I search for Emree, but the apartment is quiet. As I make my way out the door and through the living room, a piece of paper on the island catches my eye. It's a note from Emree telling me she had to leave for work but would have her phone on her and to call her if I needed anything at all. I had completely forgotten she picked up a shift today for one of the other girls who covered hers to go to one of the boys' games.

In no time, I am in my car and driving with no thought in sight. All I know is I needed to get out of there. I don't know what would hurt worse, the fact that Camden hasn't shown up or called, or if he had called or shown up. Either way, I need to get him out of my mind. I need a distraction and a place that holds no memories of us.

A place comes to mind. Somewhere I haven't been since last spring. Somewhere I know I can find peace, where I have zero memories of the man I love far too much.

TREASURE ISLAND BEACH is practically empty as families pack up their stuff after spending the day out in the sun. With it being fall, not many people visit the beach, but it is still hot enough during the day to enjoy the sun and sand. I find a spot far enough away from the water that the tide will not wash up and touch me.

As I take my seat, I inhale a deep breath, enjoying the fresh and salty air in my lungs. When I moved to Florida, I never considered liking the beach. It is a peaceful place and now that I'm settled in the sand and am taking in the ocean smell, I wish I had found more time to come out here. It is a nice place to get lost in your thoughts or a good book. Being at the beach during this time is a favorite pastime of mine considering the sun and I are not friends.

The sound of the waves helps to drown out the thoughts and images I haven't been able to escape all day. I grab the stack of letters burning a hole in my bag and place them in my lap. The familiar, perfect cursive written on the front brings back memories of my mother writing thank-you notes after any party we had. She would tell me a proper hostess always thanked their guests, no matter the occasion. As I stare at the ten letters sitting on my lap, I can't help but feel a sense of longing to have a mother who was the kind that would sit around and girl talk with me, take me shopping, and bake in the kitchen together. My mom did none of that. She was distant and cared more about her functions and parties than anything to do with my life. As long as our relationship looked good to her friends and potential donors, she was happy.

My parents were not the loving kind, not to me or to each other. Their relationship seemed too formal from the outside. In public, they had the appearance of a textbook couple with the perfect daughter, but at home they rarely spoke to each other or me. I guess that explains why I am much more comfortable by myself rather than in groups of people or at parties.

The letters on my lap start to feel heavier as they sit there, and I decide to take the leap and open the first one. It's dated August 26, 2020. It was the start of my freshman year at Braxton and more than two months after I left home. As I run my finger along the seal, my stomach tightens in anticipation of reading what my mother wrote to me long ago.

Dear Blaire,

I'm not sure how to begin this letter to you. You probably do not want to hear from me, and I do not blame you for that. In my life, I have made many mistakes and at the top of that list is how I handled the events of what happened two years ago.

My image in this town became more important to me than my own daughter, and for that I cannot apologize enough. It did not take me until losing you to realize the horrible mistakes I made. I should have been there for you. Your father and I both should have. I cannot speak for your father, as he has his own reasons for how he handled it, but I will speak for myself.

I am sorry, Blaire. I am sorry for how I abandoned you. I am sorry for not being the support system you needed. I should have stood by you in the worst of times.

Though I hope you can find it in yourself to forgive me, I understand if you do not. I am not even sure I deserve your forgiveness, but that does not mean I will not hope for it. I do not know if you will even open this letter or throw it away. If you toss it in the trash, I cannot say I blame you.

There is much more I wish I could say to you, but I will end this letter here. I am glad to see you moving on with your life and continuing your education. Braxton University is a wonderful school and I hope you make the best of memories while you are there.

I love you, Blaire. Though I was not the best mother, please know that.

Always,
Mom

My tears drop onto the letter in my hands, and I clutch it to my chest. These are the words I needed to hear as a scared sixteen-year-old. A young, terrified girl who felt abandoned by everyone. My mother's words about the mistakes she made ring in my ears, and I wonder how she would have done things differently after the rape. If she'd have stood up for me against Harvey's family and the town that chose a side.

I open the next letter and begin reading it, the tears continuing as my mother tells me again how sorry she is and how much she wishes she could change the past.

As I read her letters, my tears subside as my mother adds more to what she wrote to me. She updates me about her life, and I notice that she talks little about my father. Her functions have continued, but she does inform me that Harvey's mother has been voted out of the board. I can't help but smile. That woman was vile to me. In public, she called me a whore and said I was trying to ruin her son's life because I spread my legs too easily. Even though what she said was not true, I couldn't help but feel small as she spewed her venomous words at me.

The sun begins to set, and I have reached the final letter from my mom. Part of me feels sad because there are no more after this, but I am also curious as to what she wrote to me. After reading the first nine letters, I feel lighter and less sad about the current events in my life.

My dearest Blaire,

As you start your junior year of college, I cannot help but wonder how your experiences have been. If you have made new friends, or maybe even met a boy. I hope you are living your life to the fullest. It saddens me to not be able to hear about these experiences and I wish I had spent more time with you during the years you were here. I should have put more focus on you, my beautiful daughter. Taken you shopping or out to dinner. Talked about your life more. I cannot undo the mistakes I have made and will always live with that regret.

I do not feel good about adding this to a letter when I want to focus on how sorry I am and how life is, but I feel like you need to know. Before you read what I am about to tell you, I need you to know that I am more than sorry for what happened when you were sixteen and cannot hate myself more for how I was not there for you. I wish I could be there and hold you in my arms as you find this out.

My body shivers at her words and I'm scared to continue reading. I know I need to, but that does not stop the worry that comes over me as I continue down her letter.

It happened again, Blaire. I am so sorry, but he did it again. Harvey was accepted to Texas A&M. He has been living there for the last two years and rarely visits home. At the end of last semester, apparently there was a party at his frat house. Blaire, he assaulted a freshman girl. She was seventeen, just a year older than you were when it happened.

I hate that you are finding out this way, but

I need you to know. He is in prison, Blaire. The girl he attacked is a senator's daughter and her friend and boyfriend caught him in the act. Harvey's trial was over the summer, and he was sentenced to seven years in state prison. With the high-profile victim, the judge gave him a longer sentence.

While I am happy he is locked away, I cannot help but feel that if your father and I had stood by you and fought him, this never would have happened to this young girl. I hope she finds peace knowing she got justice. I hope you have found peace, Blaire. I do not know if this news will bring you comfort or if you wished I had not told you, but it would not feel right to me if I had kept this from you and continued my letters like usual.

His family has moved from Maskon. His father resigned as police chief when the news broke of what happened and no one knows where they went. Not much of a loss, though. I see now how wrong it was how we handled everything that happened and put our relationship with the Galloways over our daughter.

I love you, sweet girl. I am sorry I did not say that enough or show you how much while you were growing up. If given the chance, I would show you how much I care for you, my darling

daughter.
Love,
Mom

The sun has officially set, and I am not even trying to stop the tears right now. He's locked away. He cannot hurt another girl for a long time. My heart hurts for the teenager I do not know but have far too much in common with. If I'd had a support system that believed me and had taken Harvey to court, this girl never would have been raped. She would be starting college as a happy, enthusiastic freshman. Instead, I can only imagine she is blindly navigating through life like I have been for four years.

I'm sad that there are no more letters from my mother. There is so much more I want to know, so many questions I want to ask her. Do I forgive her? I'm not sure. I feel like I could, but there is still so much I want to know. I need to talk to her, not have a one-sided conversation through these letters.

I smile knowing that my hometown is free of the horrible family that is the Galloways. Harvey's father did not deserve to run the police department when his own son was a terrible offender. People who cover up crimes because they are in a powerful position and the criminal is a loved one are a special kind of evil.

As I look out at where I know the water is, but the darkness has swallowed it, I can't help but smile. My mother has opened her eyes to her treatment of me over the years and wants to fix a relationship I thought would always be broken. Harvey has gotten what he deserves, and I hope he is miserable in whatever cell he is stuck in for the next seven years.

Making my way back to my car, I pull my phone out to call my best friend. Going back to my apartment is the last thing I want to do and I need Emree's help with something. She should be home by now and I am hoping she is available.

After hanging up with Emree, who was more than happy to help with my plan, I drive toward my apartment, feeling a weight lifted off my shoulders. The heartbreak that is Camden Collins is still stuck in the back of my mind, but I have another relationship I need to focus on. One I need to fix, and I hope it helps a part of me that has been broken for so long.

Pounding on Chloe's bedroom door in the house she shares with her sorority sisters, I'm about ready to shoulder my way in if she does not answer in the next minute. When we got to the house, it took some flirting from Maddox to get inside and I was ready to shove each of the girls blocking our way to the ground if they kept blocking me. Chloe hasn't answered her door, but I know she is in there. Avoiding me and hiding.

"Chloe, if you don't open this fucking door, I will break it down!" I boom. My patience has left, and I'm done with her bullshit.

Just as I'm about to slam my fists against the door again, it swings open, and a half-naked Chloe is standing there with bedroom eyes and a smile in a sports bra and boy shorts. "Hey, baby. Long time no see," she purrs.

I shove my way into the room and push her out of the way. "Cut the shit. We need to talk."

Mateo, Levi, Conrad, and Maddox make their way in, and Chloe's eyes widen. "Listen, I get this is college and we should all try new things, but this is too much even for me."

Levi flatly laughs. "Funny, but there's no way any of us are going near your snatch anytime soon."

"That's not what Cam said last night." She smirks and my blood boils.

"Fuck you, Chloe, there's no way I would have touched you. Tell me what the fuck happened last night because I know I didn't drink enough to black out."

She pops her hip out and puts her hand there. "Blacked out? You were awake enough to screw my brains out before you fell asleep in satisfied bliss."

"Try again. I don't remember any of that, so you better tell me the truth before I get more pissed. And trust me, I can tell when a skank is lying."

She walks over and rubs her hand up my arm. I push her off and her smile falters slightly. "Why would I lie, baby? You told me you were tired of fighting me off and needed a wild night. I gave that to you. I'm sorry you don't remember, but that is not my fault."

"You fucking ruined my relationship, you bitch!" I shout.

"You mean that little virgin?" She laughs. "Don't even pretend like that wasn't some charity case. A man like you needs more. I can be that for you."

Pieces are starting to come together. She had to have done something. Planned this. She must have set out to destroy my relationship. I just don't know how she got me to black out the way she did unless... "Did—" The words get choked in my throat. "Did you fucking *drug me*?"

"Oh shit," one of the guys murmurs.

Chloe's eyes widen, but she quickly covers it. Too late. I saw the slip. "Why would you ever assume that? Of course not."

"Y-you *drugged me*. How? Why? Why did you drug me? Just so I would have sex with you? Are you that desperate?"

"I have no idea what you're talking about," Chloe says and turns to walk toward her bed and takes a seat. "Saying I *drugged*

THE ACT OF TRUSTING

you is a serious accusation, and I would ask that you lower your voice as I am sure my sisters are near and none of them need to hear your ludicrous accusations."

"You need to tell him the truth, Chloe," someone says from behind me. All six of us in the room turn our heads to the open door and a petite redhead is standing there. Her fingers are clasped in front of her, and she looks nervous.

"If you know what's good for you, you would shut up and leave, Piper," Chloe seethes.

The girl, Piper, takes a deep breath and straightens her shoulders. "No. He deserves to know. It's wrong what you did, and you can't ruin someone's life like that."

"Shut the hell up—"

I cut Chloe off. "Please tell me, Piper," I beg her. I need answers and not getting them is breaking me. Waiting for Chloe to grow a conscience could take years and I don't have that time. I need Blaire to know the truth the moment I do.

"She...she drugged you. With a roofie. I heard her talking with some of the other girls. She wanted to ruin your relationship."

Levi moves toward the girl's side, sensing Chloe's wrath coming down on Piper.

Never in my life have I ever been this angry. Grabbing the closest thing to me, I launch it in Chloe's direction. The lamp misses her and shatters against the wall. "What the hell is wrong with you!"

There is clear fear in Chloe's eyes, and I don't even care. Never have I wanted to make someone so scared of me before. Someone comes up and grips my shoulder. "Camden, man, come on. You got the answers you needed. You can't hurt her, though," Mateo says as he glares at Chloe.

"Why? Why shouldn't I fuck with her like she thinks she can with other people?" I stare at Chloe and swallow the lump in my throat, afraid to ask the last question I need an answer to. "D-did you fuck me?"

She looks between my friends and the girl I am forever grateful for standing in the doorway. She rolls her eyes. "No. Even with my best efforts, you couldn't get it up. So don't worry, you didn't cheat on your precious virgin."

Mateo's arms come around my shoulders as I lunge forward. "Not worth it, man. We'll get her back, I promise."

As I stare at the most hated person in my life, I take a few deep breaths. "I can promise you this, I am going to make your life a living hell. Just wait, Chloe. You're going to regret every choice you have ever made."

Turning, I head toward the door. My friends follow me as I pass them and together, we walk down the hallway that is filled with clone-looking sorority girls. I turn to Levi. "Grab Piper."

He gives me a questioning look. "Why?"

"One, she can't stay here. Not after being truthful and outing Chloe. And second, I need her help."

"With what?"

I look between my friends. My teammates. Four guys who have had my back for the last two years and who I would trust with my life and take a bullet for. "We're going to the police station."

THE LAST SEVEN hours have been hell. Not only did I get strange looks from every cop at the police station after saying I was roofied and assaulted, but I was poked and prodded at the hospital by multiple nurses and doctors as they collected pictures, blood samples, and swabs for their records. Even though I told them I was not raped, they said it was protocol to do every test.

The good news is that the blood test came back positive for Rohypnol. Even though Chloe confirmed what Piper said, it hit that I was actually roofied. You hear about this stuff on the news and on TV, but I never thought it would happen to me. Never have I even known someone who was drugged. Until Blaire, I never knew someone who was assaulted either.

Blaire. It has been hard knowing the truth all this time and not being able to tell her. Before we headed to the police station, I considered stopping by Blaire's apartment and telling her everything that happened and asking her to be there for me during this, but I needed to wrap my head around everything. I was also scared that if she was with me now it would bring back flashbacks of what happened to her, and I wouldn't want her to ever relive that.

The two officers who have been asking me questions and followed us to the hospital are standing in the room, once again asking me more questions.

"Looks like we have everything we need, and a deputy has been sent to pick up Miss Stevens from the address you provided us. She will be arrested and charged with a variety of crimes such as assault and infliction of bodily harm. These charges are a felony and, if found guilty, she will face a good amount of prison time," Officer McNally explains to me and Maddox, who has been in the room with me most of the time. The rest of the guys and Piper are out in the waiting room.

I don't know much about the law or how this all works, so I just nod. "Um, will I have to go to court or anything?"

"Yes. You won't need a lawyer or anything. Unless everyone decides to settle, you will be called to the stand and would need to make a statement to the jury. The prosecutor that handles the case will go over everything with you."

"Okay, that sounds fine." It feels weird talking about this stuff. Like I'm in an episode of *Law & Order* or something.

"If you don't have any more questions, you should be able to be discharged." He looks down at his notepad. "We'll go over the information you provided us with the prosecutor, and she should reach out to you soon about the case."

"Sounds good."

Officer McNally and his partner exit the room and I breathe out a sigh of relief. I'm ready for this day to be over with. I need to go to Blaire's apartment and beg her to let me explain.

"How're you holding up, man?" Maddox asks. He comes over and takes the seat next to the hospital bed I have been sitting on. They tried to get me to change into a hospital gown, but I refused. I had hit my limit for the day and the nurse understood.

I rub my eyes with my palms. "I don't even know, Mad. This doesn't even feel real. Like fuck, I was drugged and assaulted. I feel like an idiot not watching out for Chloe to try something like this." Taking a deep breath, I admit something I have been trying not to think about. "I'm embarrassed. Like shit, she assaulted me. She would have fucking raped me, dude. That shit doesn't happen to guys."

"Don't downplay this," Maddox says in a serious tone I have never heard before. "And don't be embarrassed. This can happen to anyone, and it's fucked up, but it is true. It happens too much and the fact that you reported it means a lot. That's strong, Camden. It takes a lot for someone to report this shit, especially a guy."

"I don't feel strong. Shit, I feel stupid for even reporting it. She didn't actually rape me, but the fact that she tried. That she touched me while I was drugged and passed out? I feel like I need to take twenty showers."

Maddox stands and hugs me. It's unusual because we

haven't had many, if any, moments of hugging. "You got us, man, and the moment you talk to Blaire, you'll have her too. We'll all be there with you. You have us there for support and you can bet your ass we will all be in that courtroom excited to see Chloe's ass being sent to jail."

I hug him back. Having friends like these guys is something I'm grateful for. I didn't have this in high school. My focus was my family and soccer and while I had my teammates on the field, our relationship off was nothing like the one I have with these four guys. "Thanks, man."

He pulls away, but not before slapping me on the back. "Now, let's get those discharge papers signed and head over to your girl. From the texts Conrad got from Em, Blaire has been gone all day. She needs to know what's really going on."

After signing the necessary paperwork, Maddox and I head out to the waiting room where our friends and Piper are waiting. Mateo called Jules and told her what was going on and she rushed down to be here also. As I come into the room, she jumps up from her seat beside Mateo and runs to me.

"Oh my gosh, I am so sorry, Camden. I can't believe that bitch did this. I hope she rots in jail." She squeezes me around the neck, and I feel wetness on my shoulder.

"Hey now, don't cry. It's okay," I soothe her and run my hands up and down her back.

She pulls back, wiping away her tears, but more are right behind them. "Sorry. I shouldn't be crying like this, but I just can't help it. This is so messed up."

Dropping my arm over her shoulders, I steer her toward our friends. "It's all good, guys. The police said they're picking Chloe up now and charging her. We'll probably have to go to court, and I'm sorry, Piper, you will most likely need to testify. I hope you're okay with that."

She nods. "Of course."

"Piper is going to stay with me for a while," Jules chimes in, smiling at Piper. "A few of the girls at her house didn't take the news so well and we went to get her clothes off the lawn and brought them to my apartment."

"Shit, I'm sorry, Piper. I didn't think of that."

She waves me off. "Don't worry. I wouldn't change my mind about telling you. What Chloe did was wrong and the girls in the house she told, the ones who were encouraging her and hiding it, were horrible. I don't want to be part of any sisterhood like that."

"All right." Maddox comes over and claps his hands. "We have a relationship to fix. Let's go get your girl."

It's late by the time we leave, and Jules and Piper decide to head back to the apartment. I'm grateful for Jules taking Piper in like that because I wouldn't have felt right with her going back to that toxic house. Knowing she is with someone as great as Jules makes me feel better. Piper seems sweet and I will forever be grateful to her and her honesty.

Maddox, Conrad, Mateo, Levi, and I pile back into Mateo's SUV and Conrad texts Emree to tell her we're on our way to explain everything to her and Blaire. Especially Blaire. Conrad doesn't get a response back right away, but as we get closer to their apartment, his phone goes off.

"Oh shit," he says after reading the message.

Instantly, I worry. "What? Is it Blaire?"

He looks across Maddox at me on the other side of the back seat. "Um, I have some bad news."

I hold my breath. "What?"

"She's gone."

"What do you mean 'she's gone'?"

He looks down at his phone. "Emree said Blaire asked her to pack a bag for her and took off somewhere. She didn't tell Em where she was going or when she would be back."

Dropping my head into my hands, I groan. "Fuck."

CHAPTER THIRTY-FIVE

BLAIRE

After I touched down in Austin, I then took an Uber for the two-hour drive to Maskon. After giving my parents' address to the driver, I sent a text to Emree and told her I landed and was turning my phone off. Camden had called me during the flight, and I saw a couple texts, but each went unread. I wasn't ready to hear from him. I had something else I needed to handle and then after this, maybe I would be ready to talk to him. At this moment, the betrayal felt too raw.

The drive feels like it goes by faster than it ever has before. The familiar views of where I grew up fly by me through the window. The neighborhood I grew up in brings back many memories of riding my bike down the road with friends, playing hide-and-seek at night, and sneaking out to meet boys during sleepovers. I smile at the fond memories and wonder whether life would have been different if I never said yes to Harvey and went on that date. Maybe I would have ended up at a different school, one that my friends and I talked about going to together. Although that was a dream of mine for so long, I'm happy it never happened. I learned those friends' true colors.

The Uber driver pulls into my parents' long driveway, and I smile at him and say thank you. He helps me with my small suitcase that Emree packed for me and then drives away. I stare up at the large, two-story house. The exterior is an off-white with royal blue shutters on each window. There are large pillars in the front and a three-car garage on the side of the house. This place never felt like home to me. It felt cold and distant and in the two years I have been gone, not once have I missed this empty house.

The only place that has felt like home to me was Camden's.

I shake my head of that thought. Now is not the time to think about Camden. I'm not ready for that yet. I need to handle this first. I need to talk to my mom. I need to get far too much off my chest, and I have questions that deserve answers.

Straightening my shoulders, I walk up the long driveway until I'm standing in front of the blue double doors that match the shutters. Grabbing the silver door knocker, I bang it twice and wait.

A woman in her mid-forties answers with a smile on her face. She is short and round around the waist, with long, jet-black hair and olive skin that makes her smile seem brighter. "Hello. How can I help you?"

It feels strange not to know this person who is answering the door to the house I grew up in. "Hi. Is Mrs. Wentworth home?"

She nods. "Yes, of course. Please come in and I will let Elaine know she has a guest."

The woman pulls the door open enough for me to come through and closes it behind me. She walks off down the hall toward the direction of my mother's office. I try to control my breaths as I wait for my mom to come out. I'm nervous to see her and not sure how we should greet each other.

The familiar sound of heels clicking on the tile gets louder as my mother approaches. She rounds the corner and the moment she sees me, she freezes. Her eyes widen and begin to fill with tears. Her hand drifts up to her open mouth and she covers it. "B-Blaire?" she stutters.

"Hi, Mom," I whisper.

She starts walking again, this time slightly faster than before, until she is right in front of her. She hesitates at first, then pulls me into her arms. The moment I'm there, the floodgates release and I'm bawling like a baby.

I'm crying for the girl who has needed her mom for the last four years. The girl who has felt alone for far too long. The girl who hasn't felt like she has had parents there her whole life.

I cry for myself because I didn't know how much I needed this.

Several minutes go by as we cry and clutch each other. I have cried more in the last twenty-four hours than I ever have before. My mom pulls back and holds my shoulders at arm's length. "Your hair. It's gotten so long," she says through tears. Her eyes take me in from top to bottom. "You have grown up far too much."

I laugh. "A lot has changed in two years. I feel like a completely different person."

A sad look crosses her face, and she quickly hides it. "I'm sure you do. Come in, come in. Don't worry about your things. Layla will get them." She smiles over at the woman who greeted me at the door. Unshed tears are in her eyes as she smiles at us.

My mother guides me toward the sitting room. While most families had rooms where they would hang out and play games or watch movies together, our family had a sitting room. No TV and no games. It was rarely used unless one of my parents was in there reading a book.

As we enter the room, I can't help but stop and take it all in.

Gone are the stuffy, uncomfortable chairs that were uninviting and replacing them are plush, leather sofas. Instead of the oil painting that was hung on the wall, there is now a large flat-screen TV. This room looks unrecognizable.

"What happened in here?" I ask my mother.

My mom smiles as she looks around. "A lot has changed, sweetie."

She brings us to the large two-seater sofa, and we sit. My hands are grasped in hers and I take a moment to look at my mom. She doesn't look like the woman I grew up with. Her usual perfectly curled hair is straightened and half up in a clip. While my mom typically wore either pantsuits or knee-length dresses, she is now wearing a pair of high-waisted white pants and a loose emerald green sleeveless blouse. Her countenance, which I had never seen without a full face of makeup, is mostly bare except for mascara and nude lipstick.

She looks younger and brighter. Like there is less stress overtaking her life. It seems a lot may have changed for both of us.

My mom reaches up and cups my cheek. "It's good to see you, sweet girl."

"I finally read your letters," I blurt out.

She smiles. "I'm glad. I can't tell you how sorry I am that it took me far too long to open my eyes and realize my mistakes." Her smile drops and she looks down at her hands now in her lap. "I was never the mother you needed, sweetie, and I will be forever sorry for that. You deserved much better."

"Why? Why, Mom? I still don't understand it. How could you not care enough to stand beside me after what happened?"

The instant regret is evident on her face and my mom's eyes well up with tears again. "For far too long, I failed at being your mother and it took me until losing you to realize how wrong I was. Never should I have put you behind my charities and functions. I was too wrapped up in our family's image and connections that I did not see right in front of me how much I missed." She strokes the side of my face as she wipes away my tears. "I'm so sorry, sweet girl. I can't explain to you how sorry I am. While I can't go back and change how absent and terrible of a mother I was, if given the chance, I would love to get to know this new Blaire."

Never did I think this would happen. That my mother, a woman who felt more like a stranger to me growing up, would want to get to know me. Have a relationship with me. The little girl who grew up feeling more like a burden is crying on the inside, wanting her mom to hold her and tell her everything is okay, while the woman on the outside has tears streaming down her face at the change of the person in front of me. She yearns for a mom. Someone to go to for advice, someone to gush about boys with, someone to call when she doesn't know what went wrong with the cookie recipe she attempted.

Nodding, I push away the last of the tears. "I would really like that," I tell her honestly. She pulls me into a crushing hug, and I sink into her warmth.

After we both compose ourselves, I pull back. There is something, or someone, she seems to have left out of many of the letters and our entire conversation since I arrived. "Mom... where's Dad?"

She takes a deep breath, and a strange look comes across her face. Worry, maybe? "In all my letters, I wanted to tell you, but I couldn't. This was not something I ever wanted you to find out that way." Instantly, I'm nervous. "Honey." She speaks in a soothing voice, much like someone does to a small child. "Your father, he passed away. The summer after your graduation."

Of all the things I thought she would tell me, that was not one of them. Maybe divorce or he left her for a younger woman, but not...death.

My father is dead. My *father* is dead. *Dead.* As in not alive.

Shouldn't a part of me have felt this after it happened? Like some daughter intuition that the man who shares half of my DNA was no longer breathing. No longer walking on this earth. Guilt washes over me that for over two years I went about my life not knowing he stopped breathing.

"What…what happened?"

Her eyes soften. "After you moved away, your father became sick. He had this nasty cough that never seemed to go away and continued to get worse and after a month, he finally decided to visit the doctor. He was diagnosed with stage four lung cancer." While I can sense sadness from my mother, no tears are shed as she talks about my father. "He met with several specialists, and they all had the same response: the cancer was too aggressive. He began to fall sicker until he was eventually put on palliative care. He passed away in early August. He was in no pain, thanks to the nurses and doctors."

"That's good," I whisper. Though I am sure there are many words a daughter should say to their mother when they find out their father has died, none of them come to me. Words of comfort or even fond memories I have of him would be the norm. Though, I have no fond memories of my dad. He was not the kind of man who taught his daughter how to ride a bike or threatened her prom date. Arnold Wentworth was a distant man.

My mom smiles at me as if she knows what is going through my mind. "You do not have to say anything. I understand. There was really no relationship between you and your father, and that is just another thing to add to the list of how wrong we were."

Looking around the room, I take in the changes made here. Not only with the house, but with the woman sitting beside me. "What happened, Mom?"

As if she knows what I mean, she waves around to the room that, in two years, changed from being an uptight space to one that is welcoming. "After losing you and then your father, I took a harsh look at my life and myself. My eyes were open to the mistakes I made over the years and the regrets I had. One of them was staying in a loveless marriage." She turns back to me. "Do not get me wrong, I loved your father very much, but over the years, we grew distant. He became more engrossed with his work and my need for a higher status in town overcame me.

"I was alone, Blaire. For the first time in my life, I was alone. Never have I felt sadder. You were gone and then your father. Although we were not close by any means, I felt hollow inside that my family was shattered. I knew I needed to try and fix the relationship I ruined between us. That was when I wrote you the first letter."

She had just lost her entire family and losing us made her realize how much she and my father messed up over the years. Do I wish that the realization came a little sooner? Well, sure. I can't fault her for eventually opening her eyes and wanting to get to know her only daughter.

"I'm sorry you lost him, Mom."

She cups the side of my face and brings me closer to rest my head on her shoulder. It's strange and very motherly, which I have never been used to, but it's nice. "I am too, sweetie. What I'm more sorry for is that it took losing him and you to open my eyes. What I wouldn't give to come to that realization sooner and maybe your relationship with him could have become more."

"We can't dwell on the what-ifs," I tell her. "My therapist at school told me that if I keep living in the past and wondering *what if*, I will never be able to move forward with my life. That is what we need to focus on."

"You have a therapist?" Her tone is curious, and I feel as

though any information I give about my new life is going to be interesting to her.

I nod. "Well, I did. I haven't seen her since the end of last semester, and even last year I only went to her once a month. Talking with her helped me a lot during my first year of college." Chewing on my bottom lip, I pull back from where she held my head on her shoulder. This is something I need to tell my mom face to face. "When I got to Braxton, I was scared to get close to anyone. I didn't have any friends, didn't attend parties, or do any of the typical college stuff most students did. I was still dealing with everything that happened with Harvey, my friends, and you and Dad. I never worked through my issues in the two years since it had happened and when there was an email sent out to all the freshmen about a therapist that is always on call if we need her, I took them up on the offer. She said it wasn't too late to talk with someone and helped me work through my issues and gave me the tools I needed."

Guilt washes over my mom's face. "We should have been there. We should have been better parents and I hate that you were fighting a constant battle for so long with no one there, especially me."

I grab her hand and give it a squeeze. "Remember, no what-ifs. I learned not to dwell on the past, and my life in Braxton has been amazing, especially these last few months. I have a great best friend, who was the first person in my new life I talked to about what happened to me, and this year I have met even more people. I let them in, which is something I struggled with for far too long."

"How about any boys? Do you have a boyfriend?"

I wince at her statement, and she notices. "Um, yeah. I mean, no." Really, I'm not sure how to even explain this because telling her and saying the words out loud makes them too real. "Something happened before I came here. It's what pushed me to read your letters. I still haven't processed it, and honestly, I'm not sure how to."

She pats my hands. "That's okay, sweetie. Love is never easy."

Strangely, her words are comforting. They're motherly and with everything that is going on with Camden and me, I think a mother's care is what I need.

CHAPTER THIRTY-SIX

CAMDEN

Three days. Seventy-two hours. That is how long Blaire has been…wherever she is. Each morning, I have called Emree and asked if she has heard from Blaire and the answer has never changed. No, she hasn't. Her answer also does not change when I text her in the afternoon and call her again at night to ask the same question.

I have gone to practice and attended classes, but other than that, I sit around with my mind going crazy, wondering where she is and how I can get ahold of her.

News broke out around campus that Chloe was arrested, and the gossip queens of her sorority spread it around that I was involved. The rumors range from she broke into my house to she hired someone to kidnap me. Some of them are crazy, like the kidnapping, and make me think far too many students are watching soap operas. A few times, I have heard people talking about what actually happened and I'm not sure if I'm glad about that. While I hope no one believes the ludicrous rumors, people knowing the truth makes me just as nervous. Maddox and the guys continue to reassure me that this is nothing to be embarrassed about, but I can't help it. Being drugged and almost raped as a guy sounds unbelievable.

Monday, the dean of Braxton U called me into his office to talk about what happened and inform me that Chloe has been expelled from the school indefinitely and is not to step foot on campus or any property owned by BU, which includes her sorority house. Tuesday, the arresting officers and prosecutor called me to inform me of the charges and that Chloe was released on bail, which her father paid for. She has been given a restraining order to remain at least five hundred feet away from me and was instructed by the officers not to leave the state while she waits for her first hearing. According to some of her sisters, her father has taken her back home to Miami after collecting her belongings.

While I feel like a weight has been lifted off my shoulders with most of the legal stuff handled, at least until a trial, I can't feel relaxed until I see Blaire. Until I'm able to convince her to listen to me long enough to hear the truth. I can't imagine what has been going through her head these last three days and it kills me that she still thinks I would ever cheat on her. That I would ever break her trust like that.

By Wednesday afternoon, I am ready to explode. I have been in the living room trying to distract myself with useless television, but I can't help but check my phone every ten minutes to see if Blaire or Emree have called or texted. Since Sunday, after she packed up and left, I have texted Blaire a total of forty times. Not once did I tell her through text or the several voicemails about what really happened Saturday night. I need to look her in the eyes when she finds out. She has to see me when I tell her to know that I would never do anything to hurt her.

The front door opens, and Conrad and Maddox come in. They drop their backpacks by the door and join me in the living room. Conrad eyes me and then my phone that is sitting on the cushion beside me. "Nothing still?"

I shake my head. "Nope, and I'm about ready to lose it. I can't handle not knowing where she is or what she's thinking."

"She still hasn't called Em either." He takes the seat on the other end of the couch. "She's getting more worried. Last night, she kept fidgeting in bed until she finally got up and went to her living room and started randomly cleaning it."

"Ugh." I run my hands through my hair, frustrated that no one has heard from my girl. "I can't fucking stand this."

Maddox starts to say something, but the ringing of my phone cuts him off. I grab it without even looking at the caller ID. "Hello? Blaire, baby, is it you?"

"Um, no," a familiar voice says. "Do you not check who calls before picking up? That's weird."

"Emree, unless you called to tell me you heard from Blaire, I'm hanging up on you."

"Funny you should mention that..."

I sit up straight and move to the edge of the cushion. "Don't mess with me right now or your boyfriend is going to struggle to have kids in the future."

"Touch that beautiful package and die, Collins. I mean it," she threatens. "And back to my best friend. Yes, she did call. She apologized many times for not turning her phone back on and worrying me, but she said she had something she needed to take care of and that it was too much to think about everything that happened with you and that bitch."

"Take care of? What does that mean? And where is she?"

Two sets of eyes are focused on me, and Conrad tries to lean closer to hear what Emree is saying. I decide to put it on speaker for them. "We didn't go into the details. She said she would talk to me when she gets home and that it was an emotional three days, but she feels better after her time away." She pauses. "And currently she is on a plane heading here."

335

I'm out of my seat. "Shit, Em, start with that. You had me worried she was never coming back or something. When did her flight leave? When does she get in?"

"It left about an hour ago and should arrive by six this evening."

One and a half hours. I can be patient enough to wait that long. "Okay, do you know what she's flying? I'll pick her up from the airport." I'm already heading toward the front door, where we keep our keys hanging against the wall.

"Not so fast, buddy. I don't think that's the best idea."

I freeze, waiting for her to continue.

"She is hurt, Camden. Seeing you the moment she gets off the plane from wherever she came from after an emotional three days is not going to help your case. Her car is already at the airport. Let her come home and get situated. I'll text you when she is here and when I think it is a good time to show up."

I don't know what to say. Part of me wants to argue with her that Blaire needs me, but another part knows she's right.

"I think you've left our boy at a loss for words, Blondie. We'll make sure he stays put and wait for your text. Give our girl a hug from all of us," Maddox says after he grabs the phone from my hand.

Emree says goodbye to us all before hanging up.

Heading back to the living room, I toss my keys on the coffee table and sit back in the same spot I have been occupying for the last hour. "I'm sick of this shit. I just need to talk to her."

"We know, man," Conrad says. "But you gotta look at this from her view. Imagine if you walked in on a guy getting out of bed with Blaire half naked. A guy you know has been trying to sleep with her for a while now, and is known as the college slut. You wouldn't listen to logic so quickly either and it would take you a while to even calm down enough to hear what she would have to say. Let her get home and talk to Em first. I already made sure that Emree knows not to say anything about what's been going on the last three days. It needs to come from you."

"Fine," I grumble. "I'll fucking wait. Again."

By EIGHT, I'm ready to bust through our door and the four roommates of mine who have decided to act as babysitters to make sure I don't go over before Emree gives the okay. She texted me when Blaire got to their apartment, but that was at six-thirty, and I haven't heard from her since.

Maddox put on the stupid show from Netflix and while it usually holds my attention, I can't stop staring at the clock. The minutes have seemed to go by slower as I sit here and wait. My patience is growing thin.

"You're going to get an ulcer or something, man. You need to calm down," Levi says from the single seat beside the couch Maddox and I are on.

"Easier said than done," I mumble, still not looking away from the clock.

A ringing comes from the other side of the room. Conrad pulls his phone out of his pocket and looks at the ID, then up at me, giving me a small nod. "Hey, babe," he answers. Emree says something on the other end of the line and I'm silently cursing him for not putting it on speaker. "Okay, I'll tell him. Bye."

I'm off my feet with my keys in hand the moment he hangs up. "Don't care what she said, I'm going over."

He laughs. "You'll be happy because that's exactly what she said. She and Blaire had a long talk about the last three days. She intentionally avoided the topic of you and Blaire didn't bring it up. Em said she seems to be in a good place."

"I'm out," I tell them.

All four of my roommates are out of their seats. "Oh, hell no, we're coming with," Maddox tells me. Not wanting to waste another minute, I don't fight with him and the five of us pile into my Jeep.

The drive to Blaire's apartment seems to take forever, and part of that is because I hit almost every red light on the way. The usually fifteen-minute drive takes over twenty and before I have the car in park, I'm already opening my door. The guys follow me as we walk through the parking lot to the girls' building and as I approach the front door, it swings open, and Emree comes out wearing a pair of plaid button-up pajamas with clouds on them.

She looks behind her into the apartment before saying anything. "She's in her room unpacking. We talked for a while and she seems okay, but I know she's avoiding the topic of what happened Saturday night."

I nod. "Thanks, Em. I'm going to go talk to her. She needs to know what happened."

Emree opens the door wider to let me and the guys in. As I head toward Blaire's room, everyone else stops and turns to the living room and takes up both the couches.

Her door is closed, and I lightly tap it before turning the knob and cautiously open the door. Blaire is sitting on her bed in a pair of sleep shorts and a black hoodie, looking down at a textbook in her lap. Her brown hair is tied up in a damp, messy bun on the top of her head and her face is freshly washed, looking brighter than ever.

She smiles as she looks up toward the door, but when she notices me, it is gone almost immediately. "What...what are you doing here?" She closes the book and sets it on the nightstand, replacing it with a pillow that she clutches to herself.

As I enter the room and shut the door, I don't take my eyes off the most beautiful woman I have ever seen. Five days of not seeing her, not talking to her, or even texting has been brutal, and I want nothing more than to go to my girl and scoop her into my arms and hold her tight, not letting go of her all night.

As I walk farther into her room, I gauge her reaction. She follows my movements as I grab the desk chair and bring it to the foot of the bed and take a seat. I lean forward and rest my forearms on my thighs. "You look beautiful, baby."

Her nostrils flare. "Please don't do that. You can't come in here and try to charm me, not after what you did." Looking down into her lap, she whispers, "You hurt me, Camden, more than I can even explain to you."

I clench my fists to keep myself from reaching forward and grabbing her, wanting nothing more than to comfort the woman I love right now. "A lot has happened since you left, and I need to tell you all of it. But you have to believe me, nothing, and I mean absolutely nothing, happened between Chloe and me. I would never do that to you, baby. I love you too much."

A tear falls from her eye as she continues to stare at her lap. "I know what I saw, Camden. She was half naked, getting dressed, and your pants were undone. It was pretty obvious what had just happened."

"Baby, please look at me," I beg her.

After taking a deep breath, she looks up and she reminds me of the scared, hesitant girl I first met two months ago and everything inside of me breaks. I hate that she feels that way again. The last two months, I have seen a different Blaire come out. One who laughs with our group of friends. Someone who has become affectionate and loves being touched, whether it is something small like needing to have her hand in mine if we're near or clutching me as I make her see stars in the bedroom. She has opened up more than I think she knows since we met and in a matter of a few days, it seems like that is gone.

While holding her eye contact, I muster up the strength to tell her what happened. "Baby...Chloe, she...she drugged me."

Blaire's mouth drops open and her eyes widen.

"She admitted everything on Sunday. She was getting tired of me rejecting her and came up with this disgusting idea."

"Camden...no. Please tell me she didn't."

I shake my head. "She tried. Apparently, with the roofie she gave me, I couldn't, you know...get it up." Shit, this is harder to tell her than I thought. Her eyes are filling with more tears, and she clutches the pillow tighter as she hangs on to every word. "She overheard me talking about waiting for you to get to the house when you and Em got off work, so she decided to stage it to look like we had hooked up to break us up."

Blaire shakes her head as more tears fall. She tries to wipe them away, but they're coming down faster than she can.

I continue to tell her about the events of what went down on Sunday. From when we went to Chloe's sorority house, to Piper coming to our rescue and telling us everything she heard in the house about how Chloe was going to roofie and have sex with me. Blaire gasps as I tell her that I went to the police and how many of the officers looked at me like I was playing a joke on them because a man reporting an assault is rare, but when Piper, once again, came forward with what she heard, they believed me more. As I tell her about getting blood drawn and having photos taken at the hospital, she squeezes her eyes shut as if trying not to imagine what happened.

When I tell Blaire about the police arresting Chloe and the arresting officer and prosecutor calling to tell me she has been charged and that the dean of our school called me into his office to inform me that Chloe has been expelled, there is hope in my girl's eyes. She has no more tears, but her eyes are wide as she takes in all the information I have dumped on her.

After I finish telling her about Chloe making bail and how her dad picked her up and took her back home to Miami to wait for her hearing, we sit in silence. Blaire has not said a word and she isn't looking at me. She isn't crying anymore either, and I take that as a good sign.

Finally, Blaire turns those gray eyes to me. "Camden, I—" She cuts off and clears her throat. "I don't know what to say, I just..." Before I can blink, she is off the bed and lunges herself at me. I catch her and wrap my arms around her waist, and she straddles me and squeezes my neck, burying her face in the nook.

She sobs and the sound breaks the dam I didn't know was ready to burst and I'm crying alongside her. I cry for the sixteen-year-old scared girl who had no one there for her, unlike the people I have now. I cry for myself, because until now I didn't realize how much this affected me and how much worse it could have been. I cry for the woman I love, the one who has been hurting thinking the man who promised to love and never hurt her, the one she put all her trust in, could do something so horrible and destroy what we have built in the short time we have been together.

We cling to each other, not saying a word, but I feel her love through her body as she runs her hands through my hair, clutching it. She adjusts her body as if she can't get any closer. As if she needs to be one with me after the short time apart.

After some time, she pulls away and rests her forehead against mine, her hands still tangled in the hair at the base of my head. "I'm so sorry, Camden. I never should have left. It hurts that I wasn't there for you through this." Her tears fall to my face, and I bring my hands from her waist to her cheeks, wiping them away. "I should have stopped and listened to you. You would have never done what she made it look like, and I know that in my heart, but my head and emotions took over and the image of you and her wouldn't leave my head."

"Listen to me, Gray Eyes." She lifts her head and stares into my eyes. Hers are slightly swollen and red, and I can imagine mine mirror them. "I love you. I love you so much, baby. Never would I touch, or even think about touching, someone else. It made me sick when I woke up on Sunday and the boys told me what happened. I knew it couldn't be true, but Mateo explained to me how horrible it looked. It wasn't until we heard the truth from Piper that I was able to breathe a sigh of relief."

She runs her nails across my scalp. "You should have never gone through this. Chloe is pure evil, and I hope she gets what she deserves. What vile human drugs another like this?" Her eyes drift off and I know she is thinking about the scum who raped her when she was sixteen. I caress her face, trying to soothe her.

"It's all over. She is gone and was charged. Now we wait for her trial, where they said I will most likely have to testify. I'm more than happy to if it means putting her ass behind bars."

Blaire nods. "I love you," she whispers. "You're so strong for reporting her. She deserves what is coming to her."

"I know, baby. I know."

We sit there and stare into each other's eyes. I caress her face as she studies mine. Not being able to take the distance anymore, I pull her forward and crush my lips to hers. She moans the moment my tongue runs along the seam of her lips before parting them, and I take in the familiar feel and taste I have grown to love. Blaire runs her hands down my neck, to my shoulders, and down my back. She repeats the trail, up and down. I grip her waist as my mouth explores her and slip my fingers up the bottom of her hoodie, resting my hands on her warm stomach.

Blaire begins to grind her hips against me, as if she is trying to get closer, although we are already chest to chest. I can feel her rapid heartbeat and it matches my own. She pulls away, gasping for breath as my mouth trails down her neck. It meets the top of her hoodie and I rip it off, needing my lips on her skin.

Pulling back, I take in her pale, smooth skin. She sits there on my lap, her top half bare and her bottom covered by a small pair of sleep shorts. I'm harder than I have ever been before and she doesn't make it easier as she bites her lip, looking at me. Moving forward, I repeat my earlier movements and plant kiss after kiss along her neck, her shoulders, and finally her breasts. She moans as I take one into my mouth and massage the other with my left hand.

There is a knock at her bedroom door, and I pull away, groaning because all I want is my girl naked. "What?" I shout.

"I understand you two are horny twenty-year-olds and need to get your groove on, but these are thin walls and if I have to hear Blaire let out a loud moan one more time, I cannot be blamed for using that image for my spank bank later," Maddox says from the other side of the door.

I clutch Blaire's hips as she giggles. "You think about my girl while jerking off and I'll strangle you."

"Don't have such a sexy girlfriend who is loud in the sack!" he yells back, and I can hear him and everyone else laughing.

Blaire laughs into my neck. "You really brought Maddox?"

I run my hands up and down her naked back, noting how smooth she is. "He insisted. Actually, all the guys did. I'm sure they're in the living room enjoying that little exchange Maddox started." We both laugh because it's impossible to be mad at Maddox, even when he uses the word 'spank bank' and 'Blaire' in the same sentence.

After we've settled down, I look at my girl. "You know, I've been going crazy the last three days. Where'd you go off to, Gray Eyes?"

Her face changes and her eyebrows are drawn together. "I should probably put a shirt on when we talk about this. A lot happened the last three days with me."

As she climbs off my lap, I feel empty with the loss of her and the moment she has her hoodie back on, I pull her to my lap, sideways this time so as to not get distracted and end up naked again.

She takes a deep breath and starts from the moment she left my house Saturday night to when she flew back this evening.

CHAPTER THIRTY-SEVEN

BLAIRE

I t is well past midnight as I lie on Camden's naked chest, listening to his steady breaths. The tips of my fingers glide up and down his perfect chest and down to the small patch of hair above where the sheet is resting at his waist. I have always loved his chest. It's tanned and solid, yet soft enough to use as a pillow. More than once I have told him I'm worried I am crushing him, but he reassures me that he sleeps better with me tucked into his side and close to him.

After going through everything I have been up to the last three days, Camden sat silently on my bed. He then began pacing the room and I worried something made him mad. Maybe that I went to see my mom, someone he had told me was a toxic person and did not deserve someone like me as their daughter.

After a few deep breaths, he confessed that he was happy I ended up opening the letters. I told him what they said, starting from the first and so on. I left out the last letter about Harvey raping another girl and being sentenced to seven years in prison. I wasn't ready to tell him yet and needed to gauge how he would handle that information. After I told him about seeing my mom for the first time, her telling me about my dad's passing, and our conversations and time together for three days, he seemed in a better place for me to drop the Harvey bomb.

Camden cursed, threw a pillow across the room, and slammed my closet door when I told him that Harvey raped a seventeen-year-old girl. Levi and Conrad came running into the room when they heard the commotion, worried about what was going on. I assured them that everything was okay, but they eyed an angry Camden before closing the door. He paced some more and when he was ready to listen, I explained to him that the girl was a senator's daughter who was just starting at A&M and because of her high-profile status, Harvey had several charges against him and was sentenced to seven years in state prison. Camden was happy to hear that, but angry, like myself, that it happened to another girl.

When I talked about my mom and our time together, I could tell that Camden was apprehensive about this newfound relationship. After listening to more of our talks and her confessions, he was happy my mom seemed to, as Camden put it, 'pull her head out of her ass.'

It was past ten when we caught each other up about what happened the last three days and it is hard to believe so much happened in such a short amount of time. While he held me on my bed, I realized how much I missed him in the short amount of time we were apart. Since we got together, we haven't gone a day without at least texting and not talking to him hurt.

We decided it would be rude to stay in the room all night without seeing our friends. Well, I thought it was rude. Camden tried his hardest to keep me wrapped in his arms on my bed, but I wanted to see the guys. I needed to thank them for being by Camden's side after what happened with Chloe. Knowing that he had a support system as great as them makes me feel less guilty for not being by his side.

We all hung around our living room, Camden not taking his hands off me. Maddox had ordered some pizza while Camden and I were in my room, and the moment it arrived, my stomach announced itself with a loud grumble that could be heard by everyone. We all laughed and dived into the greasy goodness. The boys didn't stay long since everyone had class the next morning, but Camden refused to leave. Conrad drove his Jeep home with the rest of the guys around eleven-thirty.

Camden and I had gone straight to bed after saying good night to Emree. Too tired to do anything else, Camden stripped both of us out of our clothes and we have been under the sheets ever since. He fell asleep rather quickly, but even though I am exhausted, sleep hasn't come. There is too much on my mind and it hasn't shut down.

"You know, if you keep doing that, I'm not going to be responsible for my actions," Camden whispers. His eyes are still closed, but his breathing has changed.

I smile against his chest. "Doing what?" I ask innocently.

He chuckles and the movement shakes me. "We have class in the morning, Gray Eyes."

I smile and my hand drifts below the sheets, gripping Camden. He hisses and I smile, knowing the effect I have on him. He's hard and I tighten my grip, gliding my palm up and down. His breathing grows faster, and I know he is close to breaking and giving me what I want.

"Blaire," he warns.

Turning my head, I look up at him through my lashes. "It's been more than three days since I've seen you and almost a week since you were inside me. Please, Camden. I need you."

Those last three words are his undoing and in a second he is on top of me in all his naked glory. Camden's lips crash down to mine as he pushes my legs apart, settling himself between them. I hook one up his hip, loving the feeling of his strong, safe body on top of mine.

His kisses along my body make me feel cherished and I stretch my neck, giving him more room to explore. Not an inch of my skin goes untouched by him. Whether it's his mouth or his hands, he's everywhere. My body feels like it is on fire with the anticipation of what is coming.

Reaching to the right, Camden opens the bedside drawer and blindly feels around for a condom, never lifting his lips from mine. Once he finds it, he tosses it on the pillow beside my head and runs his hand up and down my body. His fingers ghost over my belly button and my legs clench around his waist. His small touches are turning me on more than anything. As he looks into my eyes, he brings his head down and pulls my nipple into his mouth, biting just hard enough for it not to be painful. I cry out and arch my back.

"Please," I beg.

He kisses the spot he bit and moves on to my other breast, giving it the same amount of attention. "Please what, baby?"

I scratch at his back as he nips and sucks at my skin. "Please...fuck me."

In a flash, his face is hovering over me. "Make no mistake, baby, there will be days I fuck you and I am looking forward to those, but after the shit we have been through, I'm making love to this beautiful woman I love more than anything."

Camden doesn't give me a chance to respond before his mouth is on mine again. He kisses me so senseless that I don't hear the tearing of the condom wrapper and in no time, Camden has rolled it on and is positioned at my opening.

I feel the tip ever so close, but he doesn't move. I shift my hips, encouraging him to enter me, but he just stares into my eyes. "What?" I ask him.

He smiles and leans down, placing a soft kiss on my lips. Pulling back, he's smiling. "I love you."

Caressing his face, my smile matches his. "I love you, Camden Collins."

In the next second, he plunges himself into my body and I gasp for breath, clutching to his back. "Fuck, I missed you." Camden's hot breath is on my neck as he struggles for air. Ever so slowly, he begins to rock in and out of me, and I meet him thrust for thrust.

Our bodies are in tune with each other. They have been since the first time. Before he makes a move, it's as if mine knows what was going to happen next. His thrusts quicken, and I feel that ever-loving familiar buildup. As my body shatters around his, my nails dig into his back as I ride the waves.

Coming down from the high, I gasp as Camden pulls out of me and flips me onto my stomach, then pulls my hips up. In a second, he is back in and thrusting faster than ever. I struggle to keep up and before I can catch my breath from the last orgasm, another is coming around the corner and crashing into me. My face is smashed into the pillow as I come and Camden thrusts into me hard one last time before molding his front to my back as he comes with me.

Not being able to hold myself up anymore, I collapse onto the bed, Camden right there behind me. His large body is covering mine and, while it is a slight struggle to breathe, I love the feeling of him on top of me. Especially after we share a moment like this.

"I love you, Gray Eyes," Camden whispers in my ear before removing himself from my body and rolling to his side of the bed.

Still out of breath, I look over at him. He is lying on his back with one arm thrown over his head as he catches his breath. He removed the condom and threw it into the trash can and now is stretched out on my bed in all his naked glory. Sometimes it is hard to believe this sweet, beautiful man is mine. Mine to love. Mine to cherish. Mine to make love to. Just...mine.

"I love you more than anything in this world, Camden Collins."

He looks over and smiles at me before wrapping his arms around my waist and pulling me to his chest. He nuzzles his face in the side of my head, taking a deep breath. It's almost as if he is having the same thoughts. That I am his. Completely.

Never would I have thought this would be my life. Having the best friend a girl could ask for, a group of guys who make me laugh and feel safer than ever, and a man who loves me and has waited for me, despite my ongoing struggles with letting people in. Two months ago, I was only just beginning to open myself up to new possibilities of making friends and venturing out to try all the things I had been avoiding for too long.

Who knew that at my first party I would meet a man who changed everything for me. A man who has shown me I can trust people again and who has taught me how to love not only him, but myself. This beautiful man who terrified me as he stood in his backyard with his penis in his hand has changed my life for the better and I will spend the rest of my life telling and showing him how much he means to me.

EPILOGUE

CAMDEN

Christmas in Florida shouldn't be a thing. They should cancel Christmas because who wants to spend the winter holiday in seventy-degree weather with sixty percent humidity? I have lived here my entire life and used to dream of that Hallmark winter wonderland Christmas. The best we have is fake snow that is hard as a rock and impossible to make snow angels in.

Despite the pathetic attempt at making it feel like Christmas while people are wearing shorts and tank tops, Blaire insisted we drive the hour out to a park in the middle of nowhere that has set up a winter wonderland with ice skating, sledding, and an open field under a dome where people can play in the snow. Although they frown upon adults engaging in snowball fights and have come to tell us we have been too aggressive and need to settle down. If a few kids are in the crossfire, I can't be blamed for what happens to them. They can learn a lesson at a young age to avoid grown men throwing balls at each other.

After not having snowball fights, attempting to make snow angels in the rock-like snow, and building a snowman that pays no resemblance to Frosty, the eight of us are sitting at a picnic table, drinking apple cider and hot chocolate...in seventy-degree weather. Though the park provides snow jackets when you are in the actual snow, they encourage guests to wear warmer clothes. This only makes me sweat as we sit outside.

"This place is awesome. I've never seen snow before," Blaire says with excitement in her voice.

Maddox laughs. "Baby, this is not snow. I'll have to take you to Boston for winter next year. You would be in for a rude awakening freezing your ass off there."

Her smile widens at the thought, and she turns to me. "Oh, can we do that, Camden? Please? A white Christmas next year, maybe?"

I laugh at her high-pitched, excited voice. "Yeah, Gray Eyes. We can have a winter wonderland Christmas next year."

She claps her hands together and I lean forward, kissing the side of her head.

"Should we finish our drinks and head to the slopes?" Jules asks.

Everyone nods in agreement and finishes off what's in their cups. The park has set up three levels of slopes. There's the bunny, the intermediate, and the challenger. Each can hold up to ten people in the giant tubes, but the challenger is definitely intimidating. Even I am somewhat nervous since there haven't been a lot of people on it.

As we stand, Mateo points his finger at each of us. "All right, do we have any pussies who aren't going to go big on the challenger or are we all tough enough to handle it?"

Most of us cheer with excitement, but Blaire and Emree have concerned looks on their faces. "Isn't that for, like... people who have done it before?" Em asks.

Jules shrugs her shoulders. "I mean, it doesn't say you have to be experienced. I think it's more for adventure seekers."

My girl and her best friend give each other a look that is

more of a silent conversation. "You know what, how about we hang at the bottom and take pictures of you adventure seekers," Blaire tells us.

Walking over, I wrap my arms around her waist. "Oh no, you don't, Gray Eyes. It's you and me. We're in this together. I'm not getting on that slope without you."

She pats my arm. "Looks like you'll be down here playing photographer with us then."

I laugh and kiss her neck. "Come on, baby. Coming here was your idea. You gotta try it at least once."

She chews on her bottom lip for a while and looks at Emree, who has a pleading look in her eyes. "Well..."

"Are you seriously that gullible?" Emree asks. "He is playing you, Blaire. You can't fall for his charm and pretty face."

I can't help but laugh because Em can see right through any guy's charm.

"But look at this face," Blaire says as she squishes my cheeks in one of her hands. "How can I say no to that?"

"Exactly like this." Emree comes to stand in front of my face that is resting on Blaire's shoulder. "No."

We all bust out laughing. Conrad grabs Emree's hand and pulls her to his side, but not before kissing her.

Leaning in some more, my lips hit Blaire's ears and she shivers as my breath moves across her skin. "If you go with us, I'll do that thing with my tongue you like so much. Remember how I had you practically making a bald spot on my head? I'll do that all night, baby."

Her breathing quickens and she closes her eyes, remembering our wild night last weekend when Blaire held my head between her legs for what felt like hours. Not that I would ever complain about making my girl feel good in all different kinds of ways.

"Fine," she says, a little out of breath.

Pulling back, I pump my fist in the air. "Yes! We got Blaire in."

She stands next to me, her mouth hanging open. "You played me, just like Em said."

"Aw, baby, I didn't play you. I still promise to go down on you all night. I swear."

Her eyes widen as she looks around at our friends, and Maddox bends over at the waist, laughing.

"Oh, Blaire baby, you poor, poor thing. How hard it must be for you to exchange thrill and adventure for a little downstairs action."

Her face turns a bright shade of red at his words. Her jaw is clenched as she turns to me. "I'll kill you." She grabs Emree's arm, who has a dreamy look in her eyes after something Conrad whispered in her ear, and together they follow the rest of our group toward the slopes.

I hang back with Conrad as we watch our girls. "What'd you promise Em?"

He laughs. "Told her I'd watch the entire last season of *Project Runway* with her this weekend."

"Oh shit, you got the worse end of the deal."

He rolls his eyes. "Yeah, well, what did Blaire make you do?"

I can't help but smirk. "Sex," I tell him simply.

Conrad stops walking. "You're shitting me?"

Shaking my head, I can't help but smile. "Nope. My girl knows what she wants and I'm more than happy to give it to her."

He storms off ahead of me to catch up with Emree. My guess is he is going to try and renegotiate their deal. Too bad for him I have a feeling she won't be budging when it comes to anything related to fashion.

After taking the three flights of stairs, we wait in line behind a group of middle schoolers that Maddox is currently in a verbal brawl with. "Yeah, well, I'll fuck your mom and make you call me Daddy, you little shit."

The kid, who only moments ago felt like the toughest guy on the slopes, stands there stunned, with his jaw hanging open. His friends around him try to cover their laughs.

Maddox puffs his chest out before bending down to meet the kid at eye level. "Now be a good little shit or Daddy won't get you any presents for Christmas."

The group in front of us is called for their turn and the kid never once smiles the entire time he gets into the tube or when they push the tube down the slope. Even at the bottom, I can still see he is stunned silent. Our group is called next, and we wait for the lift to bring a tube back up.

"Did you really have to scar the poor kid?" Jules asks as she gets into the waiting tube.

"He told me I look good for a lesbian. How can I let that shit slide?" Maddox responds. "First, I'm pretty sure that's some fucked-up homophobic bullshit and second, I look good no matter what. No need to bring lesbians into the mix."

Jules rolls her eyes. "He's a stupid kid."

"Yeah, and now he's been knocked down a few notches. We need to humble them young, Julesy."

Once we're all situated in our seats, the park worker goes over the basic instructions: don't stand up, keep your limbs inside the tube, don't try to spin said tube. He sounds bored out of his mind saying these in a robotic tone, but I guess I would be too if I had to do this all night.

After we all agree to not do any of the things on the list, he tells us to hold on tight to the rope handles on the sides and pushes us down the slope with his foot. From this angle, it looks much steeper than it did from the bottom. Blaire must realize that too because the moment we start heading down, she lets out an ear-splitting scream and holds it the entire twelve seconds until we reach the bottom.

My heart is racing as we slide straight ahead to another employee waiting to get us out of the tube and I can't help but smile at the adrenaline rush. Beside me, Blaire is still gripping the handles and her eyes are wide as she stares ahead.

"Gray Eyes, you okay?"

She doesn't move but shakes her head. As I stand, I laugh because her panicked look is adorable. Bending down, I pick her up and cradle her to my chest. After thanking the park employee, I follow our friends back toward the picnic tables.

Blaire clutches my neck. "That was terrifying."

Her body shakes as my chest rumbles with a chuckle. "Is it safe to assume there will be no couples skydiving in our future?"

Her eyes widen and I get my answer in that one look. "You must be crazy."

"Only crazy about you, baby."

"Even I have to admit that was lame." She laughs and I'm glad the fear seems to be gone and she relaxes more in my arms.

We join our friends at the picnic table as Maddox goes on again about the middle schooler and contemplates following him home and finding his mom. With Blaire on my lap, I look around at our friend group.

Four months ago, I met this shy, timid, beautiful woman. Our lives collided in the strangest of ways and as weird as it sounds, I knew at that moment she was important. I didn't get her name, didn't speak a word to her, and she ran off at the sight of me, but it was as if my heart knew she was someone important.

Never have I believed in soulmates, but part of me can't help but think like that when I look at the gorgeous woman in my lap. She has been a comfort and a support. Through the preparation for my testimony in the trial coming up, she has stood by my side at every meeting. She is there to rub my sore muscles after a difficult game or practice, and not once has she complained even when I know her hands must be sore. When I admitted I was struggling in our math class, she came right over with all her study tools, ready to prepare me for our final exam.

I couldn't have asked for a better woman to love me and that I get to love. She made it effortless to fall madly in love with her and I smile knowing she's mine.

As our friends laugh, Blaire looks over at me and catches me staring at her. "What are you thinking about?"

I smile. "You."

Her eyebrow rises. "And what about me?"

"How much I love you."

Her eyes soften and she melts into my chest. "I love you too." We sit in comfortable silence as we watch our friends talking and laughing. "Thank you, Camden."

"For what, baby?"

"For making it easy to trust you. For giving me everything I never knew I wanted. What I needed."

With my arms wrapped around her waist, I pull her closer to me and rest my lips against her temple. "Never thank me for that, Blaire. I should be thanking you for giving me a chance to show you what being able to trust someone is like. Forever, Gray Eyes," I promise her. "I'm here to love you forever."

Want to read more of the Braxton U crew? Emree and Conrad's story is now available. Check out The Hurt of Letting Go.

THE HURT OF LETTING GO

Are we or aren't we? Conrad has been toying with me for too long and enough is enough. He needs to decide if he wants to keep me or finally let me go.

CONRAD DUGRAY

Falling in love was never part of my plan. I was supposed to graduate college and prepare to join the family business. My family's expectations of me as the oldest son were far too high and they were becoming harder to reach.

Emree wasn't supposed to be the girl I fell for. My family already had a future wife in mind for me and they would never accept someone with Emree's background. I tried to push her away on multiple occasions, but it was becoming more difficult each time. Once my family found out about her, they would destroy anything we had.

EMREE ANDERS

Being in love with a man who didn't seem to want to commit was a special kind of torture. Conrad constantly pushed me away and just when I was trying to move on, he was back again, claiming he couldn't go another day without me.

My heart couldn't take the tug-of-war game he continued to play with it and I feared it might shatter the next time he pushed me away. I needed to stand my ground and make him decide if he wanted me, or he would have to let me go.

ACKNOWLEDGMENTS

Back in 2017 I started this book and life got in the way and I stepped away from writing and the Book Community as a whole. Never did I think on a random Tuesday in August that I would get this sudden urge to write in a book I haven't thought much about in years. Then to my shock, I completed this story in a month. It felt like I was dreaming and it was an emotional day for me when I realized I finished this book.

There are far too many people I am grateful for that have helped me so much on this journey. The first is my friend, my cover designer, and all-around amazing human, Cassie Chapman. She is one of the sweetest people I have ever met and having her in your corner is so meaningful. She has been there to let me pick her brain and created the most perfect cover for this book and I can't wait to work with her on future projects.

Another person that I am screaming THANK YOU to is Micalea Smeltzer. She is such an inspiration and is always there to help when I have questions and ask for suggestions. Her books are part of the reason my writing motivation came back, and for that I am so thankful.

Kari Nappi-Goldin is someone I will never be able to express my gratitude to. Coming back into the Book Community and publishing my first book in years has not been easy, especially with how much has changed over the years. Kari is an amazing friend and always there to bounce ideas off, help when I am completely clueless, and to create beautiful graphics. Having her there has been such a help.

To all the other authors that have been there during this

process, thank you all. This community is one filled with some of the most amazing people, and I love how we are all there for each other. Being back and talking with so many of my favorite people has been amazing.

To my editor and proofreaders, thank you all so much. You have helped me with making this book even better and fixing my many mistakes. I promise, I will one day get it together. Probably not, but I'm glad to have each of you there behind me!

Readers, you will never know how much we appreciate you. To all the readers who have read The Act of Trusting, left reviews, shared it on your social media platforms, thank you all so much. I hope each of you have enjoyed this book and I can't wait to bring you the rest in the series.

To my family, thank your for being patient with me. I basically became a hermit while writing this book. There were many missed family events, dinners, and celebrations. Your support and love means more to me than anything.

To Rumi: thank you for being such an amazing human and don't ever leave me.

ABOUT THE AUTHOR

Lexi Bissen is a new adult and young adult romance author who aspires to write in all genres, including paranormal—which started her obsession with words and fictional characters she cares about more than real people. She's also a coffee snob, reader, far too sarcastic, and dog rescue advocate.

Born and raised in Tampa, Florida, Lexi enjoys spending time with her family, taking in the sunshine with a good book, and giving the voices in her head a story. Writing has always been an escape for Lexi, where she can check out of her life and discover new, exciting places she makes up—but not in a crazy way.

When Lexi isn't writing, you can find her binging the latest Netflix show, laughing at her own jokes, or sipping iced coffee while spending way too much money at the bookstore.

Check out Lexi's website for updates on upcoming releases, current books, and where to follow on social media: https://www.lexibissen.com/.

f